Depraved Desires

An Anthology of Dark Erotica

HellBound Books Publishing LLC

A HellBound Books LLC Publication

www.hellboundbookspublishing.com

Printed in the United States of America

Depraved Desires

Compiled and Edited by Xtina Marie

A HellBound Books Publishing LLC Book

Houston TX

Dedicated to each and every one of the phenomenal authors, the darkest imaginings of whom are captured within these very pages, creative talents who have entrusted us with the product of their blood, sweat and tears – we hope we have done you proud.

Foreword

There's something to be said for both dark erotica and erotic horror. Having started out as publishers of horror - and having only recently ventured into erotica territory - we have now sampled both sides of this literary confection.

The melding of fear and sensuality is tricky, but it also makes a lot of sense. They both get the heart pounding. Breathing shortens and the skin prickles. Eyes dilate and the mouth goes dry. These symptoms are part of man's—and all mammals'—fight or flight response when stressed. There is, however, something decadent about twisting it on its head. Not to fight or flee, but to indulge in the things that turn you up, regardless of how depraved they might be. That's the simple beauty of erotic horror and dark erotica: it plays on your subconscious reactions, daring you to look deeper into yourself.

Xtina Marie, our very own Dark Poet Princess has an expert's eye for picking out stories that at the same time shock and arouse, in addition to creating her own. Xtina's skillful construction of myriad varied voices into one volume just dripping with sex and terror speaks volumes of love of this sensual, dark genre and those who write within its borderless worlds. So, keep turning the pages, Dear Reader - maybe you should read this risqué tome alone, or maybe you're more the exhibitionist and dare yourself to read it in broad daylight, and somewhere deliciously public.

For nothing contrasts more perfectly with a warm, sunlit day than those squalid, dirty alleys where unspeakable things may well be happening right now.

But don't worry, we won't tell anyone.

HellBound Books Publishing LLC

<u>Contents</u>

Depraved Desires

Show-Off City

Shaun Avery

I was coasting along a country highway getting a blowjob from a MILF when the vampire first attacked.

Not that I realised he was a vampire, of course. Not then. I thought at first it was just some psycho driver.

Whatever he was, though, he came barrelling in out of nowhere and crashed into the side of my car. Just as I was about to come, too, but I've always been good under pressure, and I used one hand to keep her head down on my cock, telling her "don't stop, baby, don't stop" whilst using the other to keep the car under control. Thankfully we'd been going pretty slow, or it would have been a harder job.

She started using her teeth a little as I brought us to a stop, and I groaned, stiffened, arched my back in the driver seat to push more of myself into her wide and

13

wonderful mouth, only vaguely aware, in my peripheral vision, of the other car racing away from us and disappearing.

There was something about it, though. Something that struck me as strange even in the one quick view I'd had of the car.

I tried to work out what it was.

I wondered briefly why I hadn't tried to check the license plate.

But then her mouth had the desired result.

And all I thought about was her.

Ah.

And it was good.

There's nothing like a fine lipstick-induced orgasm to take your mind off everything else in the world.

But in the aftermath, with my lady friend now sat upright in the passenger seat and expecting that I do something in return for her, I couldn't help but feel a little curious, and I got out and checked my vehicle.

"Shit," I said.

He'd really done a number on the side, where he'd hit.

She came to stand behind me, placed a hand upon my shoulder, said, "Who was that guy, Dave?"

"I don't know, Dawn," I said. I looked at her. "Do you?"

You might think I sound like something of a tool here. You could even be right. But in my business, jealous ex-husbands are the number one threat.

"No," she told me, and I could see from her eyes that she was telling the truth.

So, I gave her the killer smile and suggested we climb into the backseat and I could pay her back for what she'd done with me.

She smiled and obliged.

And a short while later we were heading back into the city.

***

Ally was watching through the window, and his eyebrows shot up as I walked into the office.

"Christ, Dave," he said. "What happened to the car?"

I told him about my mystery assailant, and in doing so, it all became a bit more real to me. In the back of the car, with Dawn on top of me, it'd been easy to lose myself in her . . . and, you know, a woman of her experience, a body of that beauty, my fingers sliding up a flat stomach across firm breasts stroking erect nipples to lose themselves in her hot bobbed hair, there was a lot to lose myself in. Now, though, a delayed feeling of paranoia and worry was starting to set in. I mean, who would want to hurt me?

I thought back to what had happened.

And finally, it struck me, the odd thing I'd noticed about the car before it disappeared.

"The windows," I said to Ally. "The windows were all blacked out."

"With paint?"

"No," I said. "With some sort of masking tape."

"Shit," Ally said. "So, you didn't see what the guy looked like?"

"No," I replied. "Probably wouldn't have, anyway. My attention was . . . elsewhere."

"Ha." He smiled. "Where is the lovely Dawn, anyway?"

"Dropped her off at home," I said. I tapped my watch, an overly thick item that was actually far too heavy for my wrist but was a trapping of my success that I could not live without. "School run, you know."

"You and your mothers," he said.

"It's those child-bearing hips," I replied. "They drive me crazy."

Then I took a seat, looked at the sign on the window:

DAVE PALMER
SENSUAL ENTERTAINMENT SERVICES

But, although it was just my name on there, I couldn't have done any of it without Ally, my right-hand man and friend.

Who then said, "so what's the plan for tonight?"

"How we looking for live shows?"

"Like any other Friday," he said. "Fully booked."

"Good," I said, nodding. "Let Marshall take care of those." Marshall was our protégé, a recent University graduate who had no actual experience of stripping himself but had still somehow managed to fit right into our world, even earning the respect of the strippers themselves. "I figured me and you would try something else."

He could barely contain his excitement. "Recruitment for the special project?"

I smiled. "Yeah."

"But what about that?" Ally wondered, pointing through the window towards my battered car.

"Nothing to worry about," I responded, waving it off. "But let's take your car – just to be sure."

***

We parked that car near the train station later that night, making the rest of the journey on foot. My paranoia must have been catching, though – Ally had kept his eyes on the rear-view mirror most of the way.

"Relax," I told him, before we exited the vehicle. "Get your head in the game. It was probably just some random guy."

He nodded.

Then we left the car, started walking.

And soon enough, we'd reached our destination.

The city centre.

Where all the bars were, and even though it was still early, about ten p.m., there was still plenty going on. I'm talking public urination, against bar wall copulation – fast, frenzied fucks, those, cocks and fingers flying in and out of orifices before the drunken lust wore off – and a river of green puke flowing along the gutter to reach its ultimate eventual destination down the drain.

"Any preference to what you're looking for?" Ally asked me.

"Blonde, brunette, bleached." Three words that could be my motto. "Doesn't matter which. As long as they're beautiful."

"Yeah?" He grinned at me. "How about bi?"

And I grinned back.

Remembering.

***

Rewind thirty-odd years to the same place, the same bars, and you'd find me and Ally there, only for a different reason. Well, actually the same reason – girls – but back then we had a different use for them.

"I'm telling you," I said, putting down my drink in the busy bar. "It'll never happen."

"Oh aye? Why not?"

His words were always egging me on – he was the one who convinced me to start stripping, and lately he'd been telling me I was good enough to strike out on my own, that I was far more intelligent than my knuckleheaded manager, Shannon. Right now, though, he had his heart set on fulfilling a personal ambition of his own, and also a common male desire: finding two women who would let us watch them have sex with each other.

I had my doubts.

But it turned out he was right.

We could find them.

And back at one of their places we watched them fall all over each other, all sliding tongues and groping fingers. I was watching, stroking myself. But I never thought to look at what my friend Ally was doing.

Until one of the girls disentangled herself from her friend's nipple and looked at him and said, "dude. Are you fucking filming this?"

He was.

I thought we were through here, that we wouldn't get to see the rest of the show, let alone participate in it. But I had forgotten how charming Ally could sometimes be, and he clicked off and put away the mobile phone he'd been using to record them and grinned at the girls.

"Sorry," he then said, sliding down his pants, letting them drop to his feet. "I'm a bit of a voyeur." He stepped out of them, walked on over to the bed, slid his arms around the breast of each girl and grabbed a breast each. "Forgive me?"

They did.

And soon the girl who'd question Ally was riding him, her face all wet and shiny from her friend's vaginal juices, whilst I was buried in said friend, who, it seemed, still had plenty of those juices left for me, and my thumbs were furiously flicking both of her nipples into a state of seemingly permanent erection whilst she had her tongue deep inside my mouth, her hands just as busy on me as mine were on her, one clutching a buttock to push me further in while the other raked open my back.

Shannon just about shit his pants when he saw those scratches the next morning.

"Good God, David," he said. Arsehole always called me by my full name, drove me fucking crazy every time. "You think housewives and hen parties will pay money to see that?"

"Yeah, I do, actually," I said, and just like that the decision was made. "That's why I'm leaving."

That night, to celebrate, Ally and I called on the two girls again.

Turned out they'd decided to become a couple.

Thanked us for helping them discover their true feelings for each other.

But didn't do much else for us.

Which was when we learnt our lesson about setting girl with girl.

***

The memory made me reply, "nah. Better give the bi girls a miss."

He shook his head. "I sometimes wonder what happened to those two wee lassies."

"They lived happily ever after," I said. "So did we. So let's start thinking about tonight's girl."

He nodded, headed off towards the bars. Not to go into them, of course – the noise of the music would be too loud in there, too much of a distraction. But between bars, or outside of them . . . well, that was a good hunting ground.

I started scanning the area, too.

But at the same time, I remembered the guy who'd hit my car, and I began to get a little paranoid, couldn't help wondering . . .

Was someone out there watching me?

***

Funny I should mention that.

Watching, I mean.

That's why we were here.

See, we were a nationwide franchise now, the Dave Palmer brand a byword for a quality live stripping experience. But Ally was always keen for us to find new ways of making money, and as you guessed from that experience with the bi-girls, he enjoyed being a spectator. So it had been his idea to try and provide a webcam stripping service.

But not with any of the people we currently employed.

He wanted a totally new start.

Hence tonight.

And though I had my doubts, thinking that the stripping experience would lose something with a computer screen between viewer and performer, Ally's argument had convinced me enough that I took the opportunity to stop two girls as they headed between bars and say to them, "hey there, ladies. You ever thought about doing any modelling?"

We always call it that, at first. It seems to work better than the word "stripper." Women. Go figure.

These two women, meanwhile, were checking me out.

As well they should. I mean, I'm no dummy. I know that the words I had just spoken could have made me sound sleazy. Perhaps they even thought I was some sort of porno guy – although, do they still have porno in this online world? I don't know. I'm digressing. Point is, though, I know all about image. That's why I was wearing the watch I told you all about earlier. No one who ever looked at that would think that I was cheap.

But it wasn't enough for one of the girls.

"Come on, Beverley," she said, pulling at her friend's elbow, trying to drag her along to the next bar. "Let's go."

"You go, Cheryl," Beverley replied. "I'll catch you up."

Cheryl scowled in my direction and shook her head. But go she did, leaving me and Beverley alone.

I looked her over.

She was nice.

No dress – I like a dress – but she had flaming red hair in natural curls and the jeans she wore were tight enough and she wore ankle boots with a sexy little heel on them. And though she was probably a bit too young for me, in her mid-twenties I guessed, she was still a woman dressed up nice to go out, and that always got me going, and I started to suspect that I would be making a call on a certain matriarch of my acquaintance before I headed home.

But back to the there and then.

"Hi," I said. "My name's Dave."

"Beverley," she said. She smiled – she had a nice smile, and I couldn't help but imagine how much nicer it would be when it was all that she was wearing. "But you knew that already, right?"

"Right," I said, nodding. "And you made the right choice, staying and talking to me."

"Really?" She frowned. "I thought you would have preferred Cheryl."

And just like that I knew I had her.

"What type of modelling are we talking about?" she said, and she looked at me as if she already knew the answer.

"We'll get to that," I told her. And I brought out my phone, an echo of what Ally had done with those two girls all those years earlier. "You mind if I get a picture first? I'll have to show it to my business partner later."

"Sure," Beverley said. "Go ahead. You want me to pose?"

I cringed inside, thinking of all the awful "selfie" poses I'd seen going around recently: trout pouts, fingers in front of faces – all that stuff. Shiver.

"No," I replied. "Just act natural."

She did.

She was pretty good at it, too.

I snapped off a shot and took her number, telling her I'd be in touch. Then I sent her off to catch up with Cheryl, no doubt to brag about the one she'd just got over on her friend.

I really thought I'd found our first new stripper.

Not yet knowing that she would be dead by the next morning.

***

Blissful in my ignorance, I went to find Ally.

He'd been more productive, had more pictures and numbers than me. But then, the whole thing had been his idea.

"That's me done," I told him. "I'm out of here."

"Lazy bugger." He grinned. "Find anyone?"

"One," I said, and showed him Beverley's photo.

"Nice," he said. "Think she'll be up for it?"

"Reckon," I said, and stretched and yawned.

"How you getting home?" he asked. "We came in my car."

"One," I said, "I'm not going home." Ally smiled at that, knowing exactly where I'd be going. "Two, a taxi."

"Well," he said, "be careful."

"Always am," I said, though of course we both knew that I was not.

Then I headed towards the nearest taxi rank, making a call on my mobile as I did so.

"Hi," I said, when Dawn picked up. "You still awake?"

She was.

And she met me at the door completely naked.

"Wow," I said, thankful that the taxi driver had already made his exit, and with a pretty big tip in his pocket, as I was in a good mood. "Not that I'm complaining, but what if the kids had come and caught you like this?"

"Heavy sleepers," she explained, and put her arms around me and her tongue in my mouth and pulled me through into the front room, me shedding my clothes with one hand whilst sliding the other all over her, and soon we were on the floor and my face was between her legs, licking her, sucking her, tasting her, and her fingers were twisting their way through my hair, her mouth saying, "don't stop, baby, don't stop," a reversal of the way we'd been in my car earlier, and then one of my hands was stroking a breast whilst the other was trailing its way down a long, long leg, reaching the end eventually and stroking her toes, and then I switched positions, putting my mouth on those toes and using my hand in and on and around her vagina, and she reared her back up off the floor, presenting more of herself to me if that were possible, and by the time I was done with both of her feet there was a little wet patch beneath her but she didn't seem to mind and then we were both ready, we were both waiting, and I slid back up her body and plunged myself into her.

Afterwards we lay there panting.

"Wow," she said, her hand on my bare chest. "No one's ever done that to me before."

"Made you cum twice in a row?"

"No, silly," Dawn said. "Sucked my toes." She looked at me. "I didn't realise you were into that stuff."

Truth was, I wasn't. But I knew it was just about rare enough that it would surprise the average woman. I used to use it on them back in my stripping days, making a little extra, off-the-books money when the official show was done. A surprise would always make them pay extra. Which might sound like a cynical way to look at things. But, you know, the cash to get out from under that idiot Shannon's thumb had to come from somewhere.

"You know me," I said to her. "Master of the unexpected."

She made a contended sound then, and fell asleep beside me.

Whilst I started wondering what would happen if her two kids – one boy, one girl – came down and caught us in the altogether.

Did that thought scare me?

Or excite me?

I don't mean anything kinky by that, you understand. No, what I meant is, did I want to meet her kids? And what would it mean if I did want that?

I looked at Dawn, sleeping next to me.

We'd have to move soon, I knew. And either I could hide in her bed until her kids went out – which, it being Saturday and them being teenagers, she assured me they would – or I could be gone before they got up. Like all the other times we'd done this.

So what had changed?

Me, I realised.

I had.

Or was changing.

I guess it meant the same.

But I didn't want to think about those changes, so instead I elected to leave, and woke her up to tell her.

But looking back at her, standing in the doorway, dressed in a robe this time, I couldn't deny the fact that I found myself wanting to stay with her.

And I found that scary.

But not quite as scary as what happened when I got back home.

***

A police car was pulled up outside the house.

And when I rounded the corner – walking, this time – a familiar face burst out of the backseat and ran towards me.

"That's him!" she shouted. "He killed her! He killed her!"

Then Cheryl was upon me, slapping, scratching.

I tried to push her off, and it was then that I noticed the odd look in her eyes.

It was like she wasn't really seeing me.

Then a bearded man was getting between us, pulling us apart, and I saw that he, too, had that glazed expression.

But by the time I noticed that, he had already slapped a pair of handcuffs on me.

"Dave Palmer?" he said. "I'm Detective Grant. And you're under arrest."

***

We had a business lawyer – a slimy little fuck called Burnett – but as you probably guessed from that description I didn't like him very much, always choosing to "let" Ally deal with him. So I didn't call him, even when I was placed in an interrogation room.

But I have to tell you: there was something about the police station that spooked me.

I'd seen a few other cops when I was being led in, and they all had that weird look about them. They were sitting at desks, typing at computers, but none of them really seemed to be seeing what they were doing.

So I made no trouble, just sat there in the interrogation room. Glad that they'd removed the handcuffs, if nothing else.

Eventually, Grant came in.

Looking at him, studying his eyes, I realised what he reminded me of. Every now and again I'd have to bust one of my strippers for doing drugs on the job. This cop looked like one of those guys. Like he was strung out on E.

He had taken my phone from me, during the "arrest." Now he placed it down on the table that lay between us, along with a thin folder.

Then he pointed to something I had not noticed in the corner of the room: a camera.

"They'll be turning that on in a minute," Grant said. "But before they do, I want to tell you something."

"Oh, yeah?" I said. "What's that?"

"The guy that hit your car says hi."

I didn't gasp at that, but I came close.

Then the red light of the camera came in, indicating that this was now being recorded.

"So why am I here?" I asked him, dragging my gaze away from the camera.

"I'll ask the questions," he said. "First of all, tell me about Beverley Maynard."

"Who?" I said, then the first name struck a nerve. "Oh. You mean the girl I talked to last night?"

He raised an eyebrow. "Is that all you did?"

Then he slid the folder across the table to me.

"Take a look," he said. "Recognise her? Take a good look. Might be hard, with all her skin removed."

With a comment like that, I probably shouldn't have opened up the folder.

But God help me, I did.

He was right.

There was skin where a pair of hands – a woman's hands – were shown tied to a stake in the ground. But beneath that . . . nothing. Just a red mess.

I peeled my eyes away from the photo and noticed that Grant now had a hand on the gun holstered at his hip.

"Must have took some doing, that," Grant said, indicating the photos with his free hand.

"Right," I said. "But this can't be her. No one could have done this in the time since I talked to her."

"You'd be surprised."

And for all I knew, he was right.

I mean, a detective would know more about this stuff than me. Wouldn't he?

I began to get nervous, seeing his hand on his gun.

"So why are you fingering me for this?"

"Because of what her friend told us," he said. "You tried to talk to the two girls. They wouldn't stop for you. Then you followed them around all night, stalking them from bar to bar."

"Are you kidding?" I said. "Don't you think she's a little young for me?"

"My thoughts, too, at first," Grant said. Then he flipped open my phone, showed something to me. "But if that's so, how come her picture's on your phone?"

And I remembered the shot I'd taken of her.

"So," he continued, "you liked what you saw. So you waited, and you grabbed Beverley when she was waiting for her taxi home."

"Wrong," I told him. "I was somewhere else. And I got someone who can back me up on that."

"That so?" Grant said.

Then he stood up, drew his gun.

I leapt out of my chair, backed away from the table. "What the shit?"

"We'll have someone look into that," he went on, but just like before he wasn't really looking at me as he said it, was instead staring somewhere above and beyond me. "In the meantime, I think we'd better put you in a cell. Just in case."

Then he came around behind me, put the gun into my back and said, "move."

I moved.

All the way to a cell, where he locked me in without another word.

I sat down on the hard bed and put my head in my hands, thinking that things must have now peaked, that my day could not get any stranger.

But I was wrong.

***

"Ah, man . . . you could pull in an empty room, you could."

So said Ally to me one time, when at a particularly lame party where the women outnumbered the men about eight to one – a party thrown by Shannon, naturally – I still managed to go home with a beautiful woman. I never made an effort to live up to this claim – that would be show-off city, right? – but to this day he brought it up to reassure me whenever I was going through a dry spell sexually.

Still, never had I thought his words would come true.

But they did, that morning in the prison cell.

I was lying back on the bed, trying to work out just what the hell was going on. I had already ruled out the possibility of Dawn's ex-husband being involved, unless he was some sort of magician. So who else?

Who else could have done that to . . .?

Oh God.

Beverley.

Remembering those photos, I wanted to both scream and vomit.

But then I thought of something.

Those photos hadn't looked like the sort of crime scene ones you see on TV shows. No, they'd been grainier, less detailed, though there was still enough blood and carnage there to let you know you were looking at the remains of a body. Kind of like they'd been done on a phone, and then blown up and printed off.

My terror stepped up a notch.

But at least, I thought, I was still alive.

Unlike that poor girl I'd talked to, and now I couldn't get away from the fact that it was talking to me that had got her killed. Which made the whole thing even worse. I mean, I know I only spoke to her for a few minutes. But I've always been a gut feeling sort of guy, and my gut had told me in that short time that I liked her, that I would have enjoyed working with her. The thought that someone had killed her – more, had killed her to somehow get at me – turned my terror into anger, made my fists tense up in rage.

That's probably why I didn't notice it at first when the hole appeared in the floor.

But then I saw it happening, and I scooted up on the bed, putting my back against the wall, pulling my feet up under me, fearful that something would reach out from that hole and grab me.

I was half-right.

Something did appear.

But it just stood there in the middle of the room, as the hole disappeared beneath its feet, as the floor became solid once more.

It was a woman.

Slim.

Slender.

Blonde.

Beautiful.

Naked.

And somehow kind of familiar, too, standing there with her hands upon her hips.

I felt an erection forming in my pants, and was suddenly glad that they'd taken my belt off me.

Then her eyes met mine.

"Dave," she said, and I have to tell you the truth, I almost lost my load there and then. There was just something about her voice that drove me crazy. Soft. Breathy. But sexy. "I've come for you."

"I – what?"

She came closer. But I don't know how. By which I mean, I never saw her move. One minute she was in the middle of the cell. The next she was right there in front of me.

"I've come for you," she said again, and she stretched out a hand.

I thought she wanted me to take it.

But instead, she took me.

One hand grabbed my penis through my pants, whilst the other went about making those pants a thing of the past.

And again, I felt there was something very familiar about her, about the way she was releasing me.

"Wait," I said.

"Why?" she said.

And pulled them down.

Letting my erection pop free.

She bent over and her tongue flicked out, licked the head of my bulging penis.

Then she pulled back.

Smiled.

"Do you still want to wait?" she asked.

And she touched herself.

One hand at her breast.

The other sliding herself open at the groin.

I looked down.

She was so wet there.

So wet.

"Oh God," I said. "Oh God."

"Do you want me, Dave?" she asked, her eyes meeting mine, her mouth wide open as she spoke, an inviting hole.

I did.

Of course I did.

But did I want something else – someone else called Dawn – more than I wanted this vision that lay before me?

I wasn't sure. But still I said, "I'm . . . I'm with someone."

"Really?" She looked around the cell. "So where is she?"

Her hand moved from her chest to mine. Stroking. Caressing.

"Well?" she said. "Where is she, Dave?"

I couldn't believe that this was happening.

But now I realised why she looked so familiar.

My first porno . . . the first thing I ever jacked it to. The scene that even the teenage me found ridiculous, where the stripper sneaks into the hospital dressed as a nurse and fucks the guy who's in there because she gave him a heart attack whilst stripping for him. She'd taken down his pyjama pants in just the same way that this woman had to me – same pace, same mannerisms on her face, everything. But it had been over thirty years since I had watched that film. There was no way she could still look exactly the same as she had back then. So just what was going on here?

"A-ha!" said the woman. "I know what's wrong here!"

She clicked her fingers.

And suddenly the vision was complete.

She was now wearing a nurse's uniform.

Then she was on her knees before me.

Taking me in her mouth.

"Oh shit," I said, and grabbed her shoulders.

I meant to push her away.

I swear I did.

But she was just too good.

Sucking and licking until I was just almost there but then pulling away and lying down on the bed, her uniform gone, her body naked once again.

"Fuck me," she said. The woman in the porno had said that, too. "Fuck me, Dave."

But I held off.

Thinking of Dawn.

Thinking of those wonderful few hours we'd shared before.

"He sent me," the woman – or whatever she was – said. "You can do what you want with me. Everything.

But there's a price to pay." Then her eyes met mine, and for just a second I caught a glimpse at what lurked behind them, and it was something that was not quite human. But then she was licking her lips and playing with herself and suddenly she was just a figure of fantasy once more. "Are you willing to pay it, Dave?"

I was.

Oh, God I was.

And I banished all thoughts of Dawn and what could have been and fell onto her and into her.

And in the warm afterglow of the moment, my warm semen trickling down her leg to meet the cold floor

below . . .

That was when the cell door swung open.

***

I jumped up and away from her, expecting Detective Grant and his gun to come walking in.

But no one did.

Instead I heard a voice say, "come on, Dave."

I looked behind me.

The woman, still lying on the bed, giggled.

And then she disappeared.

This time, I couldn't keep it in: I did gasp.

I had half a mind to just stay here – I mean, you'd think a cell would be a safe place to hide out, right? But then came that voice again, saying, "come on, Dave. I'm waiting for you."

It wasn't a woman's voice.

But it was somehow just as seductive.

So I got up and I got dressed and I followed it.

***

With vigilance, of course.

But when I reached the main detectives area, I saw that I need not have worried.

There was an orgy going on here.

Women straddled men on desks; men had women bent over chairs. Tongues licked at crotches and slender fingers tugged furiously at erect penises until they exploded, cascading white all over the room. There were a few gay couplings, too – girl on girl, guy in guy, and everything in between. It was even going on back in the cells, grunts of pleasure and the squeal and slap of skin on skin coming from over that way.

And the scariest thing?

Fifty per cent of each pair – some male, some female – turned to smile at me as I passed by.

Except one.

Detective Grant looked at me over Cheryl's shoulder, her breasts, much larger than they'd looked last night in her going out sweater, swaying and rocking as he took her from behind.

"I think he's getting away," he said, one hand at Cheryl's hip, the other pulling at a nipple that didn't seem like it could get much bigger.

"I don't think so," she said. She pulled his hand up to her mouth, sucked his fingers a little. Then spat them out and nodded at me and said, "aren't you forgetting something?"

I was.

As well as my belt, they'd taken my shoes, too.

I went and took Grant's.

We were about the same size – in feet, smart-ass – and it didn't look like he'd be needing them any time soon. Not with Cheryl now pushing him back onto a chair and stuffing her groin into his face.

"Come on, Dave," came that voice again.

I looked up.

Then headed out into the night towards it.

*＊＊

And it was strange – everything seemed normal on the street. I'd thought for a frenzied second that this lust bug might have hit the whole city, but apparently, that was not the case.

I wasn't sure where to go, though.

And I was no longer hearing that little voice.

Had I just imagined it?

I didn't think so.

In my confusion, I pulled out my phone, thought about calling Ally.

But what would I tell him?

No.

I had to help myself here.

And I was suddenly sure that I had to go home.

So that's where I headed.

Sadly, though . . .

There was somebody waiting there for me.

*＊＊

I pushed open the front door, and the first thing that hit me was the smell.

On top of everything else that had happened tonight, it almost made me turn and run.

But bail out on my own house?

I don't think so.

So I went further in.

Walked into the main room.

It was dark, and I don't just mean that the curtains were closed across the windows, though they were. No, it was something more than that. Something deeper.

But not deep enough to hide the shape of someone sitting in my chair.

He had spun it round the other way, so he was facing one of those closed windows.

"Sorry about the smell," he said, that voice still smooth and seductive, making me wonder all the more about its owner. "I'm afraid we had to make a bit of a mess."

One hand emerged, pointed.

The limb was skeletal; the skin sank almost down to the bone.

Still, I followed it.

To where a pair of severed arms in handcuffs lay on the floor.

"Beverley?" I said, remembering what I'd seen on the photographs back in the interrogation room. I took a step closer to the chair, feeling anger flare up inside me. "You mean she was killed here?"

"Part of your test," said the voice. "See how you'd cope, how'd you react, seeing your home defiled this way. That's what the last few days have been about, Dave."

"A test?" I said. "What kind of test?"

"To see if you were worthy, Dave," came the reply. "Worthy of being my replacement."

And he stepped up, stepped into view.

I took a step back, shocked.

Like his arm, the rest of his body was skinny, and I could tell that this was not just his natural frame. No, there was nothing natural about him, this creature that stood before me. He was withered and wizened and skinny and weak.

Except for his eyes.

They still seemed full of power.

"Thanks," he said. "I'm glad you think so. They certainly worked on Detective Grant and the rest of his colleagues at the police station. I took a little visit there, earlier last night, just before you headed to your lady friend's. Did a little trick on them. Then the girl, and her friend – lured them both back here, told one what to believe, and . . . well – you know what I did to the other." He gave a bitter smile, and for the first time I saw his teeth, saw that they weren't natural, either. "But all those tricks, they cost me dear."

"Tricks?" I said. "To frame me? Why?"

Before he could reply, I heard footsteps behind me.

Lots of them.

I turned.

Saw the woman I'd slept with back at the cell, saw the people who'd smiled at me in the detective area.

But they looked different now.

They were still beautiful.

But their mouths hung open.

And their mouths were full of fangs – just like the man I was talking to.

Who then said, "we call them succubae. Incubi, for the male of the species. Sexual vampires. They keep on loving you and loving you, until you've nothing left to give." My doppelganger nurse stepped forward, laid a hand against my cheek. "Unless I tell them to stop, of course."

And when she touched me, suddenly I saw.

I was back with her, at the station.

It was full of corpses now.

And the creatures were closing in on the only two people I'd recognised back there: Detective Grant and Cheryl.

"No," I said, pushing her away, breaking the mental link. I looked to the withered man. "Why her?"

He shook his head. "No loose ends. You'll learn that soon enough."

"You keep talking about learning," I said, "and tests. Just what are you, pal? And what do you want with me?"

"I'll show you," he said.

And he did.

***

Like earlier, with my nursing friend, we then seemed to be moving without actually moving. Rather, the room was moving around us, changing too, becoming no longer a room but a vast and dark forest.

In which two men were getting it on.

At least, that's what I thought, at first. I mean, one of them was screaming in what I thought was pleasure. But then I saw the blood leaking away and I realised the one on top was actually working on the neck of the guy below, as opposed to his junk, and I put two and two together and I got –

"You're a vampire?" I said to the man standing next to me.

"About to be," he said.

And pointed.

The guy on the bottom, he was younger and fitter and healthier, but still . . .

"It's you," I said.

He – the version in the present – nodded.

Then the other guy in the past turned to face us.

I bent and vomited.

He was in even worse shape than my companion. Sores. Boils. Bits of skin hanging off his face. The works. And as I watched, he keeled over and died.

"God," I said. "I didn't think you guys could die."

"A popular myth," he said. "But that's all it is."

Then the him in the past stood up, and I just couldn't help but notice . . .

He looked good.

Strong.

"We live a lot longer than you guys," his present-day version told me. "And we don't age – not until the last days, when we're ready to move on. And you always know when that time is – that's when you start looking for a replacement."

"What?" I said. "Doesn't everyone you bite turn into one of you?"

He shook his head. "Another myth," he said. "What we bite, we kill – until we're ready to pass on our legacy."

Then the forest faded, and we were back at my house.

"But why me?" I asked him.

"You're strong," he said. "Powerful. Handsome. All the things a vampire must be." He paused.

"Successful, too. You've come far in this world. Now it's up to you to decide if you want to go further in another."

I thought about it.

He placed a wrinkled hand upon my shoulder.

"The first test was the car crash," he said. "Wanted to see if you panicked. You didn't.

"Then the arrest – I was watching, through Detective Grant's eyes, to see if you broke down. You didn't.

"Then the test with your new succubus friend here."

She stroked my face again, and I couldn't help but notice that I wasn't looking at her fangs with quite the same revulsion that I had done before.

"You wanted her so much," he said, "didn't you? And if you take my place, you can be with her all the time. And she can be any woman you want her to be."

To confirm this, she transformed into a dozen different women. Some of them ones I'd been with in real life, some of them ones I'd masturbated over, two of them women I'd wanted but never got. There weren't too many of them to choose from. Naturally.

"They're at your beck and call," he said. "We true vampires command this lesser breed. You can do with them what you please."

I remembered all I'd seen them do back at the police station, and I have to admit, I liked the sound of it. My stripping guys had always had their limits. With these creatures, there seemed to be no such thing.

"But what about my house?" I said, sweeping an arm around the place.

"That's up to you," he said. "There'll be no fallout from the station – your name was never recorded, and your lady friend here removed all the video surveillance." She winked at me at the mention of her name. "But I think a clean start is always better. There are always places you can find to live. They will show you the way to go."

Then he locked his eyes on mine.

"Decision time, Dave," he said. "Will you be my replacement?"

"I – I . . ."

I looked at him.

Saw all I could be. Saw more power and strength than I had ever experienced before.

"What do you have to do?" I said.

He smiled.

"Will it hurt?"

"No," he told me. "It'll be something just like a kiss."

And you know something?

It was.

***

Sunday evening.

I understood now why the vampire had used the black masking tape on his car.

We could come out when there was still sunlight, we could . . . but we had to be pretty securely protected from it. That meant blocking out your windows if you were in a vehicle – and wrapping yourself up in black clothing if you were on the street.

That's what I had done.

Now, I stood looking through a window of my own – the one that read DAVE PALMER SENSUAL ENTERTAINMENT SERVICES.

I saw Marshall working inside.

But the word "saw" meant more, much more, than it ever had in my old life.

I saw the blood pulsing through his veins.

So much of it.

"Pick someone weak," the vampire had said, "for your first meal. Someone who'll not put up much of a fight."

"Why?" I said. I flexed a huge muscle. "Aren't I strong? And powerful?"

"Yes," he said. "But you're a whole new species now. Your strength will take some getting used to."

Then he coughed and collapsed, breathed his last.

I felt a certain sadness at his passing. Guess that was my gut all over again. We'd not known each other long. But you could say that he had changed my life.

That's why I was here.

But I knew that I couldn't do it to Marshall.

Not to someone that I knew.

Instead I walked through the front door.

He looked up from his computer screen.

"Mr. . . . Mr. Palmer?" he said, squinting at me.

"It's all yours now," I told him. I noticed my voice was different now, smooth and seductive, like the vampire's had been. "Yours and Ally's. Enjoy it."

Then I was gone, my old world vanishing quickly behind me.

But something else emerging in its place.

The thirst.

***

Sunday night.

I watched her mill around the house with a dull robotic lifelessness.

I wondered if she'd tried to call me.

I wondered if she was already missing me.

I can't say that I blamed her. I knew I was going to be hard to get over. But maybe I could give her something else to think about.

We'd had a good time, had me and her. But I'd never let myself get fully inside her life. And now I understood why.

The hour grew late and the thirst inside me grew, and soon all the lights inside the house went out, leaving me in darkness.

And out there in that darkness, I grew tired of waiting, of watching, and finally began to move. And with the thirst pulsing, demanding to be fed, a living thing inside me . . .

I knew that soon I would finally be meeting Dawn's kids.

Thighs Maketh the Woman

David Owain Hughes

Not tonight, please. Not ever *again. I can't…* he'd argued with himself on his way home from work, but the sight of so many women in short skirts displaying their tight-clad legs had driven him crazy. Businesswomen, college sluts, mums, women out shopping, grannies, fatties, skinnies, curvies – they were out in force for the perverted world and its gimp to see.

Now, parked up, his body shook violently from the horn coursing through him. He yearned for sexual release, even though he'd had one in the men's toilet at the office. Glory, his supervisor, had been wearing the shortest skirt he'd ever seen, and when she sat at her desk, which was across from his, he could see up it and had spied her pink knickers.

Dirrrty bitch was wearing stockings, too!

Come dribbled out the tip of his cock – the front of his pants were slowly gluing themselves to his bell-end and nut sack. When it came to removing them later today, Anthony knew his pubic hairs would be a matted, knotted mess. The thought made his cock pulsate and ache. His hardness pushed with such force, Anthony thought the elastic in his underwear would snap, but it held firm.

The various sights up Glory's skirt and of her bending over in it had initially stirred his lust, but he'd quashed it. Anthony had thought by doing this, his journey home would have been uneventful, but he'd been wrong. And, thanks to his change in shift pattern, it meant he was leaving work at three in the afternoon at the height of summer – there would be weeks of torturous drives home and he'd already been a bad boy on more than one occasion.

His eyes flicked up and landed on the newspaper lying across the top of the dash – his hard-on wavered.

It's not my fault! Why was I cursed with a leg fetish?! He hammered his fist against his steering wheel. *Just drive off. Go on, do it*, his mind niggled. *Put the turn signal on, and pull off... I dare you!* Anthony put a shaking, hovering hand to his car's indicator, but he couldn't do it.

Tears welled in his eyes.

A knotted tightness developed in his gut.

"Just one more to add to my collection," he muttered. "*One!*" He looked up and out the car's windshield through glassy eyes – a stray tear splashed onto his cheek and slid down to his mouth. "I don't mean to hurt them, honestly…" He licked dry, cracking lips and tasted the salt from the single tear.

Another beaded his cheek. "Things tend to turn rough, that's all."

The headline on the paper caught his eye: *Stocking Strangler Slays Sixth*! But his gaze didn't remain. A cackle from across the road caught his attention. A bevy of beauties had gathered outside The Turntable pub, which was located down by the terminal ending for trains. It was a deserted site where the ladies of the night gathered, even though it was only four in the afternoon.

"Get yourself down there, mate," Gary from work had said. "Those dirty slappers will allow you to do anything to them. Fuck 'em in the arse, *anything*! They'll even gobble your gravy pipe for a fiver!"

However, Anthony was looking for a special kind of lady to add to his collection. He'd bagged a skinny, a fatty, a curvy, a college slut, a suit and granny. Now he was on the hunt for a chick with a dick – a pretty boy with a shlong looking to have a hot load dumped up her arse.

"What about boys?" Anthony had asked Gary on the quiet, not wanting to be overheard in the office. Gary had pulled a face of confusion, and Anthony had added, "You know, with tits!"

"You dirty little man!" Gary had grinned. "Look out for a woman wearing pink fuck-me boots. Her – or his – name is Francesca." Gary had then winked and walked off.

Thinking about it now, it hadn't just been Glory's ridiculously short skirt or the sight of so many tight-clad legs on the streets whilst driving home. No. Gary's information had been the catalyst. It had bubbled at the back of his brain since their conversation that morning, and had clearly chewed away at his sub-consciousness.

And then his mind emptied, his eyes clapping onto a tall woman wearing pink, thigh-high boots as she exited the pub. When she strutted, he could see she was wearing tights under her boots and a petite, flaming cerise-coloured skirt. Her make-up and hair was immaculate, and from this distance, Anthony would never have been able to tell she was a man in disguise.

Gary never said if she's had her cock cut off or if her magnificent looking tits were real... It didn't matter about her knockers, so long as the dick was there, rubbing itself against the gusset of her tights and knickers. *A new one for my collection,* he thought, rubbing his hard-on.

He started his car and pulled down to the pub where she stood. Anthony used the buttons on his door to operate the passenger-side window.

"Hey love, fancy a good time?" he asked, digging a fistful of twenty pound notes out of his wallet.

Her eyes seemed to light up, and she bent over and leaned on the door. She poked her head in and addressed him. "Sure, lover. What you looking for?"

"The works!"

She smiled and got in.

He drove her to a dark, secluded spot where the trains used to pass – but the rails had gone cold decades ago.

"Are you wet, baby?"

"Uh-huh," she said, biting her lip but not looking at him.

"I'll give you extra if you take your tights and knickers off and give them to me for my collection."

48

She snapped her head in his direction and gave him a cold stare. "It's *you*, isn't it! You're him." She grabbed the paper and threw it at him. "Some of the girls have been talking about you, the way you get them to peel their tights off…"

Fuck! He'd made the paper a few weeks ago after beating a woman and taking her tights by force. *The game's up…* Anthony thought. But, to his surprise, she rucked her skirt up and took her tights and knickers off.

"It's okay – I can play rough with the boys!"

Anthony's eyes were instantly drawn to the woman's cock growing between her smooth, muscular thighs.

"You want to touch it baby? You like the boys? I thought it was legs… That's what the papers and other girls say about you."

God, I want to run my hands up those thighs so badly. He nodded like a bobble-headed toy and reached out for the woman's penis. "You are Francesca, right?"

"The one and only." She smiled, pulling him closer. "Go ahead, put your mouth around it. You know you want to."

Anthony bent forward, his tongue protruding. "Thank you, Francesca."

"That's okay, hun…" she said, and then forcefully wrapped her tights around Anthony's neck and pulled with all her might.

As he bucked and thrashed against her, she rubbed her cock against his flip-flopping body to a pulsating orgasm. "Oh, I'm coming…" she gasped. Her thick, pearly-white jism splashed his face and found its way into his flapping mouth.

Anthony tried to get his fingers beneath the material constricting his breathing, but Francesca's hold was too tight.

"*Please…*" he chocked, spitting phlegm-like come onto the dashboard. His fingertips clawed at the silky-smooth tights to no avail. His mind scrambled, to try and think of a way out of his situation, but failed. In an attempt to elbow her in her guts, Anthony found he had no leverage, and so his blow to her midsection was weak, causing little to no damage.

The stranglehold intensified.

He then made an attempt to slam his hand down on the car's horn, but he couldn't reach it. His feet acted like flip-flopping fish out of water, and couldn't be used to stamp down on the accelerator. His eyes started to flicker and roll in his head. Dizziness set in and black spots danced before his off-kilter vision. He coughed and spluttered as the last of his air escaped him.

"Lucky number seven!" she whispered down his ear.

Dark Desires

Dusty Davis

1.

Hope Sullivan plopped the basket of clothes she was carrying down on the couch, spilling loose socks, as the doorbell chimed a second time. Fanning herself with her hand, trying to cool the beads of sweat that formed on her face, she pushed back the curtain of the bay window and peeked outside. A girl stood on the stoop. From the looks of her, Hope doubted she was even old enough to drink. She wore a short, pin striped skirt that hugged her tanned, toned legs, with a white button up blouse. A pair of black heels added at least four inches to her height. Hope let the curtain fall back into place and opened the door a crack.

"Can I help you?" Hope asked. The young girl held the handle of a luggage bag that had wheels on the bottom in one hand, and a small, black box in the other.

"Hi, my name is Desirae. I'm from the Deviant Pleasures Adult Toy Shoppe and am going around the neighborhood selling our brand-new product, Dark Desires." The girl released the handle of the bag, letting it fall to the ground where it landed with a thud. She held out the box for Hope to see. The lid was a dark maroon shade and appeared to be velvet. "This was our best-selling toy this past summer," Desirae explained as she ran her hand along the lid.

"Wait a minute, you're going door to door selling sex toys. Is that even legal?"

"Not just any sex toys, Dark Desires," Desirae replied with a smile too big to be genuine. "It's guaranteed to make your deepest, darkest desires a reality," she concluded with a smirk.

"Not interested," Hope countered with a huff as she started to close the door on the girl.

"I can give you a personal demonstration," the young girl said as she wedged her free arm in the frame to stop the door from closing all the way.

Hope ripped the door back open and stared at the girl, aghast. "No thank you. I don't need any of your products, now please leave my property," she sneered.

The smile on Desirae's face faltered as she took a step back from the door. "Yeah right, I know your type lady. Bored housewife, afraid to try anything new. You probably only spread your legs for your husband after it's been so long, you start to feel guilty about it," Desirae snickered.

"Now you listen to me, you little slut. It's none of your damn business what me and my husband do, now go peddle your sex elsewhere before I call the police and shut your operation down," Hope yelled before slamming the door in her face. It rattled the living room. She spun away from the door and stormed over to the couch and her basket of laundry. Sitting on top of the pile of clothes was the little black box with the maroon colored lid. She spun around on her bare feet, expecting to find the door open, and the girl standing there, but she remained alone. Hope picked the box up from the basket. It was heavier than she expected. She carried it into the kitchen and dropped it into the garbage can. Lifting the bag out, she tied the strings together, and took it the front door where she dropped it. Stepping over to the window, she pulled back the curtain and looked outside. The front walk was deserted. The girl wasn't anywhere on the street or at any of the neighbors houses. Hope swung the door open and tossed the bag out onto the front porch. She would have to remember to tell Doug to move it when he got home from the school after awhile.

Hope returned to her basket of clothes and carried them down the narrow hallway to the second door on the right, the master bedroom. She dumped the clothes onto the bed so she could sort them better and let her mind drift back to the girl at the door. The more she thought about it, the angrier she became, until she found herself cramming Doug's boxer shorts into the drawer without folding them first. She inhaled, taking a deep breath, and let it out slowly. Hope craved a cigarette even though she hadn't smoked since her previous marriage four years prior. She threw her last pack out along with her abusive husband and never looked back until now.

Hope made her way back to the bed and her pile of clothes, fighting the urge to smoke, when all of a sudden, she felt eyes on her back. Like someone was staring a hole through her. She spun around and found the room to be empty like it should have been. Hope crossed the small room to the single window and looked out. The front yard was also empty. The grass would need cut for the last time before it got too cold, she thought as she stared out at a white picket fence that dotted the yard like every other house on the block.

With a sigh, Hope turned back to her laundry and couldn't help but think about what Desirae had said to her. How she was bored with her sex life and afraid to try new things. *It's not boring, it's safe,* she thought as she picked up another pair of Doug's boxer shorts and tossed them into the drawer. *I don't have any desires,* Hope thought, knocking over the basket. It landed on the remote control for the television which blared to life on the wall. A couple were having sex on the screen. The girl was young and blonde, sitting on the guy's lap who moaned with pleasure as she bounced up and down. Hope scooped the remote up and shut the power off. The TV screen went blank.

She could feel her face turn red even though she was alone in the house. "What channel was that?" She asked herself, knowing that they didn't have any of the pay channels. Hesitantly, she pushed the power button bringing the couple back onto the screen. The guy was sitting behind a desk and when the camera zoomed in she immediately recognized the face of Doug. His head was thrown back as the blonde rode his cock with her tits pushed up against his chest. Shocked, Hope took a step closer to the television. The girl turned her head to face the camera and Hope saw that it was Desirae. "What the Hell?" Hope watched as she

55

climbed off her husband's lap and turned around allowing him to enter her from behind across his desk.

Hope felt like Desirae was staring directly at her, the way her eyes caught hers, and how her lips turned slightly up into a smile as Doug pumped into her. Anger coursed through her body, but she couldn't make herself shut the television off. She wondered who had recorded it and how it played in their bedroom. On the screen, Doug pulled out of Desirae who got down on her knees in front of him. Doug spurted cum over her big tits and mouth as she moaned with pleasure.

The sound of the front door closing brought Hope back to the present. She quickly shut the power off as the sound of heavy footsteps pounded down the hall. "Hey baby," Doug said poking his head in the door. "You okay, you looked a little flushed?"

"Yeah, I'm fine. I just carried a load of laundry up from the basement," she lied, unable to meet his eyes. Hope tossed the remote onto the bed and picked up more clothes to fold.

"What's wrong baby?" Doug asked stepping further into the bedroom.

"Nothing. I'm fine, just a little tired. Let me finish this basket of clothes and then I will get dinner started," she snapped.

"Okay baby, I guess I will get some work done in my office then," Doug said with his hands in the air, surrendering.

Hope watched him turn and walk away. His footsteps echoed loudly off the hardwood floor. She waited until the door of his office closed before returning to the pile of clothes, still shaking with anger.

***

Doug Sullivan dropped his bag on the desk, spilling papers out. Walking around, he plopped down in his chair. It protested under his weight, squealing with agony. Throwing his head back, he thought of Hope in her baggy sweats. He wished he would have went to her and lifted her shirt up and took her tits in his mouth, letting his tongue roam over her hard nipples.

He shook his head, bringing himself out of the fantasy as he sat up straight. Doug knew that he couldn't try something like that with Hope. It would freak her out. He had to wait until he was sure that she was in the mood before attempting to have sex with her. The last time that he tried just kissing her neck, she clammed up and didn't talk to him the rest of the night. Doug wished that she would tell him the guy's name that abused her and made her so ashamed of sex. He would track him down and beat the shit out of him. Doug always felt bad when he pushed her, but sometimes he couldn't help it.

Letting out a sigh, he dumped the rest of the papers he had to grade out of his bag, and started to arrange them when the small television on the wall behind him clicked on. He spun his chair around to face the screen and saw Hope sitting on the bed. "What the Hell?" He grabbed the remote from a side drawer in his desk and tried to change the channel but the screen remained on the bedroom. Hope lifted the grey sweatshirt over her head and tossed it to the floor. The camera panned back like someone was in the room filming it and a man appeared in front of the bed. He approached Hope casually with his shirt off. As he made his way to the bed, Hope twirled her finger around her nipple. Doug could see that it was already hard.

With his back still to the camera, the man undid his pants. Doug saw the man's ass crack as he jumped to his feet, sending the chair rolling backwards across the floor. On the screen, the man grabbed the back of Hope's head and shoved his cock into her mouth. She accepted it greedily, taking it in as far as she could before gagging. Saliva and pre-cum. drooled down her chin.

Again, Doug tried to change the channel but the screen stayed on Hope. He clicked the power button but the camera stayed on her as the man yanked her head back, pulling his cock from her throat. His hand found her neck and squeezed. The camera zoomed in on her face as she grimaced with pain. A tear slipped from her eye and rolled down her cheek, plopping onto her leg. The man then pushed her up to her feet and back against the wall. He spun her around and pulled her pants down around her knees. The man looked at the camera at his side and winked as he slipped his cock into Hope.

The screen turned to snow. Doug pressed the power button on the TV and the screen blinked out. "What the fuck was that?" He asked himself in the reflection of the television. Looking down at the papers on his desk, he knew that he wouldn't be grading them tonight. Bringing the remote back up, he clicked the TV back on and the local news appeared on the screen with the headline reading about another school shooting. Doug dropped the controller on the desk as he fell back into the chair, staring at the TV waiting for it to show him images that he didn't want to see. It didn't change.

He sat there for the longest time replaying what he saw in his mind. That was our bedroom, he thought to himself. She had on the same clothes that he saw her in

when he got home. *The video must have been recorded today, but how did it come up on the TV?* He wondered.

*** *** ***

The house was quiet except for the pounding of Hope's heart against her chest as she finished putting the clothes away. The anger she felt remained, but the trembling had subsided. She didn't know what she was going to do about Doug and his affair with Desirae. The picture of his face kept racing through her mind as she bounced on his cock. It had to be a mistake, a trick of the camera. It was just someone who looked like Doug, she thought pacing back and forth. That would explain how Desirae knew about their sex life, Hope contemplated. She paused in front of the television, wanting it to turn back on, so she could know the truth. Reaching up, she clicked on the power button. The screen lit up revealing a cooking show. Rachael Ray was making one of thirty minute meals.

Confused, Hope opened up the DVD player to find the tray empty. "How the Hell was it playing?" She whispered, her voice sounded strange. The image of Doug popped into her mind again. His mouth was open, moaning with pleasure. A tremor shook her body. She liked that look on his face and wished that it was her that made him that way.

The sound of something vibrating brought her back to reality. She looked around the bedroom and saw it on the nightstand beside the bed. The little black box was back. Hope rushed across the room and flipped the lid open. Inside a pink, phallus shaped, plastic thing vibrated against the inside of the box. She scooped it up and clicked the button on the bottom to shut it off. The vibrating stopped. Hope listened intently for the sound of footsteps on the hardwood floor outside in the hallway. None came. She placed the toy back in the box and gently closed the lid. It was made of velvet and had the letters DP scrolled across the top. Hope thought back to what Desirae had told her, that she worked for someone named Deviant Pleasures, and assumed that was what the letters stood for.

Carrying the box, Hope crossed the room to the window where she peered out, searching for the girl. Her husband's mistress. A school bus letting off children to their waiting parents were the only ones out on the street. A slight mist brought a premature dusk along with it. Streetlamps lined the sidewalks with their faint glow casting shadows on the ground beneath them.

Hope returned to the bed with the box and sat down on the edge. She flipped the lid up and removed the toy from inside. The handle was made of a soft silicone that ended with a rounded tip that reminded her of a tiny ice cream scooper. Dropping the box on the bed beside her, she examined the toy further. Dark Desires was scrawled into the handle in a fancy script. The image of Doug with his head thrown back in pleasure popped into her mind again. The vibrator came to life in her hands and she nearly dropped it.

She clutched it to her sweatshirt hoping to silence the noise. She didn't think that it would carry into the next room but she didn't want Doug to find her with the toy. The vibrations went through her shirt and she felt her nipples extending, becoming erect. Looking up at the open door, she slipped the toy under the sweatshirt. The scooped end caressed her nipples causing a moan to escape her lips.

A need filled Hope that she hadn't felt in a long time. She quickly pulled down her grey sweatpants around her knees and slid back to rest against the headboard. She slid the vibrator down her body until it came to rest on her clit. She pushed it harder into her, making herself squirm. With her free hand, she clutched the bedsheets as an intense orgasm rocked her body. She could taste blood from where she bit her lower lip as she shook with relief.

Hope turned the toy off and had the sudden feeling of being watched. She looked up to the door expecting Doug to be standing there, but the frame remained empty. Her eyes drifted to the window where a man stood under a streetlamp, in the rain, staring into the window. She felt his greedy eyes caress her skin and a shiver coursed through her body. With a yelp, she rolled off the bed, crashing to the floor. Yanking her pants up, she shoved the vibrator under the bed as the footsteps that she expected earlier finally sounded in the hall.

"Everything okay?" Doug yelled rushing into the room. Hope shot up to her feet and ran to the window. The street was once again deserted. She could still feel eyes on her, caressing her skin. Goose bumps peppered her arms. Shuddering, she hugged herself.

"Honey, are you okay?" Doug asked putting an arm around her shoulder.

"Yeah, I'm fine. I thought I saw something outside and cracked my foot on the edge of the bed," she lied as her eyes scanned the night for the stranger.

***

From the kitchen, Doug could hear Hope banging around. The smell of bacon drifted lazily through the house as he finished buttoning up his shirt. He looked over and saw the wall where Hope was pushed up against and fucked in the video. Shaking, he grabbed a necktie from the drawer and made his way back to the bed. He wrapped it around his collar but the tremors made him drop it to the floor. Doug bent over to pick it up and saw something else sticking out from under the bed. It was pink. He retrieved it and held it up to the light. It was a vibrator. Dark Desires was inscribed down the shaft of the plastic. The tip of the toy was moist like it was used recently.

Doug thought about Hope using it on herself and his erection was instantaneous. *Why is she hiding it?* He stared at the toy and wondered what else she was keeping from him, other than the man from the mysterious video. Doug shuddered and dropped the vibrator back to the floor where he found it.

He stepped into the hallway and followed the sound of Hope humming in the kitchen. She was serving up two plates full of eggs and bacon and he took a seat in front of one. "You are in a good mood this morning."

"Why wouldn't I be, I'm married to the best guy in the world," she told him with a kiss on the cheek. A smile formed on her face. Doug watched her suspiciously and tried to return the smile. He wondered if she could tell it was as forced as hers.

After a silent breakfast, Doug took his plate to the sink and rinsed it. He felt Hope's eyes on his back. He wanted to confront her about what he saw on the video and about the vibrator, but he didn't know how to approach the subject. Doug kept his mouth shut as he shimmied into his jacket. "I'm going to get going now," he told her with a quick peck on the lips. Thinking the whole time about the cock that had touched them. Repulsed, he turned away. "I might be late tonight, I will probably stay and get some things ready for the rest of the week."

"Okay baby, just give me a call and let me know for sure when you will be home," she was quick to answer with another forced smile.

Yeah, I bet you want to know when I will be home so I don't catch you with that man, Doug thought angrily as he yanked the door open. Outside was cool and breezy, but the sun was out, shining down. He made his way to the car and climbed inside. The engine roared to life and he backed out into the street. He glanced through the bay window trying to see Hope as he drove away. She wasn't in the living room. Doug drove down the block and pulled the car to the side of the road and took his cell phone from his back pocket. He wasn't going to the work today. There wasn't any way he would be able to deal with teenagers all day. He dialed the high school and told them that he wouldn't be in, that he had some personal things to take care of.

***

Hope waited until Doug's car turned down the corner and then ran to the door. She flipped the deadbolt into place and headed for the bedroom. Stripping out of her clothes, she dropped them to the floor beside the bed, and retrieved the vibrator from underneath where she hid it the night before. Plopping onto the bed, the sheets were cool against her bare skin. Scooting up to the top of the mattress, she clicked the toy on. It vibrated in her hands. Her eyes drifted to the window. The curtain was pulled back exposing the clear blue sky. The guy standing in the rain last night came into her mind. *Let him watch,* she thought massaging her already erect nipples with the toy.

Bringing her other hand down, she fondled the moist spot between her legs. She thought about Doug and how his fingers felt when he touched her there. Her mind drifted back to the stranger that had watched her through the window. She could feel his stare on her naked body, caressing her skin as she rubbed herself. Harder now, she brought the vibrator down to her clit and felt the soft plastic against her. The vibrations seemed to grow harder the closer she came to orgasiming. Just as she thought she was going to explode, the television on the wall came to life. The screen showed Doug's office with him sitting in his chair. A blonde-haired girl, that Hope assumed was Desirae was on her knees in front of him. His cock throbbed as she took him in her mouth, sucking him deep. Hope pushed the vibrator harder against her clit as she watched Desirae's mouth come free, dripping wet. She climbed on top of Doug as Hope came hard, falling back onto the bed with her eyes closed.

She laid there lazily, pinching her nipples between her fingers, and listened to the moaning sounds coming from the television. Then she felt the mouth on her pussy. She sat bolt upright, pushing herself up on her elbows. The dark-haired stranger from outside was between her legs. He pushed them further apart and stuck his tongue inside her. She grabbed a handful of his hair and pulled trying to get his mouth off her, but then his abnormally long tongue hit a spot that brought her to climax. Hope gripped his hair tighter, but pushed his face harder into her. He licked every inch of her, making her cum again, harder than she ever had before.

Hope wrapped her thighs around the stranger's head, squeezing, making him lick harder, faster. Another orgasm rocked her body making her crash down onto the bed. His mouth left her pussy and she sat up on her elbows getting a good look at him for the first time. He had curly, brown hair and eyes the color of ice. Without breaking eye contact, he slowly undid the buttons on his shirt and threw it to the floor by the bed. Hope took in his rock hard body and watched as he opened the jeans of his pants and took his cock out. It poked up towards his chin that was shiny with her juices. With the palm of his hand, he wiped his face and then hooked his hands under her thighs and pulled her back down to the bed. Straddling her right leg, he brought her left up over his shoulder, and then entered her wet pussy with ease. His cock filled her completely, stretching her.

She clenched the bed sheets tightly as he pumped into her, slowly at first and then gaining speed. She wanted to cry out with pleasure but the sound got lost in her throat as her orgasm built. He pushed further into her, putting more of his weight on her. She felt like she was being crushed. Hope could feel herself hanging on the precipice of ecstasy, about to fall off, and then it was gone. "No, don't stop," Hope pleaded as his cock slipped out of her. She turned over and saw Doug spin the stranger around and punch him in the face.

***

The words that came out of Hope, hurt Doug more than the broken hand he received by punching the man in the face. *She didn't want him to stop fucking her,* he thought as he shook his hand trying to get the feeling back in his knuckles that were already swelling to twice their normal size. Looking up, he saw the stranger staring at him, unfazed by the blow. He looked the man up and down as he zipped up his pants. Hope crawled on her hands and knees behind him on the bed. Anger filled Doug's veins, it coursed through him like fire, burning him from the inside out. He rushed at the man, tackling him to the bed, barely missing Hope. They bounced off the mattress to the floor with the man landing on top of Doug.

The wind was knocked from his lungs. He laid there under the man for what seemed like an eternity before he sat up relieving some of the pressure. His fist raised up in the air and then shot down like a bullet, connecting with his jaw. He knew that he should move, but couldn't get out from under the stranger as another blow rained down on him. His fist connected with his nose, shattering it. Blood poured down his face. Through squinted, tear filled eyes,

Doug could see it stained on the man's fist as he landed another punch to his temple.

Somewhere behind the man, Doug could hear Hope shouting, but he couldn't make out the words. It seemed like she was trying to help him, but he wasn't sure. His vision darkened at the corners of his eyes as the words of Hope pleading for the man to not stop fucking her played in his mind.

***

Hope pulled at the stranger's big arms, trying to pull him away from Doug. Over his shoulder, she could see what was left of his face, and it wasn't much. His nose was mashed into his head and covered with blood. His eyes were glazed, staring blankly behind the man. Hope scratched the stranger's back, raking her nails down his skin. She could see the angry, red welts in her wake. He swung back his elbow and caught her in the nose. Blood erupted like a volcano. She flew backwards through the air and landed hard on the floor, jarring her spine. She sat up in time to see the man bring another fist down into Doug's face as she watched through blurry eyes.

The sound of high heels clicked on the hardwood floor and was followed by Desirae walking into the bedroom with a smile on her face. "I see you played with Dark Desires," she said through her blood red lips. Hope crawled up to her knees as Desirae put a gentle hand on the man who shifted his gaze from Doug's shattered face to her toned legs. A pang of jealousy shot through Hope's body that she quickly shook off.

Desirae reached down by the bed and picked the vibrator up and ran it through her fingers. The man watched her longingly. Noticing his eyes on her, she ran a hand down his chiseled chest. "You really need to be careful what you wish for," Desirae said turning her attention back to Hope. "There are always consequences for the things we desire," she taunted with a smile. Hope watched as she wrapped her arms around the man's waist, and turned the vibrator on. It buzzed making Desirae giggle as they faded out of existence, like a bolt of lightning in a black velvety sky, leaving her alone with her dead husband.

Twenty-Six Photographs

Adrian Ludens

Jeff Granger took the day off from work just to wait for the mail to arrive.

He lounged, albeit restlessly, in his leather recliner. He sipped a gin and tonic, savoring the aroma, relishing the taste. A solo piano composition of longing, loneliness, and regret emanated from his stereo speakers- courtesy of Erik Satie's genius.

When he heard the muted clink of the mailbox lid dropping back down, Jeff strolled to his front door, opened it, and retrieved the contents the postman had left. Two pieces of junk mail, a bill and a large manila envelope made up the day's delivery. The manila envelope was addressed to him. He tossed the other mail onto the entryway table. With his wife, Heather, out of the house and at work, he could examine the contents of the envelope at his leisure. Jeff sat down in his recliner, tore open the

envelope and retrieved a lengthy typed letter. It read:

"Mr. Granger,

Enclosed, you will find the prints from the two rolls of film that I took two nights ago. Per your instructions, I used black and white film. I don't understand why you wanted black and white rather than color, but I followed your instructions to the letter.

I find the grainy quality of the prints heightens rather than diminishes the illicit nature of what took place. Why you would want to put yourself through seeing these is beyond me. Two or three photographs would be sufficient for an uncontested divorce in any court of law. Yet you were insistent that I take twenty-six. With all due respect, you are a glutton for punishment, Mr. Granger.

But I digress.

On the night the enclosed pictures were taken, I parked one block south of your residence (on the nearest cross street) and followed your wife when she left the house. I kept pace at a discrete distance. We reached her initial destination, a sports bar on Seventh Avenue. After fifteen minutes, she left the bar with a tall man with an athletic build. He appeared to be between the ages of twenty-five and thirty. He got into her vehicle and they drove away together. Again, I followed at a safe distance.

We drove about ten minutes to a residential area on the west side of town. Taking note of the driveway they turned into, I drove past and was lucky enough to find an apartment complex a few blocks down the street. I parked my sedan and moved back down the street on foot. I carried my camera around my neck with an assortment of lenses ensconced in my jacket pockets.

As I neared the house, a pickup truck approached and I had to duck behind a hedge. A tall man with longish hair, maybe 30 to 35, hurried up the sidewalk and entered the front door without knocking.

I stationed myself below the living room window, crouching, so as not to be seen. The house next door (behind me) was dark and the driveway empty. I felt safe in assuming no one was home. A thick stand of lilac bushes stood behind the house, blocking prying eyes from that direction. I found that staying concealed was not as great a problem as I had anticipated. I was able to lean against the

trunk of a large tree on the south side of the house and look directly into the living room, while remaining undetected. I chalk up to either sheer luck on my part or sheer stupidity on theirs, that the curtains remained open the entire time.

Now comes the part of my job that I take no pleasure in, but I must relate everything, just as it

happened. Inside the house, your wife, the two aforementioned men, and a stocky, dark-complexioned

third man who I presume to be the home's owner, all stripped out of their clothing. As I focused my camera and started clicking pictures, my stomach sank. Mr. Granger, I hope you'll forgive me for saying so, but your wife is the most shameless sybarite I have ever had the misfortune to encounter. My apologies for using such an arcane term; I mean a sensualist, though a word more vulgar—harlot,

perhaps—might serve in this instance.

The prints, although grainy, show in detail your wife engaging in oral, vaginal, and anal penetration with all three men, in succession and often simultaneously. You will note that none of the men used condoms. Far from being concerned, you wife appeared to take great pleasure in this detail.

I am by no means a prude, Mr. Granger, but I must question the complete lack of morals your wife exhibited, to say nothing of her three "lovers." I put that word in quotations to show that I use it with deep cynicism. The depraved and prurient actions that took place can hardly be considered anything less than animalistic.

And the sanitary concerns. I was sickened as I watched not one or two, but all three men take turns engaging in anal sex with your wife, pulling out and finishing in her mouth. I feel ill just thinking about it. Be warned: contained herein, you will find a photograph of your wife with her head tilted back in an apparent effort to "gargle" their combined discharge. It is third from last, if you wish to skip it.

Your wife let the men double penetrate her—in succession. When one man climaxed inside her (an assessment I make based on facial grimacing and other indicators), he would pull out and the next would take his place. Your wife either stroked or fellated the third man. They rotated in this way until the men completed their rotation.

When they finished their decadent exploits, two full hours later according to my wristwatch, your wife was drenched in semen. The last few pictures I took show her condition when her lust was finally sated. All four participants retired upstairs. As they returned downstairs to the living room one by one, it became apparent that they'd all showered away any evidence of their actions. They didn't know about me, or the photographs I took. So, evidence remains, and in plentitude.

In closing, I must admit I've never witnessed such a display of excessive debauchery. While some might perceive (or even criticize) you for being milquetoast, I must compliment your level-headed approach to gathering evidence to build your case. The hurt, betrayal and jealousy you must feel are more than any man should have to bear.

You have my sincerest condolences. I hope the evidence before you, does not upset you too much. Don't shoot the messenger, as the saying goes. You asked me to do a job and I did it. I'm sorry you had to see these prints. I wish you all the best in what is sure to be a speedy and successful divorce filing.

Yours,

Michael Nabors,

Jensen Investigative Services"

Jeff Granger reread the private investigator's letter. Then he rose, switched out Satie for Ravel's Bolero, sat back down, and finished his drink in two gulps. He picked the manila envelope back up and slid the prints out with trembling hands. He closed his eyes and inhaled the sweet smell of the developing solution still fresh on the prints. He counted them without looking at them; twenty-six prints, just as the man had promised.

Two days ago, Heather had turned twenty-six years old.

And though it was her birthday, his wife had arranged for Jeff to receive the present; a graphic,

transgressive photo gallery starring her, custom-made for him. All Jeff needed to do, she had said with an impish grin on her face, was supply the photographer. Jeff smirked at the thought of the investigator lurking, snapping photos, and thinking he remained undetected. Jeff guessed the man, despite his puritanical protests, had developed a second set of prints for himself. "Methinks thou dost protest too

much," Jeff murmured, and chuckled.

He sat back and looked at the photographs one by one, taking his time, and studying every detail. Heather seemed to revel in the wanton acts. Jeff studied her face, her eyes, and her expressions with rapt fascination. Perhaps, next time, they would make plans to allow the photographer entry, so that she could look straight into the camera's eye. Jeff's cock remained rigid and twitching as his eyes drank in each exhilarating new view of his wife playing porn slut. As the music built and reached its

insistent crescendo, Jeff gave in to his urges and fanned the photos out on the floor. He unzipped his slacks, took his throbbing erection in hand, and began to stroke.

Love Craft

Jason D'Aprile

Thump.
Thump.
On the wall.
I know you can hear me.
I know you enjoy it all.

Howard closed his eyes tight enough to make his brow hurt. It was madness. Uncontrollable madness. And it was infecting him. He knew he should move his bed away from that wall, that just beyond--mere inches away--was a devilment that was destroying him like a vile sickness deep within his soul.

He knew he should just move, leave this cursed old building, but he couldn't. Perhaps it was blind stubbornness, but he felt something more. Inky, black tendrils seemed to latch onto him each night as the demons just beyond went at it like some kind of hellish carnal beasts. He'd seen the man once, going past in the dark corridor and the smile plastered on that shadowy face had given Howard chills.

The man--if indeed he could be called that--moved with a bizarrely ethereal slide, as if his limbs were mere illusions and he seemed to float along the ground.

And the woman... The times he'd seen her, his gaze averted from the sheerness of her dress, but the way she moved, like a studied whore of Babylon, burned in his mind and awoke a sickening hunger. And when the two walked by him together, the man putting his hands places no decent woman would allow *right* in public, Howard's mix of disdain and disgust melded into a confusing concoction of wanton lust. He tried to stamp it down, ignore it, even deny its existence, but in the end, he was powerless.

So, he sat upright on the bed, eyes so painfully closed listening to the rabid baying of wolves against the wall behind, his right hand clenched around his own erect cock, jerking in clumsy, haphazard motions. Tears streamed from his closed lids, as he tried not to breath, to not make a sound at all.

He could feel something though, a strange cold taint to the air as the pounding continued. With a gasp and a whimper, his whole body shivered as he felt it; a cold, slimy caress against the side of his face. His head whipped back, eyes suddenly wide open, face contorted in fear, and he could see them.

She was held down, legs and arms spread wide, forced into submission by black and gray tentacles, their piercing suction cups cutting into her skin, leaving bloody circles against her wrists and ankles.

She was screaming out, pulling at her cephalopodic bondage, trying to get away, but then, as he watched transfixed, not really.

The man, if you could call it that, was almost human. Four limbs like a man's, but elongated, pocked with suction cups, ending in distorted hands and feet, each with smaller tentacles instead of phalanges. Beneath each main arm, were more much longer tentacles that rose up high, filling the ceiling like a mass of worms, before coming down to be her bondage. His skin color was a blotchy mess of white, blue, black, and gray, though his torso and head were very much still human in appearance.

He could feel his own hand tightening further around his own cock, stroking it furiously, feeling a level of arousal completely alien to him. The vision of their unholy union stayed focused within his consciousness, as he saw the man upright pushing his bizarre writhing, tendril cock deep into her womanhood. Her expression changed from surprise, to fear, to discomfort, to finally letting out a deep wanton wail, as he plunged back and forth into, leaving more and more discolorations against her skin with each motion.

Somewhere--and Howard had lost all track of his own body except the pressures against him--he could feel more of the tendrils wrapping around him too. Looking up from his bodiless viewing point, he could see more of the man's--whatever he... it was-- tentacles piercing the wall between their rooms, curving like panicked worms as they pushed through the wall.

Howard watched with sickened fascination as the... man pulled his unholy penis from within her, arched his back, and shoved himself forward just enough. Howard was transfixed by the bizarre demon's massive member. A tendril of ungodly proportions with the head of a human cock. With one tentacled hand, the creature pried her mouth open and held it, as the monstrous cock slithered up her belly, between her ample cleavage and down into her mouth.

He watched as her eyes grew wide with panic, but still the man shoved deep, back and forth, as she tried to scream and wept uncontrollably. The smile on the man's face grew ever wider as her panic increased, and then he relented, slipping his cock out again. Howard shuddered as she yelled and, pinned down as she was, lunged her mouth after it in an attempt to not let it escape her grasp.

He slapped her, still smiling, then plunged down her throat again and she responded like a brazen beast, huffing and crying, relentless to give and take his pleasure. Then, he pressed a hand down onto her forehead, pinning her head to the bed, shoved himself back off her and with barely a moment's notice, the tentacles wrapped around her flipped her over and he repenetrationed her. He fucked her more rapidly now, as Howard felt his own hand matching its pace.

Howard began to scream, as the couple did, and his vision went black with an explosion of foul-smelling dark inky effluence erupted from between her legs and her body slumped down as the demon's cock lay still again. Somewhere, far away, Howard could feel warm congealed wetness against his own taut knuckles.

For a moment, there was silence, then a raucous laughter from behind him, through the wall. Howard wanted to cry, to hide, to flee. Instead, eyes closed, head down, he cried. After an interminable time passed, he got up, cleaned himself up, and went out for a walk.

Thereafter, his nights were hounded with visions and softly spoken, sharp whispers of secrets no man should hear. He tossed and turned to nightmarish images of undying beasts of pure horror and torment burning worlds and devouring suns just for the sheer pleasure of bringing an end to all things. Sometimes, their death laden eyes stared at him as they lashed out with their tendrils.

He woke up screaming almost every night, bed robe and sheets soaked with sweat. And sometimes in the worst of it, he'd feel the tendrils come again, touch him gently, until one day he looked down, his hand against his own cock, and he saw the other. That one-eyed demon staring up at him erect for inches.

With a gasp, he grabbed it with his other hand, and in clumsy, pained motions, began stroking in tandem. His vision faded to that apocalyptic neverland, where imponderable gods crushed the fiery landscape beneath their horrible appendages. The harder he went, the more vibrant the vision became. He became aware of the stench of smoke and sulfur in the air, as his breath wavered and he coughed.

Howard struggled to return to his four walls, to the mundanity of his life, but he couldn't. The monsters turned now and were heading toward him, and he couldn't stop jerking, his hands trapped in a cycle of self-destruction. He pulled harder and harder, gripping more and more tightly, until he could hear himself screaming.

As they loomed over him, endless teeth and tendrils everywhere, he felt his climax and pulled with a furious anger, screaming louder than ever. He heard a sickeningly wet ripping sound, then an inhuman howl of pain, as his left hand pulled up holding the writhing, dismembered alien cock. The gods, he knew them older than then even the universe, looked down at him with detached bemusement, then faded away.

He was left sitting up in his bed, staring down at the still moving member in his left hand, his right hand still slackly holding his own. With a gasp, he stood up quickly, nearly falling off the bed, and rushed to his wardrobe closet. With one hand, he rifled through the small piece and pulled out a simple leather and wood box he used to hold special things. Hurriedly dumping it out, he shoved the cock into the box it barely fit in and slammed the lid shut.

Turning around and looking at the room quickly, he breathed heavily, moved to the bed and set the box down. Twenty minutes later, cleaned up and properly dressed, he left with the box held securely under one arm.

***

At the end, it was hard to write with the constant pain, but he knew he must. His last instructions were meant to be followed to the letter, not to be questioned or second guessed. There was a box, deep in the closet, sealed shut. It was a simple, small box of leather and wood. It must be put into his casket *just* before his final placement in the ground.

It was, he had said, a possibly strange request, but surely others had put upon far more burden to their survivors then he. So it was requested and, despite some questions and strange looks, so it was done. Just before the casket closed, unknown hands gingerly placed the box upon his chest and into eternal slumber with him.

***

So far beneath the ground, no one could hear the cracking of wood, but there in the dark was a strange slither and a building wet trail of thick slime moving from the broken box and down the body. Squirming beneath the body's trousers, a cheap thin fabric bit of work, they wrapped upon his now eternally erect member.

Slowly, the hollow of the dismembered piece slid down over the lifeless cock, and strands of ripped flesh began to spread out across the crotch of the body, as it completed its journey. With a gasp and a shudder, the body moved. Through every pore, rank liquid flowed out and life returned to Howard again.

He could feel his limbs stretching, bending in bizarre, unnatural ways, and felt the bumps of his skin first pop up, then expand. He smiled, as feeling returned, and in the deep black depths, Howard let out the kind of uninhibited laughter of sheer joy that he had never once known in life, as both his hands slipped down, tearing aware the fabric of his suit, and wrapped around his brand new life.

His Favorite Phantom

Matthew R. Davis

Toby had thought that everything would change now that he'd shifted himself within the world – had hoped to gain a new perspective on a life that had grown listless and dull. But when he got to work on Monday morning, everything was just the same: his fading *Revenge of the Sith* mug, the only thing he'd ever won, was already dirty in the sink when he went to make his morning coffee, and his most hated radio station droned the same inane songs and banter as if dragging him into a time loop. He forced his hands into their daily routine and told himself that these things took time. He wouldn't become a new man overnight, but he'd taken a decisive step forward by moving into his new flat.

He couldn't wait to pull up in that unfamiliar driveway, to turn that freshly-cut key and be greeted by well-known furnishings in strange rooms. To sit on his old couch and stare at the new walls, marked as his by the three posters he'd been lugging around since he'd moved out of home, drinking a beer and leaving moisture rings on his freshly-bought coffee table. To hear a voice calling from the bedroom – *Toby? Toby!* – asking how his day was, asking him to come lay himself down for a while –

Ah, but that last bit would have to wait, much as it had been waiting for some years now. But even the thought that this new flat would be just as empty of life and love as the old one couldn't shake Toby's desire to return to it, to penetrate it, to own it. When the end of another shift announced itself with a collective sigh of relief, Toby walked out to his car with less drag in his step than usual.

Coming home to all this change gave him a warm buzz of competence. He'd managed this task on his own again; he had some iota of control over his life. Toby sat on his couch and drank a well-earned beer, staring idly at the scantily-clad model on the cover of a nearby magazine and wondering if he should christen the flat with its first self-spilled milk before deciding to have a shower instead. And with that, his life fell back into its well-worn track.

After microwaving a crappy pizza for dinner, Toby flicked through his well-thumbed book on slasher movies – but it was the first time he'd enjoyed it here in these new digs, so that was okay... just as it was okay to watch *The Hunt for Candy Parker* afterward, because these walls had surely never borne witness to it before, and its old-fashioned charms never failed to make him feel at home. AJ Stanley's nude scene still gave him a swift tingle of arousal, and the shoddy FX of its axe murders brought an indulgent smile to his lips.

When it was time for bed, Toby had another subtle differentiation to enjoy. His old mattress had long been in need of replacement, so he'd been pleased when the land agent – an odd little fellow, rather vague – had eventually agreed to let him keep the queen-size that the last tenant had left behind when she moved on. The inherited bed lay soft but firm beneath him like familiar flesh, and there was a strange comfort in letting himself be moulded into the shallow concavity of an absent body. He did so tonight, and felt as cosy as a child cuddled to his mother, or a lover to a lover. Sleep came for him on swift wings.

At some deep point of the night, Toby dreamed that he was no longer alone in his new bed. A naked figure brushed smooth skin against his and whispered welcomes into his ear. He reared up to see, and there she was – her sandy-blonde hair spread out across his pillow, her oh-so-familiar eyes sparkling with happiness. He laughed in delight, realising that the bedroom around him was now the kitsch teenage one he'd seen on his flat-screen TV that very night. He was about to make love to Candy Parker, in her bed, during her nude scene. And why not? This was a dream; it was 1981 and it was now and never, and the film stock that had recorded her fictional beauty had preserved it for eternity. If this was the only way she could be his, then he would take her that way and be glad.

"Oh, baby," he sighed. "You're the most beautiful girl I ever saw."

She giggled, just the way she did in the film. *"Aw, Toby. You really feel that way?"*

"Let me show you how I feel."

"Toby?" she said, a teasing question as he pressed his insistent self against her, and then *"Toby!"* as he popped inside – a statement of declaration, of desire. It felt so real he almost pinched himself to be sure, but he knew full well this was a fantasy, one of his oldest and best-loved... and so, with her pale blue eyes burning into his, he blessed his imagination for this boon, and he took her.

But even in the dream, he couldn't manage to take her far before his own body's will broke in a sudden spasm of conclusion. It had been too long, and this dream-Candy was just so *vivid*. Her rapture-flushed face, her slick and slender body, the way she pushed back relentlessly against his strokes – it was all too much – just as always – once again he was sitting before his parents' TV with the sound right down, long after midnight, rewinding and rewinding until that all-too-brief loop of Candy in the bedroom had appeased his raging teenage urge. He fell into a deeper darkness, the pits of night at the centre of her eyes, and didn't land until his alarm clock startled him into sudden consciousness.

***

The novelty of a new home wore off faster than he'd hoped, which was just as fast as he'd expected. Coming back to the flat on the second day, he already felt like he'd played this scene out a thousand times and would do it another thousand before anything changed. Toby was working his way into the same old depression when there was a knock at the front door.

Well, this was out of the ordinary. Hoping it wasn't someone with bad news – or well-dressed young men with Good News – Toby pulled himself out of the couch to see.

"Hey man, how you doing?"

The guy standing on Toby's section of porch, grinning in welcome, was short and fit and Asian with grey seeping into the edges of his well-kept hair.

"Hello?"

"My name is Joe. I'm you next-door neighbour. I come to say, welcome aboard!"

"Oh, thanks." Toby opened the screen door and offered his hand. Joe moved a smouldering roll-up to his left and met the shake firmly with his right. "I'm Toby. You been here long?"

"I live here for five years," his neighbour shrugged. "Not so bad. Better to have a new neighbour, though."

Who had the old one been? Toby remembered the land agent telling him she had been in her mid-thirties, on welfare, a little high-strung.

"So what you doing? You having a beer? Come over, have a beer with me. I always like it to meet new people."

Toby was curious, so he locked his door behind him and carried a Heineken through the next one over. Once he was settled on Joe's couch, looking around at the silk wall hangings of tigers and the fish swimming blankly in a transparent box in the corner, his host fetched himself a beer and sat across from him with a wide grin. It was probably supposed to be welcoming, but Toby couldn't help thinking for a moment that Joe was cruelly amused, mocking him.

"So, what you do for work?"

Toby told him, trying to sound at least a little enthusiastic and failing.

"Ah, but we don't talk about the work. You like to party, have some beers and play the music?"

"Sure, sometimes," he admitted, leaving out the fact that they were usually parties of one. Joe grinned, tapped the neck of Toby's beer with his own – Tiger, what else? – and sat back, pleased.

"Good, good! Me too. Fuck man, you only living the once, you know what I'm saying? But no, you try telling that to the fat bitch used to live next door."

"Oh, in my flat?"

"Yeah. Miranda, she called. Always the complaining – my music too loud, I'm drunk, I yelling at people over the road, blah blah blah. She got nothing better to do, she just sit there and watch soapies and smoke all day. She got the asthma. No man coming around to hump-a-dump, not the way she look."

"Uh, right. So you weren't on the best of terms, then."

Joe sneered, took a swift swig of beer. "Not sad she moved on."

"Where'd she go?"

"Who know where anyone go?" Joe shrugged. "Just happy not to have to listen to her anymore."

After a while, Toby would have been equally happy not to have to listen to Joe – the man never seemed to stop talking. His beautiful and happy sons, his decades in the produce markets, his stints in jail for aggravated assault; his ex-wife, that bitch, and the parade of women that had allegedly graced his bed since – and the new immigration laws that were too lax, and the Africans he distrusted and the junkies he despised and *fuck*, did he go on. It was an hour before Toby found an appropriate juncture in the monologue to make his apologies and leave, his head ringing with tales he'd never asked to hear.

There was a more welcome presence awaiting him on the other side of consciousness. As he slipped into the cool dark pool of sleep that night, Toby felt his limbs brushing against bare skin, and the well-known feel of his favourite phantom brought his libido crashing to attention.

"You've come back to me," Candy purred, wrapping a silk-smooth hand around his rising cock. *"Toby, I've been alone for so long. Will you be mine?"*

"I've always been yours."

"Say that again," she sighed, a rattle in her breath, husky with lust.

"I'm yours," he panted as he slid deep into her hot cradle, feeling her arms and legs wrap around him. "I will always be yours."

Well, in a way it was true, wasn't it? He'd long been Candy Parker's supplicant, making obeisance to her with one hand, and on some level his fantasy had always been to somehow lay with her. And now he was, and it was inside his own head, so why should he be reluctant to say anything?

But he felt oddly reticent to say her name – as if to admit it out loud, even in slumber, would render the whole idea ludicrous and send this sad sack of a man spinning back into consciousness, to remind him that he was alone, alone, alone – the kind of man who replaced real women with wet dreams about fictional teenagers, and even then couldn't control her... or indeed, himself.

For that ecstatic explosion was building inside him, and he gasped and knew there was no going back, and he ground harder and faster as she grew around him and pulled him ever closer and deeper into her dark universal mass, and just before he jerked and cried out she pressed her dark eyes up close to his and wheezed, *"Love me."*

He only felt free from those eyes when his alarm barked at him like a disturbed dog and brought him out into the morning light.

***

The novelty had completely worn off now, and the next day was the same as his days had always been. Toby woke and worked and came home, and he'd only been ruminating over his beer for ten minutes when Joe knocked on his door and invited him over for a drink – the beginning of another routine. He sat and smiled and listened to his neighbour talk and wondered where his own, real-life Candy was at this very moment. Was she perhaps sipping vodka and listening to a middle-aged acquaintance bitch about fellow tenants, also dreaming of finding that special someone?

"You like that?" Joe prompted, and Toby nodded back into reality.

"Huh?"

"A bit of the hump-a-dump?" Joe grinned and made the accompanying gesture with his hips. On him it looked natural, possessive, virile; Toby knew that if he tried it, it would look awkward, impotent, offensive. "When you take the one-eye dog to the fish market?"

"Oh, hell yeah," Toby agreed, though the length of time since he'd had anything of the sort would have made Joe gape in amazement.

"I knew it. Hey, you a good man. We should go out sometime, get some women. You want another beer?"

The idea of hitting the tiles with Joe was a disturbing one – he had visions of shady clubs where he was the only white man, of exotic beverages that would make his head spin, of ending the night in humiliating drunken impotence atop a Thai prostitute – but as the man fetched some more beers from the kitchen, Toby decided that a night out was just what he needed. Not with his nattering neighbour, but alone – a single man out on the prowl. Why not? It had been far too long, and the succulent dreams he'd been having of late had awakened the beast in his body. It called for meat, and he longed to feed it more than scraps of memory and fantasy.

When he managed to pull himself away from Joe's monologue, Toby had a shower and threw on some of his best clothes. He made himself look as good as he could, told himself that some guys had to work with much worse, and walked down to the nearest pub.

It was quiet – well, it was a Wednesday night – but there were a couple of single women loitering about the place, pretending to be busy on smart phones or drinking at the poker machines. Toby found a street mag to peruse and quickly downed two beers, watching the women. One looked not unlike a middle-aged Helen Mirren and might possibly up for a spite-fuck to irritate an absent husband, but he'd have to compete with a mechanical bandit for her attention. There was a younger woman he liked the look of, a busty urban bohemian around his age who looked like she'd been around the block, but she seemed to vanish between drinks. The others were fat and colourless, used up, asexual animals who'd traded physical lust for a doomed and addictive avarice.

Toby pondered the wisdom of this endeavour as he drained his beer and stared listlessly at the pages before him. Maybe he should just go home, stop fooling himself –

"Toby? Toby!"

The woman he'd thought had left was at his elbow now, staring at him. At first he thought she was accusing him of something.

"It *is* you, isn't it? Toby, oh, I forget the last name, from Hamilton High?"

"Yes…?" Now that he'd been prompted, he realised that he should have known her all along. "Oh, hang on – "

"Rebecca Carroll. Well, it's Rebecca Marr now, legally, anyway. We had English together?"

"Yes, yes!" He remembered her now – a sullen, well-developed girl with the habit of braiding beads into her forelock when she was bored, which was always. "Of course. How are you?"

She sighed. "I've been better. Maybe a drink will cheer me up?"

Toby bade her sit and ordered what she wanted. They discussed their school days first, and as they spoke he snatched brief glances at her. Rebecca was no AJ Stanley, but she seemed to have retained much of her teenage figure. What he could see of it stood firm in defiance of bloat and gravity, and her face was deepened in its allure by the colourful life she'd lived since he'd last seen her. It seemed that her post-school years had not been much better than his – freefall into a hated job, the realisation that her dreams were beyond her, the wrong man that it had taken her ten years to leave completely. She liked to talk, more so with each drink, but unlike Joe she was quite bearable. When Toby next checked his phone, two hours had passed.

"In a hurry to get away?" she asked, hiding hurt behind the jibe.

"No, not at all. Just wondering how much longer we have before they kick us out."

"I'm sure we could squeeze in another couple before we go," she said, and Toby bought more drinks, thinking: *oh, wow. I think this is going to work.*

"You know," she soon declared, "you seem to be a lot cuter than I remember."

Toby smiled, pleased at this rare compliment. "Thanks! But you... you don't seem to have changed much at all. Well, what I mean is, Bec, you still look young. And pretty."

Rebecca smiled, patted his thigh. "Thank you! It's hard work being a woman, you know. So much maintenance. After a while, all this stuff just starts to go south."

She cupped her breasts, as if Toby had somehow missed them in that low-cut top. He stared, and let her see him staring, and she smiled again. Her hands slowly slipped away from her chest and away down her jeans-clad thighs. She took another sip of her drink and watched him, amusement in her eyes.

"Drink up, mister. We'd better be going soon."

A few minutes later their glasses were empty on the bar, and last drinks were called. Rebecca shook her head for both of them and took Toby's arm as they headed for the door. The cool night air only made her cling to him harder.

"Do you need a taxi?" he asked, in case he'd misread things.

"Do you want me to go?"

She stared at him honestly for a moment, smart cracks and drunken bravado laid aside, and he saw that she was just as lonely as he.

"Actually, I want you to come home with me," he said, and she smiled and snuggled into him as they walked back to his flat.

When they arrived, Rebecca went to the bathroom, then walked around and commented politely on his posters and furnishings. He saved her the trouble by drawing her beery mouth up into his, thrilled that he was finally asserting his manhood again. She moaned into his kiss and began pawing at his body. After a minute or so of preamble, he guided her into the bedroom and they collapsed onto the mattress, fumbling at each other's clothes.

As he stripped her bare, Toby worried that he'd had too much to drink. What if, after all this time, he brought a woman home only to find himself unable to uphold his end of the bargain? These thoughts muttered darkly across the top of his head as he pulled Rebecca's breasts free, suckled on nipples he'd spent one long rainy afternoon in English imagining in his mouth. The recollection helped. This was a woman he'd desired a long time ago, if fleetingly, and now she could be his. Like Candy.

Candy. Now that thought helped even more. As Toby pulled the jeans and G-string over Rebecca's pistoning feet, he imagined Candy's thrilling giggle – imagined that this shaven cunt he splayed and stroked was hers, heard her voice dubbing moans over the patient silence beneath him. Now he was hard, as hard as he'd ever been, and he couldn't bear to wait any longer. He pushed himself up, helped her divest him of his shirt, kicked away his pants. Now they lay squirming together on the bed, nothing at all between them, and Candy sighed in delight as Toby jerked Rebecca's legs apart to settle around him and yearned forward.

Rebecca didn't sound at all like his favourite phantom. She breathed in rough little gasps and swore vigorously under her breath, her fingernails clutching painfully at the nape of Toby's neck. Their pelvises slapped wetly together in a careless and impatient rhythm, and now Toby was back in English class, fucking Rebecca on her desk, watching that beaded forelock bounce about her younger face as he drove himself into her virgin flesh, and so quickly the explosion was there and waiting to happen. His whole body stiffened as a helpless moan escaped him, and more besides.

He lay there for a minute, anxious that he'd lift himself up and see disappointment in her eyes – but when he looked, he realised that what he'd assumed to be a scornful snort was actually Rebecca snoring. Reminding himself that she'd been awake during the sex – hell, she'd hardly had much time to doze off – Toby slipped himself free and lay there for a while, watching her sleep. He pulled the quilt up over her, and she snuggled into it with a muffled sigh.

So what did all this mean, then? Was she his woman now? Or would she be gone in the morning, and no number left behind? He found that he didn't really care either way. He'd broken the drought. Rain hissed down upon the parched plains of his sex life, and it turned to the applause of an approving crowd as he slid into slumber.

His dream was different that night. No Candy appeared beside him, and he lay alone in her bed, staring at the baseball pennant that the props department had pinned to her wall. But the mattress seemed hot, as if

covered with an electric blanket, and there was a curious element to that heat. It felt like anger.

***

Toby awoke naked and uncovered the next morning, his brain as parched and fuzzy as his mouth, and saw the sunlight playing across his ceiling before realising that he'd forgotten to set his alarm. His eyes jerked over to the sideboard in panic, past the huddled shape of his quilt, and he sighed in relief when the clock told him he had just enough time to get ready for work. He threw himself blindly out of bed and stumbled into the shower, and it wasn't until the cold water struck him that he remembered he had shared his bed with a woman last night.

Rebecca Marr, *nee* Carroll. A fantasy come true – he'd managed to bed one of his old classmates! It was all Toby thought about as he quickly rinsed himself beneath the spray, that and the way her naked body had looked last night, the way it must have looked back when they'd first known each other. Often such thoughts would cause him to perform an amatory ablution in the shower, but this morning he was sated and at ease with the world. He dried himself off and strode proudly naked back into his room, and discovered that the quilt was huddled over nothing but itself. Rebecca was long gone.

Toby was a little deflated, but found he wasn't too hurt. She'd provided a palpable outlet for his desires, and now she was gone without any awkward goodbyes or comparing of intentions. Why should he complain? Yes, he was alone again... but now he was reminded that he need not always be.

Toby went to work whistling, and not his dirty mug in the sink, or that hateful hit parade of pap, nor any of his workmates could bring him down that day.

He relived the previous night all through that day and all the way home. He sat on the couch and savoured his beer, remembering Rebecca beneath him – the bounce of her bountiful breasts, the gulping heat of her pussy – the way he'd pulsed his seed into her, where his primal urge insisted that it belonged. Would she be keen to have him again? He checked his phone for messages, his lounge and kitchen for notes she might have left, and found nothing.

Oh well. One night soon, he'd have another – and in the meantime, there was always Candy.

It was a pleased Toby who slipped into bed that night, a Toby who'd reinstated himself in the world – but only until he leaned over to turn on his alarm. Because that was when he finally noticed what was littering the floor on the far side of the mattress.

A black G-string, a brassiere and low-cut top, even a pair of inside-out socks – and peeping from one jeans pocket, the black screen of a mobile phone.

Toby's joy soured like old cream. But this didn't make any sense! Rebecca could hardly have been so desperate to leave that she'd jumped up and run away completely naked. So how else might this have happened?

His skin prickled – it could be nothing good. He rolled onto his back, slipping into the well-worn depression in the centre of the mattress, and frowned. This was not something he wanted to have to think about, and as soon as his queasy mind flitted away from it for a moment, he fell asleep.

Toby awoke within a dream to find a slender naked form once more beside him, and smiled. He put one hand on the rise of her hip, and she gave a muffled sigh. He thought it sounded like the one Rebecca had made when he'd pulled the quilt over her. Had the dream changed, then…? Stopped being an echo of his horny teen years, and become a reflection of his recent life? Even the scene around him had changed, and not changed; it was no longer a movie set from 1981, but a perfect reproduction of his own bedroom.

"Rebecca…?"

He tugged at her, and she came quickly – flipping about to stare at him with pale blue eyes that blazed with fury.

"That's not my name."

"Sorry," he muttered, feeling oddly embarrassed. "Wrong world. That was real… but you're my dream girl, Candy."

She glared at him even harder, skin as pale as her sandy-blonde hair in the scant moonlight.

"That's not my name."

Ah, so he'd gotten it wrong. This was not the fictional beauty after all, but the jobbing actress who, according to a DVD extra, had only taken this thankless heroine role to pad out her anorexic resume.

"Okay, okay. AJ, then."

Her hands shot out, pulled him firmly onto her. He felt her legs wrapping around him, as hot as ever – but this time it was not lust burning in her eyes.

"That's not my name!"

"I'm sorry! Why are you so mad?"

Candy – AJ – whoever she was behind that exquisite face – gave a sneer quite unlike anything he'd ever seen.

"How DARE you bring that skinny bitch into my bed! How dare you make me… make me have to DO that!"

The rage in her eyes was fierce – the implication of her words, terrifying. Toby tried to free himself, only to find that the woman had him locked in place atop her and he could not pull away. Her arms, her legs were so strong – so thick –

"I let you see me the way you wanted… let you have me the way you wanted… and THIS is how you treat me?"

"Please – "

"It's going to take me a long, long time to forgive you, Toby."

He struggled and thrashed in her grip, wanting nothing more now than to wake up.

"If ever," she wheezed.

"Let me go!"

"Love me."

"No!"

"You WILL. Now… say my name. Tell me you know who I am. SAY MY NAME!"

Toby felt those three syllables rising to the tip of his tongue, but could not bring himself to say them – as if that would make this insanity true, mean it was actually happening, and not just inside his sleeping mind. And it *couldn't* be, not even in a nightmare – her slender limbs could not be bloating around him to squeeze him even tighter, so powerful beneath their loose, flabby skin. Her eyes could not be as dark and small and unfamiliar as the hair that splayed out across his – *her* – pillow. Her huge bosom could not be pressing into his face until no air remained to be breathed, the lolling rolls of her body could not be pulling his own in so deep, deeper than any woman could possibly allow as he sank and thrashed and choked on flesh that tasted of sour linen.

But it was and they were, and as the mattress swallowed him whole, Toby did scream her name, screamed it in his mind as a final desperate plea… and from then on it was all he ever heard, an endless echo across the yawning gulf of perdition.

And he was never alone again.

The Doll

or

The One Who Will Take You Away

Matt Leivers

Leon sits in the hard straight-backed chair. In front of him on the hard wooden table is a single photograph, creased and worn from incessant handling; the emulsion cracking; the image dull beneath a patina of smeared finger marks. On either side of it Leon's hands flat against the bare wood, fingers occasionally curling against the grain as he tenses. The room is silent apart from the sound of breathing and of Leon's sharp gasps as he digs his fingernails into the table top.

Silent; apart from when the thing behind him speaks.

Please, and he can feel its long fingers toying with his hair. *Turn around.*

In front of him on the table a single photograph - creased and tattered - and he's held it in his hands so often and run the tips of his fingers across its surface so many times and pressed it to his lips so much that he knows its look and feel and taste almost as well as he knows himself.

Please, it says again and its voice is filled with so much longing that Leon feels like he is being dragged into the sky by a thousand wild horses. *Just turn around*, and Leon can feel its fingers - as cold as dead bone - on his face; on his lips; on his eyes; its mouth and nose pressed against the back of his head. *Why won't you turn around?*

A single photograph, of what looks like a ball-jointed doll and at first that is what Leon had thought it was; all falling hair and lambent-eyed and face tapering away to nothing. Just a stupid ball-jointed doll and when the photograph had come flapping out of the book to curl at his feet like a wounded bird he had given it a single cursory glance before folding it in two and using it to mark his place. Just a ball-jointed doll; polyurethane resin; late twentieth century; style of Volks. Nothing at all to catch the interest of a serious collector like him.

Please, the thing behind him sighs and he can feel its breathless mouth against his ear. *Turn around.*

***

It was really just a bogeyman story, an urban legend, something to scare novices at post-Convention parties. Leon had been hearing different versions of it for a decade, and knew of men in their eighties who could remember having been told it when they were boys. *That one's worthy of Kramer,* they'd say, nodding askance at some particularly beautiful example. *A touch of Kramer about it, that one...*

Among collectors Heinrich Kramer was the stuff of legend, only a fraction less of a myth than his book *De Simulacra Pupae et Carni.* Some versions of his story had him a Bavarian philosopher, others an alchemist; driven out of Germany, hounded and harassed and often in hiding; in and out of men's knowledge until he had appeared in Ghent at the end of the fifteenth century. Here his story coalesced into fact, for the city's Minute Books recorded that he had been burnt alive in the Korenmarkt by the doors of St Nicholas' Church, the tolling bells unable to drown out his screams and curses as the flames licked the flesh from his face. The good burghers of Ghent had burned him on a pile of his own books, ridding the world - as they put it - of his evil in both word and deed, and as Kramer had died so had all knowledge of the contents of his reputed masterwork.

But under the varying details and elaborations the basics of the story were always the same. Heinrich Kramer had been a genius – mad, probably, but a genius none the less - and had succeeded in bringing inanimate things to life. *De Simulacra Pupae et Carni* was a manual on how to make living dolls. Kramer - so the story went - had perfected his process over many years, and it was the growing number of at first very imperfect but increasingly successful results that had led to him having to flee from Bavaria. According to the story, he had destroyed all of his creations except the last, and that one he had taken with him to Belgium.

For three hundred years after Kramer's death knowledge of his book had receded, until most people believed that it was simply a fairy tale. And then a handwritten English translation entitled *Treatise on Dolls* had been found in the library of Jacquette-Célestine Davezac. After The Terror had ended, her books had entered the Bibliothèque Nationale, and there the *Treatise on Dolls* had remained. When the library moved to the Rue de Richelieu in 1868 the book did not, and once again it receded into rumour and speculation.

"But what happened to the doll?" the scoffing collector would inevitably ask.

"No-one knows. But some say that old Kramer turned it loose before the mob took him, and that it got away. Four hundred years old now, and as young as the day it was created. Some say that it's out there still, somewhere, looking for Kramer. Some say that it seeks out men who live among dolls - like Kramer did. That it hunts them down, thinking they're him, looking for the one thing that no-one will give it."

"What's that?" Leon can remember having asked the question himself, wanting the old fool who had cornered him at the bar to shut up and go away.

The old man had fixed him with a watery eye. "Death."

"Death? So why will no-one kill it?"

The old man had looked at him again, pityingly. "Would you, then? A doll that was immortal and youthful and perfect? And *alive*. Is that what you'd do to it? Kill it?""

Leon had shrugged. "So what happens when you don't?"

The old man had looked at him in silence for a moment before wandering away, shaking his head sadly. And Leon, like so many young collectors before and since, had gone home to his dolls and that evening and - for the first time ever - had felt their eyes following him as he moved around the house, and that evening - for the first time ever - he had locked his bedroom door.

***

Please, the thing behind him says again and Leon feels its chill hand against his throat; his Adam's apple duck beneath its fingers as he swallows. *Look at me.* The hand slides down over the swell of his pectorals and his breath catches in his throat; gooseflesh blooms across the flesh of his chest as it buries its face in the angle of his shoulder and neck. He can feel its lips against his skin, as smooth and cool as glass; the scrape of its incisors as it opens its mouth, the pressure of its tongue probing into the hollows above his clavicle.

"Stop," Leon gasps. "Please stop."

<u>No</u>, and Leon gives an involuntary cry as it squeezes his skin between its thumb and forefinger, through the cloth. *Not until you turn around.*

In front of him on the table is a single photograph. A photograph of what looks like a ball-jointed doll. Leon stares at the picture and even when he squeezes his eyes closed and tries to ignore what the thing behind him is doing with its fingers he can still see it. Androgynous – and even now he can't tell if it is male or female or if the words even make sense – and not young so much as ageless. Pale yellow hair framing the delicate narrow face, all bone and shadow; skin the colour of paraffin wax; bruised eyes brooding under lowered brows; lips like a fresh scar. Impossibly perfect and with nothing that appeals to the doll collector in Leon. And yet for the past days he has been able to think of nothing else; look at nothing else; dream of nothing else except this one impossible perfect doll.

Please, it says, pulling up the hem of his t-shirt; dragging its cold lifeless fingers across his tightening flesh. *Please.* Not quite begging.

***

Schuster wouldn't tell him where he had found the book and at first Leon hadn't believed it. "Just come to the shop," the dealer had insisted and Leon had heard something unfamiliar under the clipped German consonants and ingratiating tone. He was about to fly to Annapolis to view a collection of late eighteenth century Neapolitan Presepio figures, but Schuster had brushed his protests aside. "No! You must come now! This book, I will not stay with it for long." Fear, Leon realized. What he could hear in Schuster's voice was fear.

"No!" the dealer had hissed, when Leon - standing amid the incredible clutter of objects that was Schuster's shop - had reached out a trembling hand to open the book. "You will not read it here! Take it! You must take it and go!"

Leon had tried to protest; had tried to press money onto Schuster, but the old man had shaken his head wide eyed and frightened. "Just go! And tell no-one where you got it!"

***

The book was ancient and quite obviously valuable, but Leon was a collector of dolls not of books so he hefted it up onto his kitchen table and turned the creaking cover back without a second thought. If he had thought about it at all, he had expected it to be Jacquette-Célestine Davezac's English translation, the *Treatise on Dolls*. But it wasn't. The heavy type on the title page read *De Simulacra Pupae et Carni.* An engraving of a man flanked by two smaller figures and a dolphin wrapped around an anchor carried the words *Aldus Pius Manutius cum gratia et privilegio, ut ex decreto Heinrich Kramer Venice MCDXC.*

Leon's Latin was rusty, but Kramer's name was unmistakable. The Latin original. Whatever else it was, it was priceless, and Leon suddenly felt a thin tendril of dread uncurl in his stomach. How could this be here? How could it even be? As he turned the pages, poring over the incomprehensible heavy black type, something slipped from between two of the leaves onto the floor. Almost without noticing what he was doing, Leon picked it up, glancing at it only momentarily before he folded it into his pocket.

***

Early the next morning, once Leon had finally stumbled to his bed, he lay in the lifting darkness, trying in vain to sleep, thinking about what he had read. Kramer's book was indeed an alchemical tract, and Kramer's obsession had been with the creation of life. As far as Leon could tell, Kramer had been in search of the secrets of the golem, and the first parts of the book had been filled with glosses on rabbinic lore

"גלמי" is *my unshaped form* as Adam was when his dust was kneaded into a shapeless husk". Kramer had collected a huge rambling mass of this stuff, and Leon had struggled for hours to understand his endless references to a thing of sun-like brightness whose skin was a bright garment, shining like his nails so that the angels in heaven were filled with wonder and awe at the sight of him. From his ramblings, it seemed that Kramer had believed that the key to attaining the ability to animate a golem lay in an ecstatic experience, the secrets of which were contained in the Jewish *Book of Formation.*

Leon had battled his way through a hundred pages of Kramer's tangled, obsessive language by this point and was struggling to keep his eyes open. About to close the book, he looked around for something to mark his place, and pulled the paper that had fallen out of the book from his pocket. Glancing at it, Leon frowned. It was a photograph, and to his exhausted eyes it looked like a ball-jointed doll, polyurethane resin, late twentieth century, style of Volks. Shrugging at the incongruity, Leon folded the picture in two and stuck it in the book to mark his place. Just a ball-jointed doll. Nothing at all to catch the interest of a serious collector like him.

***

Leon sits in the hard straight-backed chair in front of the hard wooden table. The thing is behind him, saying nothing because it has its open mouth pressed into the angle of his shoulder and neck and he can feel its lips against his skin, as smooth and cool as glass, the scrape of its incisors, the pressure of its tongue probing into the hollows above his clavicle. One of its hands is chill against his throat, and the other is plastered against the exposed flesh between the hem of his t-shirt and the waistband of his jeans. Leon can feel the need pulsing out of it in waves, pushing him up out of the chair. Being next to it like this is like standing in the exhaust of a jet turbine, deafened and battered by the invisible blast. It is futile, trying to fight it, and Leon knows that before too long its fingers are going to tighten around his throat and choke the life from him, or that it is going to draw a blade across the jugular in his neck, hungrily sucking down the lifeblood that pumps relentlessly out of him. He can feel it trembling in its desperation, feels its fingers fumbling at him, gasps as it drags its hand across taut cloth. *Please,* it says, lifting its mouth from his neck. *Look at me.*

***

When Leon wakes there are only two thoughts in his mind. One is that whoever had translated the *Treatise on Dolls* for Jacquette-Célestine Davezac knew enough Latin to see the obvious meaning, but not enough to catch the subtleties of the language. Every word in Kramer's book seemed to have multiple meanings, and while he slept his brain had deciphered its title. *De Simulacra Pupae et Carpi* did translate as *Treatise on Dolls,* but that literal reading failed to catch the hidden sense of what Kramer's book was actually about. Another reading had occurred to him while he slept, one that he did not quite want to think about. Because if Kramer had wanted his book to simply be called *Treatise on Dolls* he would have titled it *De Pupae.* Why use three different words for doll? Because rearranged, his title said something quite different. As *Carpes simulacrum pupa* it meant *will you pick dream-figure doll? Will you pick phantom doll?*

The other thought is about the photograph that had fallen from the book. Leon makes himself a cup of coffee and sits down at his kitchen table, pulling the folded picture out from between the pages, unfolding it and ironing it flat beneath his fist.

It is a photograph, quite new, and at first glance it does look a little like a Volks Super Dolfie. If it is male or female Leon can't tell, and it could be anywhere between early adolescence and late twenties. It is androgynous and ageless, pale yellow hair framing the delicate narrow face, all bone and shadow, skin the colour of paraffin wax, bruised eyes brooding under lowered brows, lips like a fresh scar. Impossibly perfect, and with nothing that appeals to the doll collector in Leon. But there is something about it that isn't quite right, something about the finish of the face that makes him almost certain that what he is looking at isn't any sort of synthetic polyurethane resin. Frowning, Leon brings the photograph closer to his eyes, peering at the pale features of the doll, the falling hair, the lambent eyes, the face tapering away to nothing. For all the world it looks like porcelain, and the skin texture is realistic enough for it to be bisque rather than china.

What is it? Leon is very far from an expert on twentieth century dolls, but he knows an idiosyncrasy when he sees one. He knows that there are people who manufacture porcelain ball-jointed dolls - very expensive hand-made things - but as far as he can tell this isn't the work of any one of them.

Leon puts the photograph down and picks up his

coffee mug. He is about to get himself some breakfast when he notices something else. In the photograph, the doll is dressed in a high-collared black vest with a heavy silver zipper, the arm nearest the front of shot bare from shoulder to gloved hand. The shoulder and elbow are both clearly visible, and at neither is there any sign of an articulation.

Whatever it is, it is a very fine piece of workmanship. Leon licks his lips, frowning slightly at the sudden dryness in his mouth. Perhaps it isn't a doll at all? Perhaps it is just a single piece figure, a plaster model very skilfully painted. Leon picks up the photo again, peering at it, wondering why his heart is suddenly racing. A very fine piece of workmanship... What is it doing in that book?

Leon flips the picture over, scanning the back, but there is just a string of letters and numbers that don't mean anything. Turning the picture over again, he looks at the doll - surely it is a doll? - wondering what it might be. And then, where it might be, because suddenly Leon wants it. There is nothing about it that appeals to the collector of dolls in him, and yet he wants it more than he can remember ever having wanted anything. "A very fine piece of workmanship," he mutters to himself.

***

The thing behind him has one hand under his chin, tipping his head back and up, trying to make him look. Leon has his eyes screwed shut, and can hear it pleading with him, begging him to turn around, to look at it. *Please,* it says, and its other hand is at Leon's thigh, clawing at the fabric of his jeans. *Please. Please. Please.*

***

Schuster won't answer his door, so Leon kicks it down. Schuster won't tell him where he got the book, so Leon takes him by the throat and lifts him against the wall, watching grimly from inches away as Schuster kicks and chokes and pleads and claws at the muscles tensing in Leon's arm. "Algh... alright..." Schuster gasps, and Leon lowers him to the ground but doesn't take his hand away from his throat until Schuster has given him the name. To his surprise, Leon recognizes it. Fabian Demal is a collector of early twentieth century Italian felt salon dolls living in Chicago.

"Why do you so badly want to know?" Schuster croaks, and Leon pushes the photograph toward him, watching the colour drain out of his face. "Holy Mary, Mother of God, pray for us sinners, now and at the hour of our death" Schuster mutters, crossing himself. Leon wants to know why Schuster is so scared, but Schuster won't say, and whatever it is that Leon has in his heart it isn't murder.

***

It is three days before Leon can get to Chicago, and he has moved through that time like an automaton unable to think of anything, look at anything, dream of anything except this one impossible perfect doll. The photograph is creased and worn from incessant handling, the emulsion cracking, the image dull beneath a patina of smeared finger marks and he has held it in his hands so often, and run the tips of his fingers across its surface so many times and pressed it to his lips so much that he knows its look and feel and

111

taste almost as well as he knows himself.

By the time he gets there he also knows that Fabian Demal is dead. At the apartment building the concierge tells him how Demal had been found, throat cut and bloodless, sprawled across his desk inside his locked apartment, over a month ago. Leon hands the concierge fifty dollar bills until the man mutters "Christ, alright" and agrees to buzz him in.

Inside the apartment it is dark, the drapes pulled against the light, the power off. But Leon can feel it, pulling at him like a magnet at iron filings, and it is only a matter of minutes until he is standing in Demal's study looking at the thing he has been imagining looking at ever since he woke up four days ago with a Latin phrase in his head and a question about a photograph on his lips.

In the photograph it is beautiful. In reality it is beyond words. Leon reaches out with one shaking hand and sticks it under the thin cotton of his t-shirt, over the thick muscle of his chest, against the beating of his wild and hammering heart. Runs.

***

Leon sits in the hard straight-backed chair. In front of him on the hard wooden table is a single photograph, creased and worn from incessant handling, the emulsion cracking, the image dull beneath a patina of smeared finger marks. On either side of it, Leon's hands, flat against the bare wood, fingers occasionally curling against the grain. The room is silent, apart from the sound of Leon's breathing.

Beyond the photograph, lying flat on the table, is the doll. Leon has been sitting here for a time he has lost the ability to measure, staring at it, sometimes picking it up and moving its head or its limbs, but for the most part just looking at it, trying to understand how anything can be so beautiful. He can't work out what it is made from - not wood, not composition, not wax or porcelain, certainly not resin - or how it articulates, or how it is making him feel what he is feeling. Suddenly, he wants very much for it not to be there, this peculiar wonderful horrible thing, lying on his kitchen table, mocking him. It is only about two feet long, but it suddenly makes Leon feel very small and very stupid. What kind of idiot lets themselves be infatuated by a doll?

"Come on, then," Leon mutters. "Do something. Come to life."

***

It is dark when Leon wakes up. At first he doesn't know where he is, or why he is so stiff, but then he realizes that he has fallen asleep in the kitchen chair. The moon is shining in through the window behind him, casting pale shadows across the table, bathing the photograph in mercurial light.

Leon is still only half awake when he realizes that the doll is gone. He is fully awake by the time he realizes that only one of the shadow figures on the table in front of him is his own.

***

"I can't," Leon says, through gritted teeth. "I can't do what you want. I can't kill you."

Of course you can't kill me the thing laughs as it fumbles at Leon with its still stiff fingers. *How could you kill me? I'm immortal.* Leon's breath hisses through his teeth as it slips its hand over his skin, lifting his head higher with the other, stroking the long length of Leon's throat.

"What do you want?"

Open your eyes. Turn around. Look at me, it pleads.

"But you'll kill me if I do."

I'll kill you, it whispers, both of its hands moving over his flesh, *if you don't.*

"I don't understand."

Open your eyes. Turn around. Look at me.

"But..."

Do it. Please. Begging now. *I need you to. I need you.*

"I don't understand," Leon says again. "What do you want?"

I want to live.

"How?" Leon can't think; tales of the golem and Kramer and the cursed doll tangled together in his mind; the almost unbearable feeling of the thing's fingers against him.

Ecstasy, the thing whispers, running its fingers up over Leon's chin into his mouth. *The scarlet or the white. Ultimate pain or ultimate joy.*

Leon can't think, doesn't know what he is being asked. All he is sure of is *please, turn around, look at me.* "Alright," he mumbles, around a mouthful of fingers. "Alright." Clambers to his feet, sees the doll - life-sized now - take a step backward before it pushes him back against the table, impossibly strong for something so slight, forcing him backward.

"Wait!" Leon cries. "Who are you? What are you?" But the doll has its mouth full and can't answer.

***

Afterwards, they lie together, the doll's fingers - warm now, and supple - tangling in Leon's hair while Leon drinks the breath from its mouth, feels the heart beating beneath its ribs, the blood pushing through its veins.

"What just happened?" Leon asks, finally, in the pause when they rest.

You gave me life. The doll smiles.

"But..." Leon pauses. "Aren't you?""

The Cursed Doll? The doll nods. *They gave me life, too. Like I said, the scarlet or the white, it makes no difference. Life is life.*

"So you're not going to kill me?"

I'm not going to kill you.

"I don't think I'd mind now." Leon is almost surprised to hear himself say it, but the doll smiles again.

I've existed for a very long time, it says, *but not always alive. Kramer thought he created me, but he was a rather stupid man, for all his opinion of himself. Too stupid to realize that all the blood I drank from him could have been spared if only he could have loved me.*

"So you killed him?"

He grew scared, the doll nods, *and was going to give me away. Like I said, he was stupid, so I watched him burn.*

"And Demal?"

And Demal. And countless others. Most of them chose red.

Leon is silent for a moment. Then "who are you?"

The doll smiles. *Who am I? I've had a hundred names. Hadrian called me Praelium. Kramer called me Nubis. Pick one.*

Again, Leon is silent for a moment. "I didn't ask your name. I asked who you are."

So you did. I can't tell you, although Kramer tried. What was it he called me? Shadows, plaything, flesh? Nubis, Praelium, a hundred names tucks a stray lock of hair behind Leon's ear.

Leon makes a small choking sound.

Deadhead

Larry Hinkle

Two years ago, I met the love of my life. Ten months ago, I made her my wife. Two weeks ago, I chopped off her head. In my defense, she tried to kill me first. But I don't hold a grudge. How could I? She's the love of my life.

Ours was a romance too fantastical for fairytales, too cheesy for Nicholas Sparks. And the sex? Jesus. You know the kind of sex middle age housewives in the grocery store checkout lines think Brad and Angelina have every few hours? Trust me, Brangelina's sex life was like your grandparents compared to ours. I don't tell you this to brag, though; I'm telling you so you'll understand why I did what I did.

Even before the deadheads came, we never had much food in the house. So it wasn't long until we were down to a sleeve of crackers and some mustard. Neither of us wanted to go outside, but what choice did we have? I couldn't just sit there and watch her starve. Like I said, she was the love of my life.

Unfortunately, our first run didn't exactly go as planned. We found some food, but the deadheads found us on the way back, and she got bit. We knew it was a death sentence.

That night, I caught her trying to sneak out. Said she didn't want to burden me. I held her and told her everything would be okay, that I'd love her forever, no matter what. I kissed her on the forehead, then on the mouth, and then, well, it should come as no surprise what happened next.

In the middle of it all, on tiptoes and bent over the couch, she turned. La petit mort, indeed. I couldn't see her face, and just took the increased moaning and thrashing as a sign that I was doing something right. Imagine my surprise when I turned her over and she snapped at my jugular. Take it from me: if you've never tried fucking your wife while she's trying to eat your face, I wouldn't recommend it.

I pulled out, ran to the door and grabbed the axe we'd kept there since Matt Lauer went deadhead on Al Roker's surgically deflated stomach on national television. In one swing, it was over. Her head rolled across the floor and hit the wall, biting at the air the whole time.

I fainted.

When I came to, her eyes were locked on me, her teeth still snapping at the distance between us. I got up and placed her now lifeless body in the bedroom, put on some heavy gloves and carried her head to the kitchen table. Then, using a pair of rusty pliers, I ripped out her teeth, one by one.

That was two weeks ago. The skin around her gums has pulled back a bit, and her left cheek has sloughed off. She's also missing an eye. But she's still my wife. She's still beautiful.

Especially her smile.

I can't stop thinking about her smile. About her mouth. About the things she used to do with it. I see her tongue, licking over shriveled gums. I try to hold out, but I'm only human. Slowly, I unzip my pants and place my hand on top of her head. She opens her mouth and takes me in.

I'm not proud, but I don't think she minds. She's still the love of my life.

Memoir of a Death Maiden

David J. Gibbs

As far back as he could remember, he had always held morbidity close. It was inescapable. The call from within was undeniable. When passing a car accident on the highway, he would always pause, eyes lingering over the twisted chassis or broken windshield, looking for what he assumed everyone else was; that dash of red dancing among the tiny shards of glass. He was hopeful that perhaps he would see a spattered crimson pattern stretched across a ruined dashboard or maybe a cracked or torn face creased by jagged lines of red. He longed to see a prone body covered with a bloodstained sheet as it awaited the arrival of the coroner's van along the road.

It wasn't until much later he realized that not everyone held the same fascination. At an early age, his lust for the macabre lured him to movies filled with gory tales of campfire murders and unstoppable stalkers. During a time when most of his classmates read ridiculously simple young adult fiction, he buried himself for weeks at a time amid the folk tales and legends of faraway lands. The darker and more twisted those tales the better as far as he was concerned.

Everyone, even the sacred few he claimed as friends, made fun of him. Of course, he had been foolish to believe that anyone would have understood what he had come to know. But he had been young and naïve at that time, but not anymore.

And in part, it was probably due to them making fun of him, that he slid even further down the stepladder into the depths of his thirst. It was as if death had somehow seduced him, she the alluring temptress of the unspeakable and he the insatiable student of all things dark and disturbing. He gave himself piece by piece to his loving, whispering temptress.

He began to realize that he would never be free of the dark embrace or the sweet solitary perfume of her enticement, the pair intertwining to the point that there was almost no discerning where he ended and she began. The entanglement of her undeniable single mindedness was almost painful. It was so incredibly intense, that at times he felt overwhelmed. And for that, he was forever thankful.

As he distanced himself from friends, and the fragments of his family, he began to retreat ever deeper into his lover's embrace. He experimented with the occult on several occasions, once even agreeing to meet with a strange group of people from the next county, who supposedly conversed with the dead. The fact that he had backed out did little to curb his appetite. If anything, it merely hastened him along the path he had somehow managed to find.

Graduating at the top of his high school class, he surprised everyone by deciding to not attend college. He more than disappointed his frail and sickly mother, not that her concern made him waver in his decision. He had toyed with the idea of joining the paramedics or fire department, but found that brought him too close to his obsession. Instead of heightening the experience, which is what he had assumed would happen, it instead seemed to rather nullify whatever magic occurred while in the throes of observing. And so, he found himself at twenty-six, a coroner's assistant. He drove the so called 'meat wagon' to and from each scene to pick up and catalog the dead.

While some might have felt compassion for those he delivered, he did not. They were merely empty containers by the time they arrived. And though some might have found him to be a cold person, someone with whom death had pulled the strings to his empathy closed, that was not the case. There was a certain amount of pleasure that coursed through him when he worked with those that passed. It wasn't purely sexual in nature, although it was at times painfully arousing. Aside from that, he felt a profound sense of contentment.

As he pored over their bodies, his eyes would take in each detail of their passing. Mortal wounds gaped and beckoned with lingering allure. Infected and decayed limbs were pliable and swollen in his grasp and they all whispered softly to him. Flesh pulling away from the soft tissue beneath always held his attention. The bloodied stumps that remained from severed limbs brought him a wave of sickly sweet serenity. All of them seemed to whisper bliss to him in their own wicked way. It seemed he couldn't satiate whatever hungered for death inside of him. He remained erect almost constantly, as his fingers danced along the edges of death.

Many times, over the years, he had tried to find the foundation from which his desire spread, and each time, he had not been able to even come close. In the thick volumes he read, frequently detailing the study of criminal behavior, there seemed always to be a singular event that triggered something within each case. And yet, there was no such event. There hadn't been tragedy early on in his life. Neither parent had been taken from him while he was growing up, and all four of his grandparents were still alive and well. He hadn't been victimized in some random violent act, nor had he lost a sibling in a bizarre accident.

And yet, despite that, he had always been drawn to the darker side of things. He began reading ancient texts by questionable authors he had secretly checked out of the public library. Every chance he could, he would sneak downstairs to watch late night horror movies that had whispered to him while growing up. All of those things never answered his question, but rather, only succeeded in staving off his need before he had to act.

And act, he had.

Determining what his calling was to be wasn't the difficult part. The difficulty came when he tried to determine what he was to do with this calling. He had floundered for a long time. As odd as it may seem, he had studied men of the cloth and their descriptions of their own calling. It was certainly something similar in nature.

At least to him it was.

They were dedicating themselves to something that was unseen and unknown, and yet, deep inside, it had been whispered to them to follow. It was truly a blind decision made to something that couldn't be verified by any means, something that had to be taken quite literally on faith.

And so, that was how his calling came. It was a steady decline toward something that had existed since the beginning of man. It wasn't something that he could discuss with anyone else, so it came slowly at first. He would catch himself staring blinding at the anatomy books. It had very colorful pages and was his favorite medical text.

While in high school, he had become somewhat fascinated with serial killers and their crimes, or more importantly the descriptions of their crimes. Anything from how they chose their victims, to what they did to their quarry once it was cornered, to how they disposed of the body to end the game. At times, it was as if he was the one speaking of these things. He was the one that stood nude over them and bathed in their spilled blood. He was the one that knew at which exact moment the victim's last breath would come.

He had never really understood how death had come to court him or even why. But, he had taken those darkly sweet first kisses in stride, and come to relish the wet, stinking breath that filled him to the core. Though their courtship had taken years before they had become familiar lovers, each and every moment shared together unforgettable, he now could not picture himself without his loving temptress.

Though they were secretive lovers, and no one knew of their love nor the strength of their bond, he was not foolish enough to believe that no one would become aware. He was always careful, perhaps impossibly so. Beneath the pale lights bathing his work table with their clean white light, he gazed upon the prone body of a young woman who had taken an overdose of her ailing mother's medication. Not a single mark marred her beautiful skin. To all who would have gazed upon her likeness, she was beautiful and appeared very much alive. Her breasts full, her hips holding a lovely curve, her hair teasing her shoulders with blonde curls. To most, it would appear as if she were merely sleeping on his cold metal table and that made his member pulse thick and hard.

The quiet calling of the cold skin, the perfect alabaster beneath his fingertips was always something that soothed his soul and tantalized him. It didn't matter if the skin was ruined or the body fouled with putrescence, but there was definitely something to be said about death perfection. It somehow held a more profound hand around his heart, when someone such as this beautiful creature arrived on his table, untouched, undamaged.

He could take as much time as he needed in the quietness of his secluded abode. Death was profoundly and starkly beautiful to him. And, he knew that the seductress that he had so easily taken as his own, so many years before stood by his side, each and every time a body was placed on his table.

Each time he looked upon them in their death visage, he could feel her beside him, taking his hands and letting him explore their bodies. She allowed him to take his time moving over her pliable bounty and

125

relishing the quiet moments between her legs. The arousal he felt was beyond the physical and his lover knew that, softly urging him on and whispering tender words.

Every spent seed was a consummation of what he felt for his temptress and a new step toward confirming what he already knew to be true. Though in many circles what he was doing was reprehensible, and in still others criminal, he did not think himself as either.

Unfettered by the tidings of an uncaring and unwilling society, he experienced freedom to a level previously thought impossible. By not recognizing the laws and morays of the city and people around him, he had complete and absolute freedom. His decisions weren't guided by the few in societal power, instead he was guided by whatever curiosity teased his mind at the moment. And, at the moment, he was most curious indeed. Curious to know the true extent of the love he had come to cherish in the darkness of his stained heart.

Carefully he disrobed, letting his lover gaze upon him with her unseeing eyes. Everywhere around him, he could feel the tender sensuality of her presence. The electricity of her touch running the length of his spine, her teasing lips around his member made him tremble with sensations so strong, he was certain beyond any doubt, that no one had experienced anything close to what he had with his chosen soul mate.

She whispered to him as she always did, her voice a loving caress in itself. He paused, her hands moving across his body, enticing him even further. His body trembled as he started the IV line in his right arm. The coolness of the steel table kissed his back, as he lay down on the table beside the girl's beautiful body.

They would share her together soon enough; he and his death maiden. His left hand moved between the dead girl's legs again, making his throbbing member pulse and thud, as he felt the solution course through his veins. The fire danced along his arm, as he felt his heart rate slow. His curiosity fueled his need and his need fueled his decision. He knew, in order to truly court his maiden, he had to get ever closer to her. They were meant to be one, and to be one, he knew what had to be done.

And so, as the darkness swept him under its thick, sensual blanket, enveloping his desire, he felt his fairest maiden's gentle breath against his neck and the gentle brush of her hand. With each, ever slowing beat of his heart, he felt her legs entwined with his, he felt her lips cover his own, and her soft wispy hair caress his bare skin.

Finally, they were together as one, as he slipped inside her, bursting with lust and desire, their insatiable hunger feeding one another.

Flow the Junction

Roger Leatherwood

I was next but no one was keeping track. The lights were above us casting long dark shadows even as they burned in our eyes from either side. Although there were only 10 or 12 others in here it seemed packed, hot and oppressive.

But that I had only a jockstrap on and was already erect, the hot stink of earthworms and menthol cigarettes and, strangely, of ginger. Of a spice in the air.

There were towels and buckets of pink water outside the bead curtain and I could hear them inside, breathing heavily without words. The heat itself was causing my cock to rage upright, straining. The lights were high, not bright but not a dark sexy vibe and I could see the hairy guy behind me and openly looked at him fingering himself, almost as old as me but heavier, also with a wedding ring.

There were two guys in tight black dance shorts filming her with handheld digital cameras, with no lights. They handed out thumb drives at a desk through the hall. They'd been here since 11 this morning, and it was now 2. I'd be out by 3, back home for hours by the time my wife got home from Sunday's visit to her mother, which never put her in a good mood, right around the time they shut this interaction down. Until the next time.

The word had spread the way the others had, through whispered talk, nods and casual acquaintances who could be trusted to be quiet and disappear after. Each location was different, though within the 20 mile radius of Oceanside. And the circles were never the same, new strangers and some repeaters who managed to overhear the new grapevine of not so spontaneous arrangements.

It was never posted, not on twitter, or any internet. Jace, in accounting looked at me a long beat last Thursday at work and told me what to do today if I wanted to again.

I hadn't seen him, wouldn't, might have left 2 hours ago or not had the balls to even show up. I recognized one other, a guy standing in the hall ahead of me with the leftcurvy cock.

Natasha Furlough was her name, not her real one. I'd been here before in summer and wanted to return one day, after I'd lived off the pearl of shame, cleaned off the memory on the backwall of my secret desires. She didn't care if I came back because there were others enough. Just to find her. Was she here for us or were we here for her?

Her organic swell of need, a monthly swinging private adult party; the red flow of blood throbbing within her. The lust of anonymous acceptance to her carnal blooms. Natasha, we heard had a deep-seated and impossible desire to fuck, to seed, for cock, a gangbang of ejaculation and discharge but not for the faces.

If there was one person who would feed her the aerobic, the cummy nutrition, the chemical attention- we would not be here in this dark cave of sweating surrender, in a den off Glaser in the suburbs of Oceanside.

Guys of all stripes stood in other rooms, just out of the hall or preparing with eye contact, grunts and questions. Heavy and married 40-year-olds, two college students, all of us looking for the thing, the different thing, the other side of the same thing; she didn't like the guys with too many tats, the gangsters, the motorcycle hardcore and were turned away.

She nodded to the rest. She understood our desire for our own personal damage. She was the wounded.

Bleeding, she bled from her cunt, she bled, but it wasn't from hurt. Only women bleed, the first cut is the deepest, she was the bleeding woman, a biological and physiological anomaly healthy and known to few and studied on a monthly basis by those up on the hill in the research wings of the campus, without panic or alarm. Grants were pending.

Her time otherwise, was her own and she filled it with the pursuits that pleased and kept secret from the neighbors, that fed and revealed her to herself. In a different house each month. That there were a cadre of strangers who arrived all day and she needed them again and that passed through the flow of her personal history was of no consequence and no lasting impact.

In the room, she lay in a plush seat upright, her legs in open stirrups on fabric of a thin non-absorbent toweling all underneath. Her ass propped on the wet layer of seat and 3 men, all naked, one with a leather belt with round Indian buckles around his girth cut above the thick patch of pubic hair over his erection. Around her legs and on the towels, was a foamy layer of blood and scum, dripping around her pussy and down the inside of her thighs down to her feet. Her period, a thin flow, had been going on for weeks now, simple and constant, wrapped except when she opened herself up and capitulated in open-legged abandon; the woman who did not stop flowing.

Two helpers quietly and unobtrusively wiped her thighs and under her naked ass, heavy and round, and slick. Not perfectly clean, that wouldn't do, just a basic swabbing. Her pubic hair was trim, a thin carpet in light triangle above the crease that dripped even as the one ahead entered, a thin spunk of red watery juice covering him, mixed with the ejaculate of the previous visitors, slick and swollen and ready for him as he sighed, hard and drowned, watched and filmed.

She looked past him, at me, a smile on her face. Tired but not forfeiting to exhaustion as her constant flow poured out and strung the source of sexual excitation. A throbbing reminder of her womanhood, her potent and fecund mother-lust, the lifegiving substance that slowly dripped out of her, been doing so for years, endless she said, they said, endless and drew us, like a menthol nectar of sticky life and fuck and birth and cunt.

Him and him and them and those of us who heard; to do her. Give her the seed, to rub and to feel the flush of her constant need and emission and a cumming kind of leaking corrosion, a bodily spilling, an overflowing ruin.

* * *

Natasha Furlough had almost been raped in the back pulpit of the St. Margaret's Church by the youth minister, who was only 22 and recently married. Natasha was 13, and already filing out.

She lost her virginity, technically, to Mary Hopkiss in 9th grade, during a sleepover while watching Heath Ledger movies late into the night.

Her periods were heavy and lasted 6 or 7 days, longer than her friends, but painless. As she grew and became sexually active, first with her own lithe hands, then small finger dildos, then with the two redheads who always read science fiction in the library- her flow would last the entire month, only changing in consistency and pungency over the weeks. She wore dark-colored cotton underwear and kotex and experimented with every style of tampons. And was shy and sighed to herself a great deal.

And she had a voracious appetite. The doctors found nothing wrong with her but encouraged her to keep her iron and nutritional intake high to avoid anemia during what was considered a developmental phase.

Her blood ran 3 or 4 degrees hotter than everyone else, and as the stream from her cuntflower became heavier- she fed it; eating 5 meals a day, exercising, talking in the dark nooks of the hallways, giving those outcasts with refined and outré tastes a feel and a fingerful.

She dropped out and spent her 19th year in bed with needles and LED and ultraviolet grow lights over her naked skin. Nothing could slake her physical thirst but to be massaged deeply, and fucked and receive tablespoons of seminal fluid that were absorbed and seemed to hormonally interact with her perimetriual walls.

The protein snot of their cock ardor would splash and stick to her spongy endometrium and cook into a voracious broth that entered her bloodstream in macrophagic thrusts. The biomolecular carrier agent crawled and coagulated into her venal pockets and stayed her heart. The flow thinned, momentarily adhesing within Natasha's greedy, open womb. Endorphins and endomines filled her with a feeling of deep love and a wet blanket of affection, which passed when her legs were closed again.

Natasha was handled by 2 Korean doctors and a nurse from Canada, who had her own agenda. And she watched as the men, none identified and none wearing condoms, began to come, first in pairs and then in organized meetings, and entered her one by one and slowly. One every 20 minutes in polite order. And the Canadian nurse would assist in Natasha's pleasure as well as with the men's while the doctors mopped up at the side, and took samples and measurements.

And the juncture of her sex and her science, the flow of 10 thousand days and the bloodlines of 10 million spermazotes, released and discarded into the bottomless need of Natasha in the den of Glaser in Oceanside, the nurse played within the pool and the folds of her wet wonder.

* * *

I was next and she shifted in her damp seat- sore as she opened, dribbling, his spunk before, a dark lumpy soup with dark clots for my penetration.

She pushed me back as I slipped in like a sausage in gravy.

"Deeper," she oozed, and her ass spurtled against the towel in a sexy splish. My balls dripped with a thin mist, the nurse pulled my buttocks apart with a gloved finger, pushing me into Natasha.

The man looked at me through a box the size of a pack of cigarettes, the single eye recording the hard, wet slop spreading her with black bleeding passion.

"Cum, you gonna cum?" The bleeding woman looked over my shoulder, to whoever was behind me. Her forehead, beautiful and pimpled and lined with sweat, the brown hair wet and curled around her eyes, sexy, her ears damp, open, her breasts heavy as if laden with milk.

I looked down on her, the light bright on her heaving stomach, my cock, all the cocks, inside her, full of red cum and tomorrow's flow, here for a moment as my balls heaved, cradled by the hand I didn't see--

Hot, burning, a boil rising within my shaft. And I shot a wad into her, like marbles passed through my pisshole. Up. My sacrifice. She bit her lip but held her breath.

Too quick, a wet blood fuck like none ever again, to keep me company in the quiet cool nights between my sheets at home, when over my wife. Who waited. I was pushed in kindest polite fashion from the woman who could not.

Was wiped off, told to dress, and smiled at as they handed me my flashdrive with the file and showed me to the afternoon outside and told me to not pass this way again.

Curse

Duana Monroe

She crept into his window, pulling the lacy silken train of her gown over the sill like a whispered breath. Her bare feet silent on the cool wooden floor as she crossed the room toward his bed.

"Beautiful," she said, as she gazed at the man lying on his side, tangled in the blue satin sheets so dark that in the night's gloom they looked like the vaulted inky sky.

His legs, knotted with muscles and thick with brown hair, were drawn up like a baby's. His arms wrapped in a cross around his chest.

He was the one, she was so sure this time.

She paused beside his bed, for just a moment. Long enough to drink in the squareness of his jaw, the thick hair that swept his forehead, interrupted by a cowlick-- so handsome, yet boy-like in the peace of his dreaming.

She lightly climbed into the bed with him, squeaking the springs, but he didn't wake.

She'd thought of him all day-- planned what she would do to make him want her. Finally, her need would be fulfilled. What man could say no to a warm, shapely body in his bed. No man could resist her.

She reclined, leaning on one elbow, next to his sleeping form. She touched his hair, clean and thick. Ran her fingers through it lightly, enjoying the rustling texture in between her fingers. The tension in her body was like an over-tightened violin string, ready to sing or snap with a twang. Her hand quested further, down the gruffly whiskered cheek, the relaxed tendons of the neck, the curving collar bone. His skin, bronze and healthy, smelled of soap-- sweet and clean.

"Wake to me, my love," she said, her voice like a melody.

"Mmmm," he mumbled, not fully waking but rolling on his back.

She sat up on her knees and quickly pulled the gown from her body, the silk floating in waves to the glossy wooden floor. She climbed up onto him and sat astride him, running her hands along the plains of his chest. The thick pecks, his ribs, the curving cage around his abdominal muscles all melted hot beneath her her hands.

He grew hard beneath her.

"You are dreaming of me now aren't you, love? Dreaming of this body? Don't be shy, you can put your hands on me," she said, her voice a sigh full of jagged breath.

"Lilith," he answered, still deep in dream, but his rough hands found her hips, naked and soft. His hand traced the curve upward to her waist and then to her breasts. His breath came quicker in sleep, as his hands cupped her breasts, kneaded them softly.

She directed his fingers to her nipples, brown and wrinkled like raisins. He twisted her nipples and groaned loudly, finally emerging enough from his dream to participate. He pushed himself up on the bed, pulled her onto him. His mouth found one nipple and he sucked it in as if he were starving.

She gasped as he worked at one of her breasts with his strong questing hand and the other with a vapid mouth, biting and licking with deft.

"Oooh, you've done this before," she said, breathily in his ear.

He answered with a growl and a nip on her tight nipple.

She replied by pressing tighter against him, pulling his face against her and grinding against his thigh.

"You want me. Tell me you want me now."

"Mmmm, I do. I want you," he said, a voice deep and gravely. Lust heated.

She rose a bit, worked him free of the covers that held him like a chastity belt. She fumbled with the covers, but held his head to her, unwilling to break away from his questing tongue. Her body, slick with need, slid against him leaving a hot trail.

Her body ached in that moment. It was a deep need that could only be eased by him, by his body inside of her. She angled her hips so that he prodded against her, savoring the blunt head against her, the promise of fulfill- ment.

His own need had taken over. He grabbed her hips and pulled her onto him, penetrating her with a quick yank, using her weight to impale her on him.

137

She gasped as he forced her open, driving deeply into her.

They clung together for a moment, this moment of first joining like the dawn of a new day-something to savor in silence. She hugged his face to her neck, fluttering breath against her sensitive ears. Then she began to move.

Her body like liquid in a bottle, surged forward. On one knee and one foot, she squatted on him, arching back on a hand. She could see his chest heaving with jagged, lusty breath and the hair of his body that crowned their joining, as she rocked on him, making him gasp in delight.

His eyes, heavy lidded and clenched, didn't meet her own.

She felt it. It was a hot lump of lead in her belly, stretching out its tendrils and burning her thighs. It built on itself, doubled and meandered, curling her toes and clenching her muscles. She fought back her orgasm, wanting to prolong it, wanting more of him.

He grumbled as she pulled off of him, but she silenced his protests with a kiss. Her tongue probed his mouth, questing like an adventurer. His own tongue met hers, though it fumbled to keep up with the lighting quick acrobatics of her mouth.

She turned her back to him and climbed again onto him. She leaned back on her hands and began to rock against him.

"Touch me, damn you. Touch me and make me fly," she demanded.

His hands snaked around her, running up and down her sides, tweaking her nipples and brushing the undersides of her breasts. Finally, one arm wrapped around her waist and another found her center:

pinching, pulling, brushing. His rough finger-tips tore at her, demanded her release. Her rhythm merged with his, a hunching jerk that buried him in her depths in a way she'd never felt.

"It's coming, baby. You too!" She said, a whimper.

He mumbled something into her back, but it was lost in the rising sound of their heated embrace. His teeth raked her back and his arm bruised her waist, but she answered this pain with tightening muscles and an arched back. She raked her nails along his thighs, making him drive deeper into her.

"Lilith," he screamed as the crashing orgasm drowned them. "Lilith!"

She howled an answer, stretching her arms to the sky. Defiance, deliverance in their act washed over her, a hot wind soothing the shuddering muscles of her legs, back and wings.

Quickly she jumped off of him just as the semen began to jet from his cock. She caught him in her mouth and began to pull for it, lips wrapped like silk, ass in the air, wings fluttering a breeze across his face frozen in shock. The jets of cum, salty and hot, filled her mouth, nearly spilling out onto the sheets.

She sucked until it stopped jerking, load safely caught between her lips.

"Lilith?" He asked, fully awake for the first time, his eyes wide with terror.

She stood quickly and pulled her gown on over her head and adjusted the back holes so her wings slid freely through. From the pocket, she pulled a small flask that shone like amber in the night's half-light. She uncorked the flask and spit his seed into the bottle. She smiled tenderly at him as she put the stopper back in the neck of the bottle and slipped it back into the pocket of her gown.

A pounding at his locked bedroom door had begun to sound more like tearing wood. They were trying to save him. She hissed at the door, but knew she had time enough to finish.

"My love," she said, spreading her dark, leathery wings out behind her. Her raven hair, crackled and undulated on an unnatural breeze and her black eyes emanated a life all her own. "I've been watching you train. Your teachers warned you about me, but your eyes would glint when they described my charms. If men like you didn't want me, it would be so hard for me to meet my daily quota. You know I was the first wife to Adam and I wanted so much more than to be his sex slave. I wanted to feel lust and heat, not just lay quiet and let him do his business and give him babies. I wouldn't stay with him, so..."

"So, you are cursed to bear the demons who torment men and women in their dreams."

"What's a few stained sheets among friends?" Lilith asked. "You wanted me when they told you about my tastes. You hoped I would come."

The young man's face paled as she spoke. It was true- both knew it.

She crossed the room and grabbed the uniform he'd so revered his entire life. She knew it was a uniform he felt inadequate in. After the romp they'd had, she understood why he questioned his calling.

She took the white collar, starched and so clean, and dabbed it along her musky lips, giving it a kiss filled with the juices of their coupling. She ran her tongue on it, showing him that it didn't scare her, that it wasn't a secret talisman against evil and lust.

Finally, she used it to wipe away the wetness between her legs.

The door was beginning to groan against the combined weight of the men who'd sheltered her lover. She had to go.

She leaned into him for a quick, chaste kiss, then turned to the window and leapt outside. As she fluttered away, she glanced back in time to see him raise the collar to his face and rub it on his cheek. With a smile, she turned back to her flight. She would meet her quota, with some to spare.

Betty the Cambion

Ralph Greco

Between the muted mauve tableaus of stucco walls, the sound of Betty's barefoot fell. Dressed as lightly as she was, a ruby red paper-thin sheath hanging from her wide collar, sides split from her neck to her ankles, the chalky October breeze undulating through the deserted house blushed a cold shiver cross the young woman's rising sheen of sweat...though, not an altogether uncomfortable sensation.

Hesitating on the Italian marble floor, the freckled-nosed girl bit her lip and stared down the empty hallway to the solid wooden door that faced her. Betty's plan, such as it was, was to open that door, cross beyond the threshold and become a woman of legend among her peers, to break the pattern and remember this night as those who had come before her had not. But the pretty college sophomore secretly feared she'd come to love what happened to her in that room beyond the door- as much or more as her sisters before her had- and she'd be sent from this house unable to recall what had transpired, while a longing urge and a sinister comeuppance haunted her for the rest of her days as it did the young women who had dared try this walk through this house and the horror it held.

*＊＊

Julia's tape made the rounds through school; from freshman to seniors (though the older girls acted as if the secret of Delino house could never entertain their 'mature' sensibilities), some teachers were even rumored to have heard it. Played nightly for rapt live audiences, even downloaded into e-mail, Julia Bents' secret recording of her "time in the room" kept every girl who heard it in a perpetual 'state.'

A junior at the private college, lanky Julia had secreted a mini-tape recorder under the flouncy flower-patterned skirt she had worn her night in Delino House. Her plan had been to close her thighs hard- as she had done-engaging the record button to hopefully capture what would engager her after she closed the wooden door and faced whatever it was all the girls before her had but had not been able to remember. After being picked up in the woods behind the Pizza Hut, as every one of the girls before her had, Julia produced her 'secret' tape.

Of course, Julie didn't remember ever producing the scream and low taped 'mewing' let alone recall activities that could have caused her to do so. As every one of the girls before her had, Julia's only proof of her ordeal was the requisite nickel-sized scar dead center of her right buttock, a similar shape just over her right nipple and the deep sensation (and low ache) of having been 'filled' with something, the size of which she could never have imagined. As with the other eight girls who had ventured beyond that door in Delino house, Julie only remembered crossing into the small room at the end of the hallway, closing the door behind herself then waking up in the parking lot silently nursing an ache she could not remember the cause of.

Julia became addicted to her oratory submission though. Returning again and again to her tape she was quickly driven mad by the things she heard that reminded her of the things she could not remember.

Betty arrived the very day the ambulance came to 11 Norton Way to 'escort' Julia from the dorm.

***

Man or beast, Betty Fect- for that was who she was-was going to know this cool leaf-blown night just what it was that was bequeathed in this house of her uncle, the wily exiled Antony Fect Delino.

She stood at the door then, wiping the palms of her hands on the material of the smock tickling over her knee. Despite her fear, Betty still felt a dollop of wetness between her legs, saw and felt her little nipples poking far out from under her sheath. There was a pull in her belly, like the gestating coil of a snake that will neither strike nor sleep. Familiar only with clumsy rumblings in backseats and family-room groping (and only with one boy, as a matter of fact) the Virginia native was rattled with how hot she was just standing here. In fact, Betty suddenly stepped right up on tiptoe and pushed her wet pelvis into the fat doorknob.

Spreading herself so her bare mound below the material could flatten hard against the knob, Betty was amazed at her sudden brazen masturbation; in fact, she couldn't be sure she wasn't dreaming. She had not heard of any of the girls before doing this (not that anyone would admit it), but Betty pushed and shucked until the sheath was sticking heavy to her front. Like the proverbial wave crashing against a rocky shore, the young woman climaxed in seconds.

Writhing, Betty came off the doorknob shaking with as much fear as she was with lust.

***

The Delino family had lived four generations in the red brick house until Antony Delino Fect, a distant cousin to the original owner and supposedly the only Delino living in the country now, donated the house to the college in the summer of nineteen ninety-five. The Delino family had amassed a sizable fortune, their money gaining the family both recognition and reputation on the east coast.

But the house quickly fell to a strange state of stasis. Not disrepair- with college maintenance keeping up appearances, the school simply didn't seem to want the place. It was rumored that the money the Delinos had made, especially of late, had come from rather nefarious dealings (it was reported that Antony Delino Fect had to leave the country) and the college administration grew skittish of such a 'questionable' donation.

So the house stood quiet and uninhabited that year…and the next.

Stories began to be hung on the quiet Tudor-like the dark shuttered windows it wore. Every new girl who passed through the tree-tunneled streets of the suburban Massachusetts college campus heard the tall tales as much as they did gossip about freshmen and teachers. In the fall of nineteen ninety-six, Delta Ti Delta, the premier sorority on campus held their hazing ritual on the lawn of Delino House. Daring new members to take a celebratory walk through the 'haunted' house as the very end of pledge week, but by the fall of that next year, after four school seasons of this specific sorority hazing, Delta-Ti-Delta 'tired' of this new ritual. It was rumored that for the girls who had entered the house, both the pledges and older sorority sisters alike, the Delino place really 'spooked them.' All the girls reported feeling an unmistakable 'presence' in the house, even in the middle of the muted sexual mayhem and mind-numbing drinking of pledging.

That October, the quick cold breeze carried leaves and courage away, as Delino house was more or less left to its own devices.

***

"Shit," Betty sighed.

Settling her breathing, letting the after-shock of the quick orgasm wash through her, Betty stood back and placed her hand on the warm doorknob.

'Get a hold of yourself!' she scolded silently, managing the single step, turning the knob, and pushing the door in. It made no sound as the darkness bade Betty forward.

The room was devoid of smell, the only light pouring in from the doorway Betty was framed in; the room had no windows, very much like a large walk-in closet. It was just an empty room in an old house with four high walls, a deep stained wood floor, and the thick wood-beam ceiling that she had spied throughout the house.

It really was just a room.

Betty's breasts ached, though, a heavy fullness to them as if she was getting her period. She didn't feel as frightened as she had when she had walked down the hall-certainly not as wild with abandon as with that damn doorknob! -but she was ill at ease. This dread both excited and scared her…because it excited her so much. As she took another step into the room, she reached for and lifted the two thin parts of her sheath-dress up and off her voluptuous pale body. Having taken her cue from what she had heard of the girls before her doing, she did regard this all as a most pagan ritual.

She only hoped she had gotten all dressed-up-then undressed-for something!

***

It wasn't until the spring of nineteen ninety-eight that Patty Ebberts and her twin sister Rachel ventured into the house to find what was, if anything, living there. Their vowed, "duty" (both girls were physics majors) was to dispel rumor and reputation. Armed with video recorders and foodstuffs, the Ebberts girls planned the entire week-end; silent, sexy sentinels supporting their scientific sit-in.

Patty was first into that room beyond the door at the end of the hallway.

Rachel had turned away for the briefest of moments when Patty called to her but by the time Rachel turned, her sister was slamming the door at the end of the hallway. Rachel reported (and Rachel's would be the only true accounting) hearing Patty's guttural moans beyond what she ran to and found a suddenly locked door. Forgetting her video recorder (and some would later scold her good common sense), Rachel was torn whether to run for help or stay. The thinner sister stood pulling and pounding for fifteen minutes, reluctantly recognizing in Patty's pleas-though Rachel would only ever admit this to Patty! -a sexual abandon so visceral Rachel grew aroused enough herself, she thought she was pissing herself in fear. Thankfully, Patty's moaning subsided as quickly as it began and the single wooden door swung open a smidgen for Rachel to dash to her sister's aid.

Rachel had stumbled into the darkness of what she could only describe as a small wooden-floored room, and like her sister- and, every other girl since- she had turned to close the door behind herself for no reason she'd later understand. The next thing Rachel knew she found herself in the Pizza Hut parking lot with no further memory of her time in that room. A weeping Patty was waiting on the gravel roadway to regale her brave sister with the same experience.

It wasn't until the next night, when the twins noticed the scars on their respective right buttock and over their left nipple, that either girl would admit to the soreness in their vaginas. In the cruelest of sexual temptation, the girls were left with the knowledge that they had experienced a moment they'd never fully recall nor relive. Like a fluttering memory hovering on the peripheral of their mind's eye, the twins would agonize together and separately on what they couldn't remember.

A legend was born that night. When Betty Fect saw the Internet posting and connected the house to her relative, she knew that when she could manage the grades and was old enough, her fate lie in Massachusetts.

***

The rush came on her so suddenly.

As her dress fell to the floor, Betty felt a pushing deep in her belly, a yearning to turn and close the door. It was a palpable sense of wanting to be alone, wanting to accept, wanting to be open and ready. She felt eyes watching her, inspecting her body, like electric tendrils tap-tap-tapping her skin; her inner thighs were wet with a flood, her eyes were tearing; she felt a blood madness taking her, as if she was a thing of liquid, to be thirsted upon, drunk...drowned in; she was frightened to her marrow for how much she wanted to release.

There was a bulbous, pulsating crotch just out of her reach...God, Betty could taste it! A live thing from the body that surrounded it; Betty brought her hands to her inner thighs and pried them apart as she stood there, willing that thick phallus to find her; like a fleshy worm periscope the picture she conjured in her mind was nearly comical if not so dangerously seductive. How can there be such power in the world,

Betty ached to understand. One second she had been standing here naked, a little cold, but breathing steady, now she was a girl unhinged.

Could she keep that door behind her open much longer?

Arching her back, Betty threw her head back and grabbed each big breast in hand, smushing her diamond point nipples through her wide fingers, kneading her flesh.

'Feast' she said in her mind, knowing fully well this thing could hear her loud and true. 'Feast.'

***

The house was guarded by a small, yet efficient college security contingent and it was only on those busiest of school nights, when extracurricular activities abounded, that a girl would even try to pass onto the Delino lawn. Julia had been the last, armed as she thought best with her recorder, but it had cost her her sanity.

What Betty was hoping was that her lineage, her family history, would allow her a 'leg up' on her sisters before her.

Grandmomma couldn't be more specific, but those northeast Fect's had always courted a smuggler's past; it was rumored Antony Fect's business dealings became shadier as they became more lucrative. The man had been described as odd, to say the least, handsome to a fault, bearing some of the same strong facial beauty as Betty, with a thin nose, high cheekbones, and dark, deep-set almond-shaped eyes. But although women were attracted to the man, he never took a wife and held no mistress for long enough for them to report much about his sexual proclivities.

No, Antony Fect Delino, it was said, was a man concerned only with money. It was even whispered among the family that the curly-haired man had made a pact with the devil to gain more of it.

Of course, Betty's grandmomma didn't support such idle talk.

***

"Pretty little one, close the door," the low liquid voice taunted from the dark center of the room.

At first, Betty thought she was going to faint, but clutching her big breasts harder, she eased her breathing, quelled her fear and held onto the idea that here she was, naked before this thing- which she hadn't accepted truly as a thing- yet she was holding her ground. The young girl had what the wieldier of this voice wanted, here deep between her wet legs, here in her heavy breasts. Sooner more than later, Betty feared she'd give herself to that thick pulsing cock she could just about smell, the hot breath she could just about feel, the skill this thing possessed she was aching to know, but as of yet Betty had not closed that door behind her wide quivering ass.

Yes, Betty reasoned, her lineage might be allowing her these few extra moments a girl like Julia hadn't been privy to.

"Who are you?" Betty groaned through her thin-parted grimace.

She felt her vagina parting as she stood there, her clitoris engorging; the thing was not touching her, but her body was reacting beyond her reason. She held herself tighter, the weight of her chest scaring her so much she feared that maybe her breasts were growing for this thing.

"I have no name," the thing teased and this time Betty swore she felt a cool breath tickle her belly.

She leaned to the source in the center of the room.

"Close it," the male voice boomed and Betty even slightly turned to the door but stopped herself in time, stood straight up, re-grabbing each breast so the pain pulled her back to what she was about.

"You cannot resist me forever," the thing said. "You need me."

"I don't need you," Betty tried, but even then, she felt her will easing out of her, like a good steam heat. God, she wanted to lie down on the floor, feel the unforgiving hard wood on her full ass as she spread her legs and just let this fiend do what it would.

"Tell me what you are…please," Betty said.

Her eyes were adjusting to the light, and she discerned a shape. It was about her height, wider if she could see right, but to her surprise, definitely human in form. The fear in her head subsided a bit; some solid ran back to her squishy body.

"In your tongue, I am called a Cambion," the thing said and the very utterance of this word slightly cooled Betty's roiling body. She stopped kneading her breasts…but kept her hands on them.

"I don't understand?" she said.

Good, feeding her curiosity was keeping Betty from feeling as light-headed as she had been. She was still flooding, her nipples achingly hard, but she was focusing her mind now, feeling the cold air of the hallway behind her ass as a reminder of what was real, outside of this room.

"You need to see," the Cambion said and from out of that center of darkness, the thing stood tall.

For all intents and purposes, he was mostly a man. Standing as tall as Betty's five foot nine height, maybe a smidgen taller, his human face was unlined and featureless, quite an unremarkable-looking man in his early thirties, Betty'd guess, if she didn't know better. There was no luster in what should have been tantalizing green eyes, no true purpose in his strong square chin.

Not wanting to, but losing the battle to curiosity, Betty's gaze drifted downward.

The creature's long neck was mottled red flesh, not scaly really, but certainly a leathery surface. Across its broad chest was a coarse plot of matte black hair, the same color as that on its head, but deep in color and texture, much like the bristles on a horse's mane. In the center of this puke of tuft hung a sight Betty could simply not get her mind around but knew all the same what it had to be.

"In the end, it was a good trade, I'd say," the naked Cambion added, noticing Betty's gaze to his ancient makeshift necklace.

Around its neck, the creature wore two tiny petrified testes on a thin yellowing cord. Betty knew whose they were. What kind of a deal had her great uncle made to grant this thing residency here in this room, to rend daring young women? Were his business dealings that important that he would trade his manhood? And what dastardly machinations had this thing, this Cambion, granted her fated evil uncle?

"Jesus Christ!" Betty exclaimed.

"He was a man more given to money than sex," the demon continued. "I came when he called. I am always available."

"But you don't want to know of my history, pretty little thing, you want..." the demon continued and stood back as Betty's eyes fell involuntarily to the erection jutting out from between the Cambion's thin hairless legs.

She had yet to see a cock that beautiful, even in her late night online searching. True, Betty had never been with any men beyond Brody and that time with Jon when they had been playing a sixteen-year-old version of 'show and tell' but she assumed this perfect thick erection to be a good eight and a half long. Strangely enough, Betty thought, for the briefest of seconds that it wasn't as big as she had thought it might be from all the tales told about the sensation the girls felt afterward...but God it was a great looking cock.

But then a clutching fear hit her even deeper than any had before. The Cambion's skill, its evil brute power was what rent girls not only sore and wanting, but forgetful. This was a thing not of the clean 'play-by-the-rules' world outside. This was a creature sporting a supremely aesthetic member but more dangerously, a demon's lust and skill.

"It will not hurt, but you will ache," the Cambion assured and it was then that Betty saw both the thing's middle fingers. They were flattened, wide, and sizzling for Christ's sake! The Cambion noticed her gaze lifting and smiled his thin red lips.

"One for your tit, one for your ass- to leave my mark," the thing explained. "Your memory will not allow much else, even one as strong as you."

"Why?" Betty asked but even then, knew she was losing control.

She feared the thing's hands more than its cock. They were so alien to her and therefore so unclean, like freed reptilian things, slithering and repulsive to her very sensibilities as woman and human. It unnerved her to look at them, but she couldn't turn her gaze away even with that fantastic cock wagging below her.

"I need to know," Betty pleaded, but even then, felt her knees quivering. She was trying to stop herself, but she could feel her body twisting even then so she could reach behind her for the door.

She could just shut the door and not see those wet fingers.

"You will not remember anyway," the Cambion said and took another step to her.

Betty looked down at the clipping sound and saw the things three-toed blunted feet. The Cambion's large erection was just touching her bare thighs now!

"Please, tell me more of what you are," she pleaded as she turned. "Please."

This close Betty could feel the heat off the thing; she dared not look down at that jumping cock below her. She eased herself to face fully forward, steeling all of her nerve to face the thing head on and know it...if it would tell her. She had now been here longer in looking at this thing, standing before her, then any girl had been before; would that help her remember?

She needed to remember.

"Sweet Betty Fect, it will just make you miss me all the more," the Cambion snickered, and Betty fell to the floor.

The thing could read her mind.

"Yes, I know who you are, little pretty one," the thing seethed over her.

Betty was terrified. The trump in her stunted juvenile deck was in keeping her identity, her lineage secret…and her thoughts to herself.

"Yes, your blood has allowed you to get this far," the thing over her sneered and Betty looked up, though she feared to do so. Damning her senses for it, she began to salivate for the thick erection bouncing just above her bent head.

Betty could not get up from her supplicant spot under that swaying cock as much as she didn't want to. Reaching up she grabbed the alive warm thing in both hands as the Cambion groaned.

"Yes," the thing cooed from above her. Betty leaned back her head and opened her mouth as wide as her lips could stretch.

"Any way you like, little pretty one," the thing cooed and Betty pulled at the warm thick shaft, stretching the sweet, warm flesh to a fraction away from her lips. Scooting her behind down hard, she opened her legs, rolling her pelvis forward, attempting to smush her fat squishy clit to the wooden floor, planting herself in that impossible dark of the room and her mind.

"This will be a first for you young girls," the thing jested and Betty began to cry with the realization that she was so lost now and needed so deeply. She stuck out her tongue to lap at the head of this creature's hardness.

"History is a demanding teacher," the demon continued standing as still as stone, willing the girl below him to begin her complete submission.

Poised with the big round head in her two fists, feeling the hot tears streaming down her face, the hot juices out her vagina, Betty looked up and smelled smoke and opened her lips even wider to accommodate.

It was then that she noticed the door to the room was still open...

"A small matter," the Cambion said. "Close...

"No," Betty moaned, sitting back away from that fleshy trunk in her fists.

The slanted bit of light, the cold air from the hallway, her knowledge of what this thing had revealed it was; Betty knew that there was a world outside that door and this thing, this Cambion (whatever the hell that was) could not venture into it. She knew. She knew. She kn...

In the Cambion's priapismic pride, in its tease for this 'unique' oral copulation, in equating Betty with all the girls before, it just assumed Betty would simply shut the door just before she took him in her sweet soft mouth. The demon could not perform until she did, until he truly had secreted the girl in this room and Betty, like all her contemporaries, had to be the one to close the door.

Betty had no way of knowing what the ritual was that this demon had secured with her uncle all those many years ago. In exchange for acute business acumen and unprecedented wealth, Fect had assured the Cambion this one single room in his house. He had allowed the demon to castrate him to show his loyalty and sexual disregard, but the Cambion, being a great wanderer of the earth, the half-human-half-animal offspring of a succubus and female, was bound by the deals he struck. Fect had assured the creature he would have plenty of human females for his picking (the private girls' college was just down the road, for Christsakes!) but he made the Cambion promise not to leave this room. Only the creature's supernatural sexual animus (aided by Fect's very manhood around his neck) could send out a scent.

The Cambion was a patient creature and had waited; his picking, while few, had been wonderfully nubile and spry with those who had come so far.

But, the demon could not perform until that door was shut, until he truly had secreted the girl in this room completely and she had to be the one to close the door.

Betty sensed all this, if not the particulars. The thing's massive penis released from her hands, it brushed her legs as she stood.

"I will remember," she said, keeping her distance from the thing. If she had been strong enough she would have reached down for her dress; as it was, she let the bastard get his last look at what is being denied him, she thought.

"It will be worse Betty Fect," the creature said. He was still raging, hard, glistening, and dangerous if she got too close, but Betty could sense some of his seductive strength dissipating. "Your longing will be worse, little pretty one."

'Read my mind all you want, you fuck,' she thought hard, looking at the creature, 'you will not have me.'

"Do you think you will be able to live the rest of your days not knowing?" the thing said. "Even the others sense me in their dreams. Their memories won't allow what you have seen and will see now, want for the rest of your days. Do you think your puny males will ever be able to satisfy you now that you have seen, touched, me?"

The Cambion stood back then, into the darkness of the room, deliberately obscuring its face and body until all Betty could see were the tops of its knees and its perfect huge cock bouncing there in the light; it retreated into a darkness of its making, she knew, not the darkness this room held. Betty stared at that erection for a very long time, wanting it, aching deep in her belly for the sensation of having it in her, but she didn't move.

"The rest of your days, pretty little one," the Cambion whispered. "The rest of your days, you will wonder."

***

Tammy's cell rang as she sat with Jill in the Pizza Hut® parking lot. Smiling in her shock, the tall red head steered her lime green Echo out of the gravel lot giggling with Jill all the way back to their dorm.

***

"You just have to believe what I say," Betty regaled her two best friends as they sat huddled in her attic room.

Nobody but Jill and Tammy knew about Betty's outing, the prevailing thought being that the fewer people who knew if you were planning a trip to Delino house, the better. And though Betty still wasn't sure how many she would tell about her experience, she'd share what she could with her two best friends now.

"It's the half-human offspring of either a succubus or incubus mating," Tammy said from the computer screen. She had logged on the minute Betty began telling her tale of what the thing called itself.

"Or it's a real guy with a huge cock that hides out to fuck girls' brains out."

"Could be that too," Tammy agreed, and they all laughed.

"Whatever the hell it was, it was kinda sad," Betty agreed and Tammy turned from the computer screen to look over at the girl with the wide eyes, as did Jill.

"I mean, just standing there waiting, the anticipation must be almost too much to bear."

"And you didn't even give him a piece," Jill coughed, and the trio laughed again.

But Betty Fect knew she had given the Cambion her curiosity and in a way that was worse than giving up her loins. As sure as she knew she was sitting there with her two best friends, her Pearl Jam T-shirt and thick blue sweats covering her body, Betty knew that there was a supernatural thing living there in Delino House. And she knew that she would be venturing back to again meet that thing in that room. The creature had been right: "the rest of your days you will wonder."

There were so many questions one could ask of a creature like a Cambion. Betty wanted answers to who Antony Fect Delino was and how he had come by this creature that now occupied his house. And she wanted another chance to stand in the light from that open door-way, face a darkness, not of this world and ache for what she knew sooner or later she had to break-down and give herself to.

The Release

Patrick Winters

Timothy Weathers sat in his car, heart racing and bladder aching. He stared across the emptied lot and to the corner where the lone lady of the night was pacing along at her station. He wondered if she'd be willing to engage in his odd indulgence. If not, then he'd been downing Mountain Dews these last couple of hours for nothing.

Timothy couldn't remember exactly when he decided that he liked urinating on women. All he knew was that it had long since become his "thing."

It had started with a web search or two for some "entertaining" sites a while back. He remembered being rather appalled the first time he saw a clip of pee play; however, his morbid curiosity had been peaked, and he ended up looking for more. He would have happened across Tina Tinkle's domain shortly after; that little vixen had helped fuel his interests in the act a good bit. But he never "did it" himself until a few

161

months ago, when a business trip to Japan took him through some shady districts with plenty of pleasures to offer. By day and night, and at an affordable price, he had relieved himself on a number of fine foreign women.

Having a woman kneeling before him—or, even better, lying on her back underneath him; the rapture of the release; the trickling sound; the feel of it flowing out across a luscious chest, or onto a pretty painted face, streaking mascara and makeup; making something lovely into something dirtied. He had to have more of it. He'd found Number-One Nirvana, and he'd kept on looking for it ever since returning stateside. So far, he'd had little luck in finding prostitutes who'd go along with his proposals.

"Oh, darn it all to heck," Timothy cursed under his breath. He took one more swig of soda for luck and got out of his car. He waddled along down the street, keeping his thighs tightly together and straightening his jacket. He glanced about, making sure that there was no one around that might see him. Luckily, the streets were dark and quiet at the moment.

He sidled up to the girl, a rather thin, black and blue haired twenty-something in a skirt and a tank top. She was pretty, her face coated in a layer of makeup; Timothy thought it would make for quite the pleasant target.

"Hey, sweetie," she said with a flirty voice. Her once-over of his suited and pudgy frame forced her smile to drop a tad. "Looking to have a fun night?"

"I do endeavor to," Timothy said with an awkward grin and a shaky nod. He shifted his balance from foot to foot, as much in apprehension as in discomfort at his tumbling gut.

"What did you have in mind?"

"Well, my tastes are perhaps . . . exotic and bizarre to most." He gave an anxious little giggle. "Quite bizarre, I'd dare to say. I should perfectly understand it if you were to deny my request . . ."

The young woman's eyebrows peaked and she crossed her arms. Her head tilted in a show of bored aggravation. "Yeah? Spit it out already."

Her demand and another pang in his innards made Timothy get to the point. "I'd . . . very much like to urinate on you . . ."

Her face didn't twitch in the slightest, nor did she recoil from him, as he'd expected her to. She thought on it for a quick moment.

"On?" she asked for clarification. "Just on, right? Not in my mouth or anything?"

"Oh, no. That would be disgusting."

She rolled her eyes and sighed. "Yeah, okay. I can help you with that. But it'll cost you more than my usual rates."

"Of course," Timothy said. "It is a strange request, after all . . ."

"Yeah, but not exactly rare," she said with a shrug. "I've been peed on before. No big deal, but leaving the corner and passing up other business to take a shower afterwards is. Judging by all the dancing and prancing you're doing, you've already got one in the chamber, huh?"

Timothy gave another giggle and nodded.

She pointed across the street to a dim alley. "Unless you've got something else in mind, what do you say we head over there and get to it?"

"Oh, yes. That'll be fine. After you, dear." Timothy motioned her on, trying to be charming. He wasn't succeeding.

The girl strode across the street. Timothy shuffled along after her, feeling like he was about to burst.

They went in a short ways, just enough to be out of sight from the street. The girl stepped into a niche between two big, rusted old dumpsters and faced him again. "Okay, let's do this."

She tossed her purse out of the way and set her hands to her shirt. She pulled the top up and over her head, her little breasts bobbing out at him as she arched her back. Her light pink nipples were hard, and Timothy stiffened a bit himself as he ogled them. The girl tossed her shirt onto her purse and knelt before him, her knees situated on wadded-up newspapers. "Aim low enough to miss the hair," she said as she pulled her locks back and out of the way, "but high enough that you don't hit the skirt. And if I say stop, for any reason, you stop. Got it?"

Timothy nodded, keeping up his little to-and-fro dance to keep his bladder at bay.

"All right then. Let's see what you got," the girl said, sticking her chest out and setting her hands to her heels.

Timothy unzipped and fiddled with his underwear until he had a hold of himself. His champagne bottle was about to pop its cork any second. He pulled his penis out, took quick aim, and let it out with an orgasmic sigh.

Unfortunately for them both, the moment his less than impressive member was out, the girl couldn't help but grin and give a hearty chuckle; instead of a hose, he was working with a tap. And in his eagerness,

Timothy didn't much care that her mouth was open a little too far. His warm stream sprung onto her chest, but as the pressure rose all the more, it shot up and across her chin. She gagged in shock as it got into her mouth. She ducked her head as she coughed, her hair getting drenched as the stream slipped past her outstretched hands.

"St-- stop!" she shouted. But there was no stopping it for Timothy; he felt lighter than air, lost to the release and that gloriously guilty pleasure he had so longed to feel.

The girl fell back onto her rear as the downpour got into her eyes, streaking her eye shadow. She was hollering now, unable to contain her disgust.

"Stop, you fucking freak!" she half-yelled, half-choked out.

Timothy moaned at her protests and the sleek look of her now glistening skin. He smiled and tilted his head back as he kept on going.

Desperate to stop the shower, the girl took aim and kicked out at Timothy's crotch. Her hard kick connected straight on, smashing into his penis and squashing his testicles.

Timothy gasped as pain shot through his gut. His smile shattered into a wordless gasp, and he started heaving as a vomitous roiling rose up inside. He stumbled back a step as he fought to stay standing. He wasn't successful.

He fell backwards, his head slamming right into the edge of the dumpster behind him with a crack and a clang. His body crumpled into a pile before it, his head lolling over his chest.

The girl got to her feet, shaking the urine off of her head and hands. She kicked Timothy's leg, a torrent of curses on her tongue. They came to a stop as she noticed the wet red color against the brown lip of the dumpster, where Timothy had hit his head. She gave a little squeal as she saw the blood pouring out of his wound, and how his eyes were half-open in a dead stare.

Not knowing what else to do, the girl put her top back on and grabbed her purse. She knelt down by Timothy and slipped her hand into his back pocket, fishing out his wallet. She pitched it into her purse and then started huffing it towards her apartment. She'd need a shower first, and then a plan for getting out of town—and quickly.

At about the same time as she was packing her clothes for a late-night bus ride, a mangy boxer came sniffing its way through the city streets. On the hunt for food, it came across Timothy's cold body. It gave his dirtied crotch a sniff before realizing that the little sausage poking out was not a treat.

It lifted its hind leg and peed on the body before continuing on its way.

Hunger for Warmth

Kenzie Kordic

As I walked down the street, I scanned the area to see if anyone was around. Yeah, it is a bad part of town, but I like it here. I don't see anyone on this round, so I just aimlessly wander. It is about two in morning. A bench is close to the corner of the next intersection so I walk over and sit down, pulling out my ancient book. Having quiet nights can be both good and bad. Good, because I have time to myself to read and think, bad because I don't get to have any fun. I get so hungry at this time of night. All I want to do is feed but I always should wait until the time is right. Lame. Hanging around in the bad neighborhoods, or what you would call the bad parts of town, is easy pickings. It seems more exciting than the typical club nightlife that everyone goes to in this day in age. Too many people mean too many witnesses.

I brush my dark brown bangs out of my eyes, pulling my book out of my shoulder bag. I open to the middle of the book. I have memorized everything in the book up until this point. It will help me out a lot in the long run when I need to know something on the fly. I have endless time to memorize this. Right as I started reading, I see an old, black two-door car pull up in front of me. I sigh, annoyed that I must put my book away, but finally something is happening. The passenger side window rolls down, a man in the driver's seat.

"How much for an hour?" He calls out. I smirk, readjusting my stockings. I stand up and walk over to the car, leaning on the door. "Honey, whatever you've got is fine for me." I said, raising a curved eyebrow and smiling happily. "Alright baby, go ahead and hop in."

I open the car door, and slide into the seat. I place my bag on my lap while pulling the door closed. He pulls away from the curb and drives heading northbound, into a worse part of town. Almost to the country. "Where are we heading to? There aren't any motels in the area." I said, placing a hand gently on his thigh. "You don't need to worry your pretty little head." He responded, staring intently out of the windshield.

About twenty minutes later, we arrive at an old, decrepit looking house. The type you see on documentaries about impoverished areas. I sigh and roll my eyes. This man couldn't be any classier if he tried. I opened the door and got out quickly. When he got out of the car, I noticed he walked with a limp. "What happened to your leg?" I asked.

"Mind your damn business, sweetheart." I laughed and rolled my eyes. He grabbed my hand, leading me to the front door of the house, pulling out a pair of keys and sliding a key into the lock. It didn't budge. "Damn rust." He muttered. He turned the key and rammed his body against the door. He pulls my face towards his and kisses me roughly, very sloppy. I can tell he is very new to this but I don't care, I need him now. I roll over on top him, pulling my lace top off and immediately removing my bra. His eyes light up as soon as he sees my breasts. I rub my breasts along his chest, moaning in ecstasy as I can't wait to breathe him in. My body gets hotter as I feel him pulsating beneath me. I unbuckle his belt and pull off his pants roughly, he tries to complain but I urgently kiss him, biting his bottom lip. I lift my skirt, not wearing any panties underneath, and rub my clit against his hard, pulsing cock. I slide down onto him, bouncing on top of him and as I do, his eyes light up in pleasure and he lets out a series of moans. I giggle and can feel it coming from me rapidly. I can't hold it in anymore, I need to release.

I lean over and kiss him softly. I pull away and whisper quietly, "Just think of all of the pleasure you're experiencing, and nothing else." He looked at me confused, but I didn't care. I kissed him hard and took a deep breath. With that, my fire released from me. I loved the way his essence tasted. Yes, it was cheap tasting but good enough for now. As I ingested his sexual energy, I could feel my headache going away. The longer I ate his energy, the more afraid he became. He tried to fight back by pushing me away but I just pressed his body into the ground and could feel his life slipping away. He looked up at me terrified as I drained the last of the energy out of him. He went limp beneath me and I climbed off him. His eyes staring at the ceiling, now lifeless, made me feel a rush of adrenaline.

Damn, he tasted like a mix a weed and dirt. Not my best choice. I pulled my clothes back on and reached into my bag, pulling out a piece of gum. 'That's better.' I thought. I grabbed my book and flipped through the pages, stopping on the slave page. I am so hungry for a group of devoted followers that will do anything I want. And I mean anything. Maybe pleasing me at a moment's notice, or draining them until death. I read the page and smirked, learning how easy it is to use my powers of seduction to control people. Who knows, maybe I won't stop there. I put my book back in my bag and started to make my way back into the city.

About an hour of walking later, I felt such energy coming from a house nearby in a decent neighborhood. I walked into the house easily enough, and saw not only men, but a group of women as well. I scanned the surroundings, there seemed like there was at least fifteen people here. A drunk frat looking guy came up to me, wrapping an arm around my shoulder. "Who are you, baby doll? Want something to drink?" This should be fun.

Beauty Box

Emerian Rich

Eve's parents schooled her from an early age to protect her Beauty Box. She was to guard its purity with her life, but she never quite understood the power of her chastity until her sixth birthday, when Bobby Lewis wanted to see it. Years later, when she was thirteen and he wanted to touch it, she thought it a joke. It seemed such a ridiculous request. Yes, her Beauty Box was precious, but she thought it was only important to herself and perhaps her family. No one else could have want or need of it. Why would they?

Bobby did. He seemed to want to touch it more than he favored his own life. No matter how many times she said no, or slapped his hand away, he came back to the spot. She finally had to ask him to leave.

"Can't guard it all your life, Evey. People will start calling you a tease," he'd said.

Tease. It was something mom did to her hair, not a name for a young girl at the brink of womanhood. Yet, it became her nickname, Evey Teasey. Bobby spread word faster than word of Mr. Atkin's prize winning horse giving birth to a two-headed calf.

Sixteen years later, a nickname like Evey Teasey still followed her. Mom and dad had died two summers ago. All Eve had was the broken-down farm house they left her and her perfectly preserved Beauty Box.

She sat at the kitchen table, a freshly baked chocolate cake in front of her and blew out twenty-nine carefully placed candles. You weren't supposed to tell your wish to anyone, or it wouldn't come true, she knew that. But there was no one there to hear it but Felix the cat, so Eve said it aloud.

"I wish there was someone I could share my Beauty Box with."

After all the years of safeguarding her dearest possession, Eve was lonely. And she felt an ache between her legs she couldn't quite relieve.

There was no one in town she even liked, let alone someone special enough to share her Beauty Box with. She was ruminating on that when Bobby entered the convenience store where she worked. He looked tired and worn out. His skin was sun burnt and sweaty. His back-wards baseball cap mussed his hair so a chunk pushed out the hole in a mess. Eve had seen Bobby working out on the road near Johnson's farm and knew he was the joke of town, but hated him just the same. Did he know what pain and chastisement he'd caused her with the nickname Evey Teasy? Something told her he didn't.

"Hey, Evey." Bobby plopped a bag of corn nuts down on the counter and guzzled a beer he'd already opened.

She keyed his total in and sighed. "Nice breakfast."

"Shit, this ain't breakfast! I haven't been to bed yet. Dumbass Rick hit the water main and we've been patchin' it since yesterday. I have a mind to kick his white ass from here to Kentucky, 'cept he's my brother-in-law and ma would tan my hide."

Eve stared at Bobby blankly. She could no more scrounge up sympathy for him than fly to the moon.

"Five-oh-three."

When Bobby opened his wallet, she saw a faded photo of Bobby's short-lived wife and two kids. The marriage had failed after four years to no one's amazement. Loraine had been prom queen and daughter to the mayor. How Bobby ever thought he measured up was a wonder to Eve.

She handed back his change and Bobby grinned, showing his tobacco-yellowed teeth.

"Thanks, Evey. Lookin' good." He winked suggestively and sauntered out the door.

Looking good? She was dressed in a polyester convenience store uniform and her hair hadn't been washed in three days. She wasn't foolish enough to be flattered. She rolled her eyes and went back to reading the entertainment magazine she'd been enjoying before Bobby came in.

The men in the magazine were the kind that would open car doors for you and send you flowers on Valentine's Day. She closed her eyes and fanaticized the beefcake model kissed her. Yes, he was the type of man special enough to share her Beauty Box with. Not some balding hillbilly who dug trenches for a living and spent every night at the local dive bar hoping for a quickie in the parking lot.

She had the next two days off and a whole chocolate cake in the fridge, but her shoulders sagged. PJ's. Cake. TV. What was last weekend's agenda? PJ's. Chips. TV. And yet she fell asleep on the couch, chocolate drool staining her red gingham pillow as the tube played infomercials into the early morning.

A knock on the door startled Eve awake and she sat up, bolt straight. The remote control stuck to her cheek for a moment before falling, strewing batteries across the floor.

A second knock sent her tripping out of her afghan to open the door.

"Oh, hey Eve. You got a package." Tom Randolph handed Eve a clipboard to sign. Tom had been a year behind Eve in high school and just a tad lower in social standing, if that was possible. They were both outcasts, but hadn't seen the use in banding together.

"Yeah, thanks." Eve handed back the clipboard and accepted the package.

Door closed, Eve inspected the return address. Her best and only friend, Jen had moved to LA to be a movie star, but became a porn star instead.

Eve popped open the box and read the card.

Eve,

I know your Beauty Box is special to you, but you're 29. Time to let someone have a look.

I guarantee you'll find Mr. Right in this. Wear it with those heels I gave you last Christmas.

Jen XOXO

Inside the box was one of Jen's work perks, a sleazy red dress if folded properly, would fit inside a tic-tac box. Under it, a fancy set of lingerie no woman in her rural area of Kansas would wear, including garter belt, G-string, and thigh-highs.

Eve rolled her eyes and stuffed it all back in the box. She didn't feel like dressing up like trash and heading for the local (and only) dive bar in town. Throwing the box in the closet, Eve decided she needed more supplies, having finished off her cake the night before.

At the grocery store, Eve picked up a cheap box of wine on sale. She didn't normally drink, but what the hell, she needed to celebrate her twenty-nine-ness somehow. A box of lasagna, brownie mix, and she was in line before anyone realized she had come to the store in her PJs.

"Oh, Evey! What a surprise," Tammy said from behind her, snickering with her friend Pamela Sue, who'd been attached to her hip since high school. They were both preggers, in similar sundresses. "Stocking up for the zombie apocalypse?" Tammy looked down her powdered nose at Eve, daring her to come up with some witty come-back. Pamela Sue giggled. "Lord knows you haven't a man to feed all that to."

Eve let the put downs roll off her as she paid cash, grabbing the bags and darting for the door.

"Better watch out eating like that. Don't wanna turn into old Mrs. Halston. They had to bury her in a piano, you know?"

Eve closed her eyes, letting out an infuriated sigh as she made it to the parking lot. She wanted to yell back that she'd be happy to end up like Mrs. Halston, but back talking to Tammy only inspired her to spout more nonsense.

Mrs. Halston was nowhere near as fat as Tammy hinted at. She'd been a sweet old widow who indulged a bit with the gourmet cookies she made. She'd been buried in a normal coffin, Eve was one of seven at the funeral.

Eve spent the afternoon cooking and after a tasty birthday dinner and half a box of wine, she was feeling quite good. She stepped in front of the tall mirror in her bedroom. She looked rather sexy, if she did say herself. Her long hair was mussed as if she'd just got out of bed from a nice dream. Her tank top strap hung off her right shoulder, revealing the swell of her breast. Twenty-nine and hot, she felt she should be going to the bar to get some attention. But the local bar was nothing but old men and cheaters. The most she could hope for was a tourist on their way to Kansas City. Her town was dwindling and with only one exit on a secondary highway, she didn't see it growing anytime soon.

"Tonight's going to be different, Eve. You'll see," she said to herself. Grabbing the box her friend Jen had sent, she pulled out the red latex dress. "Yeah. This will make it different."

***

Eve stood in front of the local watering hole, Mal's in her city-girl outfit. She lived around the corner, but already had blisters from the outlandishly high stilettos. The shoes were all anyone could see of the outfit, since she'd donned her dad's old army-issue trench coat over. Still, she felt self-conscious with her hair and makeup done up and knowing what she had underneath the coat. The worst thing she could think of was someone seeing her trying too hard.

The front door of Mal's burst open, causing Eve to pop out of her daze. She took a deep breath in and backed up into a parked car.

"No! Hank. It's enough. I don't want to hear it!" Tammy screamed, hurrying to her car. She had a hard time finding the right key as her husband caught up to her.

"Tam, come on...she's means nothin' to me, babe. I swear." He grabbed hold of her arm, and swung her around.

Eve couldn't help watching the crushing scene. Even Tammy wasn't awful enough to wish an unfaithful husband on.

He planted a sloppy drunk kiss on Tammy's mouth, hugging her tightly to him. But instead of pulling away, Tammy sunk into the embrace, tears ruining her black mascara.

"Come home, baby," she whimpered, smoothing back his unruly grown out butch-cut. He nodded and she helped him into the passenger seat, despite her being so pregnant she could barely fit behind the wheel.

Eve couldn't help but let out an exasperated sigh. Tammy heard it and looked up. Her broken-woman expression disappeared and she slammed the passenger door with a vengeance.

"Don't you dare judge me Evey Teasy...don't you dare!" she screamed, shoving Eve as she went by. She got into her SUV and sped out of the parking lot, spraying dust into the air as her tires accelerated.

"Don't pay her no mind." Bobby stood by the front door, lighting a cigarette. "She'd just pissed because her old man's fucking the biggest slut in the county."

"Leeann?"

"That'd be her." He let out a puff of smoke and grinned. "I ain't never seen you here, got a date?"

Eve didn't want to answer. She didn't even want to play nice with Bobby, but her body ached to be near someone. Was it truly that bad to want the man who'd been the cause of her exile in town? The word "desperate" stamped in her mind.

"I get it, you don't want to talk to me." Taking another drag, he dropped the cigarette, stamping it out with his toe. "That's fine." He made to go back into the bar, but paused, turning back to her. "You're lookin' real nice tonight. Be a shame to waste it." He held out his hand, motioning for her to take it. Cocky smile and sexy eyes didn't make it easier to deny him.

Eve's body screamed in her ears. She had to have him and urgently.

"Why don't..." She glanced at him shyly. "Why don't we go to my place instead?"

Bobby's expression was priceless. His mouth popped open, but he was clearly speechless.

"Unless you don't..."

"No! I do. Wait...wait here."

As Bobby disappeared in the bar, Eve panicked. What had she done? Invited her arch-nemesis, the man who had made her uncomfortable adolescence even harder, into her home? Before she could bolt, he was back with his coat in hand.

"Let's go."

The walk back home was short enough for the awkward silence not to grow to an unbearable level.

She led him in to her house and locked the door behind them. Removing her heels and coat, as a force of habit, brought on a stare from Bobby that told her she wouldn't have to beg for it.

"Wow." He gasped, smiling and then plopped his jacket down on the table. "I can't believe you were gonna wear that into Mal's. Do you know how many men would've...well, you woulda started a brawl for sure."

She blushed. Suddenly she was thirteen again and he was telling her how he wanted to touch her Beauty Box. But her body reacted differently than it had sixteen years earlier. Something between her legs uncoiled, and a tingle of pleasure licked up her spine.

Bobby stepped forward slowly, holding out his hands as if approaching an unknown puppy. She let him advance and he placed his hands on her hips.

"Man, I've wanted you so long, Eve." It was the first time he'd called her Eve and not Evey since they were little. There was real longing in his voice and Eve understood then, why he'd been so mean. She'd denied him the one thing he wanted beyond anything, to touch her. He wasn't forgiven, but she understood his longing as he moved his right hand over her backside and his left up her neck. Kissing him was opening a door to passion she'd denied herself for sixteen years. She couldn't help grabbing his back and massaging him closer to her.

Yet, fear entered her mind from all those years of hurt. Would he have sex with her and then tell everyone in town she was a whore? Evey Teasy would turn to Evey Easy. She heard the echo of chant in her ears and pulled back from him. She stared into his eyes, connecting with what she thought might be the compassion inside him.

"No one will know?" she whispered.

"Nah."

"I mean it. You tell one person and I'll slash your tires, burn down your trailer, the works."

"I swear. It'll be our little secret."

She studied him, running her hand along the back of his neck, smelling the maleness of him close her in.

"Come on, Eve." He kissed her and ran his hands over her backside. "I can't wait. You've got me so hard."

She felt him against her, hard and long, wanting to stick himself where no one had ever been. Her body trembled with anticipation. She stepped back from him and unzipped the latex dress all the way down, allowing it to slide off her shoulders and to the floor. Not needing a bra with the tight latex dress, she stood practically naked, with just the G-string, garter and thigh-highs on.

The sight of her kicked him into high-gear. He yanked off his shoes, threw off his shirt, and unbuttoned his jeans. Eve took off the G-string, a little self-conscious about not being waxed, but her mother had told her not to let anyone near her Beauty Box and so she'd just given it a nice trim.

"Hell Eve, you've got a hot bod. Your tits are fuckin'..." He didn't finish his sentence. Grabbing her boobs, he sucked on one nipple and then the other as his hard dick pressed into her leg.

Eve remembered seeing Bobby's dick when he was young. They used to play naked in the kiddie pool on his front yard, but little Bobby had grown into a man since then. She reached down and stroked it, so hungry for it, she wanted to put it in her mouth, but it belonged somewhere else. Her Beauty Box throbbed with wanting, wet, and begging to be violated.

"Now," she gasped, gripping his shoulders to pull herself up and wrapping her legs around his waist.

"Condom?" he asked.

"I'm on the pill." She lied. "Now!"

He obliged, guiding his dick into her Beauty Box. It slid in easily, her juices paving the way deep inside her. Contrary to what the magazines said, it didn't hurt. No, it felt like his hard shaft was the thing her body had been missing forever. Like it had been cut from her as a child and only now joined back into its rightful place.

He grunted, his eyes closing in pleasure and she bit her lip so not to call out. Staggering over to the couch with her still attached, Bobby plopped her down and for a moment they lost contact. Eve scowled, how could he leave her unsatisfied? But a moment later he plunged back into her and the feeling of wholeness returned. She moved her hips, loving the sensation of him pushing, poking deeper inside her with each thrust.

She cried out. He thrust harder.

"Oh, yeah...want it harder, baby?" His speech was straight off a porno, but she didn't care.

"Um-hum..." she whimpered.

"Like that?" He slammed deep into her, his cock growing harder and plumper with every stroke.

Her Beauty Box swelled too, determined to keep him inside, wrapping tighter around him, but she wanted it harder, faster than he seemed able to govern. She shoved her hips up, causing him to topple to the floor, with her on top. Looking down, she enjoyed the mix of shock and enjoyment covering his face. His hands planted on her breasts and as he played with her nipples, she rode him. She liked being in control, his thick shaft hers to command. Yes, she would choose if they went front, back, sideways or deeper. She placed her hands on his abs and pushed herself up, slamming back down on him with a force that pleased them both.

He gasped and moaned, gripping her ass and pressing her down on him. When he started to shake, she knew he was close to release. She'd never reached orgasm with someone inside her, so she didn't know what to expect, but she wanted it so badly. Her body moved faster toward something...a satisfaction she couldn't fathom. Heat radiated inside her like the sun on a hot summer day and she wondered if being attached to his hot dick would give her a sunburn on the inside. When he clutched her ass to him and she felt a gush of warmth inside her, her own body shook with desire. She rode the wave of ecstasy, body sensitive and tender as if any slight movement of her hips would break her in two. She looked down at him, a smile prominent on his face, his head rolling back and forth as she thrust.

And then it popped. The big bliss ball inside her exploded, sending fireworks of light to her closed eyelids. She shivered with delight and her legs squeezed tight against his groin. The pleasure was all consuming and she didn't realize the ringing in her ears wasn't from orgasm, but from Bobby's scream. There was a jolt and she fell off him, against the Lazyboy, her Beauty Box open and exposed.

"Fucking bitch! What the fuck? Shit!" he screamed.

She didn't understand why he was yelling until she looked down at his crotch where blood covered him. Perhaps she should have told him she was a virgin, but to be fair, he'd deflowered half the cheerleading squad in high school, he should've known blood was part of the deal.

He continued to scream as she gasped for air, her orgasm still rolling silently through her limbs. He grasped his crotch. The blood seemed to be coming from him, not just on him. Then she realized his dick was missing. Her brain slowly digested his insane tirade.

"You fucking bitch! You broke my dick off. You fucking asshole piece of shit!" He tried to pull on his jeans, but blood spurting from his crotch kept him grasping to block it.

Broke it off? She didn't think someone could do that just by having sex, but then again, she wasn't a pro at the whole thing. She looked around the floor. Where had it gone?

A slurping sound came from below and she looked down to see his bloodied manhood sticking out of her. It slowly slid out and despite the morbidity of what was happening, she found herself aroused. She wanted to push it back in, deep inside her, to feel the thrill of orgasm again. With it disconnected, she didn't need him at all.

As she yearned for his dick, it slid back into her and her body tingled with delight.

"What the fuck? How are you...are those...teeth?" His eyes went wide with horror.

She looked down, arching her back so she could see her Beauty Box fully. Well, they certainly looked like teeth. The teeth latched onto his manhood and undulated, pulling his dick further into her. It disappeared into her warm depths and the teeth snapped shut, devouring the piece she'd claimed. Deep inside, she felt her body consume him, throwing her into another fit of ecstasy. She closed her legs and rolled, squeezing them tightly together. Oh, it was better than anything she'd ever felt before. Her insides swallowed him whole, chewed him up and then assimilated him into her core, nutrition she didn't know she needed.

"You fucking bitch! Help! Help!" Bobby staggered up, his jeans around his ankles and reached for the door. His bloody hand slid from the doorknob and he tripped, knocking his head on the entry table. He fell to the floor with a final thump.

Eve couldn't help herself from rubbing her clit into another orgasm as his still body lay quiet enough for her to enjoy it.

***

The day after Eve's birthday, she woke with such a content feeling, she didn't know how she'd ever top it. Oh, she had ideas, but she'd have to try them to see if they worked. Her Beauty Box was awakened, and a whole new world opened up to her. The only question...where to start? Who deserved to be her next meal? Tom the postman? Tammy's cheating husband? Whoever it was, she knew, her Beauty Box could never be denied again.

A Dark Love Story

Helen Mihajlovic

In the night, he comes for me while I peacefully sleep. He disturbs my dreams. He resembles a demon, a beast and a wolf. He whispers in my ear, 'Adele, my name is Duncan.' I wake in a sweat, my heart racing as I breathe heavily.

It has been a year since this creature entered my life. With him he brings constant torment and unrest, yet he is hard to resist. My safety can only be assured during the day, for he never ventures during this time. He lurks in shadows of my dreams, never allowing me to see his face in complete light. He reveals little of himself and that which he says could be a lie. Yet he is very persuasive and can lure you into his world where all is dark.

The morning has come and I am glad it is day. The sun shall keep him away from me. I put on my pretty white dress and brush my long ebony hair.

After breakfast, a black carriage waits outside to take me to a suitor. As the carriage brings me towards him, I know the suitor is not the man my heart desires. He is tall and very young. He wears the finest suits and hat. We will dine with the most superb cutlery, eating poultry and the sweetest desserts. There will be silence; we have nothing to say. I feel like running away. I search for true love, yet in seeking it, all I find is torment.

The day is coming to an end, my suitor waves goodbye and it is a cold farewell.

The carriage takes me home to my mother's warm smile and she hugs me. My eyes fill with tears as she recognizes my absence of love yet again. She assures me not to worry, that someday, the right one will be there for me.

I enter my bedchamber and I look around in fright. Will the demon come tonight? I slowly drift into a nightmare. I hear him whisper to me.

'It is Duncan.'

But he's nowhere in sight, except for a trail of blood on the cold ground. I follow it to a gothic gate that opens as I approach. A staircase leads to a dark dungeon. I am shrouded by darkness. I stumble on the stairs, cobwebs clutch me and I rush into Duncan's sharp claws. He grabs my waist and my heart clatters in my chest. Duncan lowers his claws to my upper thigh and scratches my skin as he tears my dress.

He presses his chest against me, his hair coarse, his odor sour. He tantalizes me with his knowledge of history, literature and philosophy. The conversation with him leaves me elated.

Nearby, a table sags under the weight of any sort of food one could desire.

Duncan grabs the meat and pushes it in my mouth. I eat ravenously. He places rice and dates into my mouth. I ask him where I am.

'Macabre origins onus,' he says.

'Leave me alone. Free me!' I plead.

'No, it is impossible,' he whispers. 'Follow me.'

We arrive at a room with red walls and gold ceilings. He takes a sweet from a dish on the table and puts it in my mouth. I experience a sense of pleasure on my tongue. His sharp claw circles my nipple. I awake.

I can smell smoke on me. It smells similar to the room Duncan had taken me to. The room had fires everywhere, as if they were keeping Hell warm. But how is it possible that I can smell them on my clothes? Duncan only exists in my nightmare!

My mother meanders into my bedchamber carrying my breakfast.

She tells me of a possible suitor that I could visit today.

'I'm tired. I've been looking for love for years, only to find pain! I want to stop looking for a while. I want to forget love,' I say.

Mother places her hand on my shoulder, smiling warmly.

'I don't want to see a suitor today.'

'Very well,' she says, leaving my bedchamber with a gentle smile.

I peer out a window for most of the day. I feel alone.

Night emerges. I am sleepy; I need to go to bed early. As I sleep, I hear a whisper.

'It is Duncan.'

His claw traces the side of my face and neck. He reaches for my nipple; caresses it, leaves small scratches. I scream as his sharp claws shred my dress. But my heart races as I feel desire. I lie in front of him naked. Every angle of my body is visible to this evil being; yet it excites me. Placing his body on top of mine, he begins a motion that gives me pleasure.

This monster can never love me; he can only give me fleeting moments of delight. This monster is not my true love; he is an illusion of happiness. Does this evil spirit even know how to love? I hope to one day find a good suitor, one that really cares for me. This monster from the pit only cares for his pleasure. Yet I cannot end my desire for him. I shut my eyes. He kisses my lips. I awake.

I am tormented throughout the day. I try to hold back my tears when my family is near. I dislike Duncan for all the suffering he causes. I think of him and the passion we have. He is an evil spirit that may enter thousands of women's dreams in one night. What can I do to be rid of him?

I hasten to our library, looking for literature on ridding an incubus. I desperately search and I find a prayer. I recite it before going to bed.

'I withdraw all invitations and permission to all incubuses. I command you to leave my dreams and allow me to rest.'

He is gone for eight months. There is peace. I am taken to meet many suitors.

One by one they all go wrong. One of the suitors is abusive, the other fills the time with mindless conversation. One is too young, the other too old. One doesn't see me as fit to be his wife; and, many whom I don't see as fit husbands. To be with them would be a waste of a life.

I cry myself to sleep. As I drift off to dream, I hear a whisper.

'It is Duncan.'

My heart beats faster. I am aghast! We are in a room filled with naked people and they all touch one another. Duncan tears at my dress. We sit on an antique chair; the couple sitting opposite caresses one another. Duncan spreads my legs, between which the couple can see. He strokes me between my legs with his claw, I am afraid he will hurt me. The man opposite us touches his partner's voluptuous breast. My monster lifts me, places me on top of him and he is inside me. The man opposite us is also inside his partner.

When we are through, a woman comes to Duncan and places her mouth between his legs and begins a hungry suction. To my surprise, I am not jealous; watching this act excites me. After hours, we are all tired.

I ask Duncan, 'Why won't you free me? I never want to see you again!'

'I can't. You keep calling for me.'

I realize this is true. Perhaps it is my loneliness or it is the lure of darkness that makes Duncan hard to resist. The forbidden that makes it so enticing. He cannot resist my call either. But there is misery in this evil.

Each night as I drift to sleep, I am frightened to dream

The Safe Word

Ken Goldman

safe·word (n.): a word serving as a prearranged and unambiguous signal to end a potentially dangerous activity, such as between a dominant and submissive sexual couple.
-- The New World Dictionary

Laurie waved to Cricket from The Trophy Room's dance floor, the girl's highly suggestive undulations Laurie's patented interpretation of vertical intercourse set to music. From the look she gave her bestie seated on the bar stool, it seemed that Laurie planned to remain in slut mode tonight and that Cricket would need to find another ride home. This had been their agreement, and finding transportation usually proved easy with some subtle eye contact and a smile. Like her pal, Cricket had developed her own moves. She scanned the room, her eyes drawn to two attractive young men at the far end of the tavern. Although their attention seemed elsewhere, she couldn't hide her grin. Either of the two would do nicely. Cricket jacked up her skirt, crossed her legs, and watched them.

No stranger to the bar scene, she recognized the men's pick-up routine as it unfolded, the game guys played to fool women inside singles' taverns like The Trophy Room. Maybe some naïve twit would miss the cues, but Cricket had observed the familiar hook-up gambit enough times to spot it coming a mile away.

The rules were simple. Exercising their cojones once a likely catch was selected, two Type-A males conspiratorially agreed upon the good cop/bad cop ploy designed to create a rescue-me-from-this-creep scenario. First Guy then makes himself as obnoxious and off-putting as humanly possible for several minutes, thereby enabling Second Guy to swoop in and save the pestered fair-haired damsel. First Guy conveniently disappears into the night, leaving a clear field for Second Guy to have the young woman's panties adorn his bedpost by midnight. It wasn't a very creative variation on the designated wingman approach, but even intelligent women bought the ploy if the act seemed convincing enough. Of course, should the game be followed by some questionable Bill Cosby brew, things could get out of hand. Cricket knew enough not to let any testosterone-fueled horn-dog's subterfuge get that far. Instinctively, she never lost sight of her wine glass.

Tonight's First Guy may have seemed convincing to a novice, but Cricket was not stupid. She felt secure enough to play along, having noticed the man with his partner-in-crime chug-a-lugging beers together not an hour earlier. During that time one aborted mission involved a long-legged blonde who was in no mood for such bullshit. Cricket would get a kick out of yanking both guys' respective chains. Rubbing her finger along the rim of her wine glass, she smiled like a school girl and turned away shyly as the more sharply dressed First Guy approached the vacated stool alongside hers.

"This seat taken?"

Simple and direct, yet smooth. Cricket offered a half smile, knowing the dance had begun.

"Nope."

"Bruce," the man said, offering his hand. She took it, and her smile broadened. Men were so predictable, bless their pointed little heads.

"Cricket."

With that minimal introduction, the game was afoot. Somehow the guy's seeming lack of effort must have worked on other women, but usually such women's intentions didn't differ much from the men who pursued them. The dark-haired stranger grinned like some Cheshire Cat, but his eyes beading in on Cricket's rack told a different story. Here was a jungle cat stalking his prey, but first checking her out close-up to determine if she were edible.

The young man leaned close.

"Cricket, eh? Like that insect that chirps by rubbing its legs together?"

Cricket couldn't stifle a huge grin at the veiled innuendo, and she understood the ping and pong of this ritual. "I'm not telling what makes me chirp. So -- Bruce, huh? Like Spielberg's Great White Shark?"

The man's teeth practically gleamed. "That depends, little fishy."

It was a terrible line. Amused, Cricket sipped her merlot. "So, I'm shark bait, am I? Tacky, Mr. Bruce. Very tacky." She could spar with him, show the guy she was in control of the situation and not some bimbette he could win over with smiles and suggestive repartee. Still, Cricket had to admit the man wasn't hard on the eyes. She expected his next words would somehow be both charming yet mildly offensive. Sure enough...

"So, what does make you chirp, Cricket?"

That had to be among the worst follow-up lines she'd ever heard, but she knew the man had intended that.

"You're mixing your metaphors, Bruce. Am I an insect or a fish?"

Bar talk seemed ridiculous to her, but how else could she answer a remark so loaded with insinuation? She said nothing more; instead, she took a final sip from her wine glass, her long fingers caressing the stem purposefully. Cricket expected this man would raise the ante to clear the runway for Second Guy, who had been watching them. She was ready.

Bruce with the pearly whites continued working from his well-rehearsed script, eventually pulling out his smart phone to hit a key for his next bit of entertainment. "Want to see whom I'd like to take home with me tonight?" He held up the phone's screen for her with the reverse photo option turned on, stroking Cricket's bare shoulder as if they were already lovers. She felt some relief that the guy wasn't uncouth enough to next scroll to a photo of his manhood, although had that been his move she wouldn't have been surprised. The photo bit earned a giggle but not her approval, and of course Cricket's indignation regarding his expectations was part of the plan.

"Very clever. If you order me another drink, I'd enjoy watching you get your hopes up."

The man nodded and got the bartender's attention, pointing to Cricket's empty glass. Now having invested actual cash in the evening's prey, ol' Bruce became uncomfortably touchy-feely with every increasingly inappropriate comment regarding his quarry's long legs and shapely behind. His remarks were tacky and, as planned, a little disgusting.

Looking over the man's shoulder Cricket spotted the tall jeans-wearing Second Guy appearing right on cue. Men could be such adorable idiots. Time had come for this shark's pink slip.

Cricket knew her part in the upcoming duel of the penises.

"You've served your purpose. Thank you for the wine, Bruce. So nice meeting you. Really."

With her kiss-off, the man's dopey expression disappeared along with his wise-ass confidence.

"Listen, Cricket, I--"

"I prefer to drink alone, okay?" She almost added a fluttering "Shoo!" motion with her wrist, but decided a theatrical flourish would be too much.

"Cricket, I didn't really mean to offend -- Shit! What I'm trying to tell you is--"

Sandy haired Second Guy stepped up behind them, tapping his pal on the back as if preparing for some barroom brawl that neither had any intentions of seeing through.

Polite as hell, he spoke in a low voice to his colleague, "Excuse me, but I believe I heard the lady here suggest you leave."

Any veiled threats that added "or else" probably would have sounded too cheesy so soon.

Instead, the man in jeans added, "Why don't you say 'Goodnight' to the nice lady and take a walk, okay?"

Succinct and to the point. And, to any woman with one active brain cell, stupid, really stupid.

Bruce's reaction wasn't what Cricket expected.

He turned to the guy who stood behind him.

"Freddy, listen. I'm calling it off, okay? We're not going to hustle this woman." He turned to Cricket. "I have to apologize, all right? I know what you're thinking, but it isn't like that. I mean, I was being an annoying putz, I know, but just now I realized that I--"

Pal Freddy seemed confused. His mouth opened, but no words came. His buddy wasn't sticking to the script. Cricket had no idea what to say. This was a variation she hadn't expected.

"Apologize?"

Smiling Bruce turned to his pal, who remained silent as a tree stump.

"I'm sorry, Frederick. Game called. You okay with that?"

"Hey, we agreed--" The man stopped himself.

"Yeah, fine, Bruce. I'm okay with it. Fuck, I'll just take my ball and go home. You owe me big time, buddy."

Poor Freddy didn't wear his frustration well. He disappeared into the crowd.

Cricket felt oddly flattered. "Some hero, your pal Mister Fred. The ass of a horse, that was supposed to be your part in the scheme, am I correct? Your pal was going to save me from the obnoxious asshole, meaning you."

The guy sat without uttering a word, as if measuring what he would say next. "Okay, yeah. We were setting you up, my friend and I. I figured you knew that. Right off I could tell you were no dope. Listen, I want to start over, but I'll understand if you still want me to leave. I know I was being a jerk. That's done, okay? What do you say, clean slate?" He extended his hand. "Hello. I'm Bruce Collier." He paused, running his thumb along the back of Cricket's hand. "See how charming I can be? No smart-ass follow-ups. This is genuine sincerity you're seeing here."

"Hmmm..." Cricket removed her hand from his. This time her fingers slid more quickly along the wine glass stem, and her sudden smile spread. "Oh, I don't know about that. I kind of enjoyed our smart-ass repartee, at least a little. But okay, I'll play along since it seems my bestie has disappeared into the crowd like your Freddy. And I do have this wine to finish. So, hello, Mr. Collier. I'm Cricket Cullen."

She offered her hand again.

"Pleasure to meet you."

The merlot encouraged her response, accompanied with a sly grin.

"Chirp!"

Seventeen minutes later Cricket climbed into a cab with Mr. Bruce Collier headed for the man's midtown apartment.

* * *

Once past the doorman, Cricket had difficulty concealing her impression of Collier's digs. The place exceeded anything she could have imagined, a 72nd

Street penthouse on the West Side that took up the entire thirty-second floor and had its own private elevator access. Somehow, she restrained herself, as if taking in a three-hundred-and-sixty degree panorama of Manhattan and its burroughs were an everyday occurrence. Extravagant almost to the point of embarrassment, the apartment probably contained a dozen rooms, maybe more.

"Some wine?"

Cricket nodded, even with several Trophy Room merlots already inside her. She turned to Collier as he chose a bottle from the lengthy rack. "All this white furniture is too lovely to sit on. Maybe I'll just stand here and look at it." She was joking, but not really.

He returned with two glasses and a bottle he quickly uncorked with a connoisseur's precision.

This version of Bruce Collier seemed far removed from the faux jerk introducing himself an hour earlier.

"We don't have to sit, then. Let's visit the balcony. The view is something to see."

"I won't need my pepper spray, will I?"

"Promise." He wasn't all over her the moment they were through the door. Cricket liked that. No, she loved that! It made her want to be all over him. Collier led her outside into the cool night, where the city surrounding them sparkled. She felt she had stepped into some Harlequin novel in which the dark protagonist might reveal himself as some royal prince who had decided to move to Manhattan and live incognito. Like Audrey Hepburn just back from Tiffany's, Cricket waited for whatever beguiling words might come from her host, but the man said nothing and stared at his wine glass. In another minute, she feared the silence might prove awkward.

Standing close to him, Cricket couldn't let that happen.

She sipped her wine. "You know, the first person who breaks a long silence usually says something stupid."

"I hear the same is true of the one who speaks first after sex."

He had caught her off guard with that one. Another awkward moment followed.

"See? I was right," she finally said.

"But you spoke first."

"And you said something stupid. Anyway, who remembers anything they say after sex?"

Collier's smile became a smirk. "That remains to be seen, doesn't it?"

Ping...and Pong...

Locking eyes with him, she felt a flirt coming on.

"We'll see." He reached for her hand. "Hell of a view from up here, don't you think?"

(...but he was looking at her.)

"You're speaking of the city, of course." He pointed to the sky and managed a really lousy English accent. "'The envious moon is already sick and pale with grief...' That's Shakespeare, you know."

Cricket knew. "That's Romeo babbling beneath Juliet's balcony while admiring her killer rack, I believe. 'Arise, fair sun, and kill the envious moon.' Poor bastard."

"What some guys will do to get laid."

Damn, he was good looking...

"Why, Mr. Collier, are you trying to seduce me?"

He pulled her gently to him and planted a light kiss on her lips. "I'm assuming I already have."

He was right, of course. Cricket giggled, her reaction more nervous than playful. Against her own will she found herself flirting outrageously with this guy. He knew it too. Christ, she didn't want to sound like some pickle brained Scarlet O'Hara. Sipping her merlot, she bought a few seconds to make sure she didn't.

"Listen, Bruce, I didn't mean to sound so forwar--" She almost burped her wine.

He seemed not to notice "Are you feeling chilly. It can get cool up here."

"A little. Yes."

She was shivering, and she knew what was coming next. Sure enough, he pulled her closer.

"Better?"

"Better."

Much better...but...

That was a lie. She was feeling a little spacey, although the balcony's dizzying height could've had that effect on her. And there was the wine. Still...

The glass fell from her hand. She barely heard the tinkle of broken crystal on the patio.

Dammit, I'm not making a very good impress—

"Are you all right?"

The wine! It was the wine!

She wasn't all right.

"I'm feeling--I'm--"

..so dizzy...things spinning...

Cricket passed out in Bruce Collier's arms.

* * *

The coldness awakened her, a numbing chill on her skin especially uncomfortable because she'd been stripped naked. Cricket had the sensation of having been trapped inside some shadowy meat locker, although the smell wasn't meat but the unmistakable stink of raw sex. She realized her wrists had been tied together above her. The rope wasn't very thick, but it was strong enough to restrict much movement. It knotted around the back support of a huge brass bed, and Cricket could only struggle like some helpless fly caught inside the web of a spider. She had no idea how much time had passed. It could have been an hour, maybe many hours. The room was poorly lit with only a few bulbs of low wattage above her, and there were no windows to indicate day or night. She wanted to scream, but her mouth had been taped shut. Maybe this was some Play Room like in that shitty novel, or maybe this was some sick fuck's version of a killing room. Would some homicidal goon in leather soon be wrapping her in plastic and making his idiot speech before plunging a knife into her gut in a revolting scene like on Dexter? Maybe this chilly enclosure was meant only for effect, a sharply dressed American Psycho's sick joke intended to scare the bejeezus out of her. If so, it was working.

A low whisper...

"Welcome back."

"Huh?...What?..."

"Will you tell me you love me, little Cricket." The voice (a man's) seemed to come from inside her head, but in the grey shadows stood a tall figure not far from the bed. He approached, tore the tape from her mouth and put his finger to his lips. "Shhh...You love me, remember?"

"Wh-What? Where am--? What is this?" She pulled against the cords of rope.

"Let me hear you say that you love me. A simple love ya will do. It can be your safe word."

Cricket strained to see the man's face. She could see only that he was shirtless. The voice didn't sound like Collier's.

"I don't under-"

"Your safe word. The word that will make all this stop. After we get started, of course."

Her head ached, and she knew anything she said during the next few seconds would make no sense. "That's more than one word and I don't know you," she answered. Her remark sounded ridiculous. She didn't even know why she said it. It seemed irrelevant if this psychopath intended to torture her, but none of this seemed real and she wasn't in control at the moment. "If I say I love you, you'll untie me?"

"Just the word 'love' will be okay. A slave must love her master, you know. Of course, if you prefer another word, that will be fine. Dinosaur. Marmalade. Jellybeans. Anything will work. But there's something you should understand first."

"I love you, okay? I fucking love you and dinosaurs and jellybeans..."

"No, not yet. I have to explain the rules first. You're in no danger right now." The man stepped closer. His sandy hair looked familiar, but he wasn't Bruce Collier. It took Cricket a moment to recall.

"You-You're that guy in the club! Your friend Bruce, he called you Freddy." The guy's name sounded like it belonged to some sweater wearing frat boy, not this Marquis de Sade wannabe. None of that mattered. What mattered was, she was naked and helpless writhing on some strange bed in this dank place, wherever it was.

"Where's Bruce?"

"Bruce? Oh, he's not here. He asked me to fill in for him."

(SHIT!)

"Untie me, okay? I don't want to play, so fucking untie me!"

"But you will want to play. You may want to play all night! It may hurt a little, but I do guarantee a fine time. I know a gamer when I spot one. Call it my 'sixth sense' -- I see submissive people! From that movie. Get it?"

Cricket didn't see the humor in any of this. "Others saw you in the club. They know you spoke with me. You can't hold me here against my--"

"They saw my friend speak with you. If anything, they saw me walk away. And ol' Brucie, he's already back at the Trophy. Has been for over an hour, as if he never left. I believe he intends to whisk away your foxy friend, the one you came with. The plan is to separate her from whatever poor schmuck who was hitting on her. Brucie is good at that sort of thing. Are you following any of this?"

"No."

"Well, no big thing." The guy grinned wide and leaned close to Cricket's face, attempting to kiss her. She pulled away, and he smiled even wider. Grasping her cheeks with both hands, he planted a long and hard kiss on her mouth. Sliding down her neck with his tongue, he nibbled at her breasts. "Great tits, little Cricket. Really great. My compliments."

She wanted to wipe his kiss from her lips, but her wrists were tied behind her. She considered spitting into his face, but he had the distinct advantage. Instead, she spoke as calmly as she could.

"I have a safe word for you. It's FUCK, as in FUCK YOU, FREDDY!"

He went face to face with her. "'Fuck' isn't a good word, Cricket. The safe word, it has to be random and unrelated to sex. Something like Granny Panties. Well, that's two words, but you get the picture."

"This whole thing is unrelated to sex!"

"Maybe. Maybe not"

"Fine. Granny panties! GRANNY FUCKING PANTIES, GOD DAMMIT!!"

"Nah. I think we can do better..."

"Pick a damned word. I don't care what it is!"

He smacked her face. Not very hard, not enough to draw blood. It seemed more of a tap, but the suddenness of it scared her. The slap probably was the beginning of something much worse, and if the guy brought out the nipple clamps, she would have to scream.

"Bad little Cricket! As I was saying, it's better if you pick the word. You know, something totally opposite and unrelated to what we have going on here, but I'll accept something exotic or romantic. Honestly, I prefer it."

Cricket's brain felt scrambled, but a word came. "Liaison! How's that for completely unrelated to what's going on here? Is that romantic enough for you, you sadistic shit?"

"Great, Cricket! Like in Dangerous Liaisons. Yes, that old novel works for me! But you can't keep berating me, okay? The slave doesn't get to do that!" She twisted away from him but he managed to slap her bare ass. Although playful, this time his slap hurt more. "No pleasure without pain, that's what Freud said. But Sigmund got it wrong. The pleasure is the pain!"

Cricket winced, although the pain wasn't much, nothing as bad as her father's spankings given during her childhood for reasons she never understood at the time. For the slightest infractions, he would take her over his knee and redden her naked ass, and... Jesus! Why did that unwelcome memory enter her mind now? This jerk, this Freddy -- his toothy smile didn't differ much from her memory of her father's expression as he whacked her behind bare handed, and God forbid she protested. The man had been dead ten years now, drank himself into his grave, and that remained her most vivid memory of him.

Christ, how could her thoughts drift at a time like this?

"Are you going to hurt me?"

"You have your safe word now. This isn't only about pain, Cricket. You'll see."

"You can go to jail for this, you know. This is kidnapping! Where am I, anyway? This can't be that apartment I was in --"

"It can be anywhere, can't it? Maybe it's just some old storage locker somewhere in Jersey, or maybe it's the netherworld itself. But you're free to leave. Just say the word."

Cricket knew it couldn't be that simple. "You said there was something you had to tell me first-- something you had to explain."

"Oh, yes! Almost forgot. See..." He leaned close, stroked Cricket's hair. "My friend Bruce, he's really a decent guy. He could be standing here now instead of me, or even here with me, but he chose not to. Know why?"

"I don't give a shit! Decent guys don't drug women! You're both freaks, if this is what gets your rocks off. And if you don't let me out of--"

He shook his head (Nuh huh!) and covered her mouth.

"I need to tell you this, and you need to listen. He liked you, you know. He was attracted to your tits and that magnificent ass -- and what man wouldn't be? But he liked you. Of course, the original plan was for him to bring you here for me, after that act we put on for you, so that much didn't change. He's much better at the Jerkyl/Hyde thing than I am, although I wasn't certain he wanted to stick to our plan back at the Trophy. But he's an honorable guy, so here you are -- and here I am. Who knows? If you're good, maybe he'll join us later. I owe him." He removed his hand and stared at her. "No screaming, okay? But I wouldn't mind a little noise later..."

"He... Bruce brought me here for -- for you?"

"All for me...you're my own little trophy."

"LIASON, dammit!"

He leaned close, pressing his weight on her. "Not yet. There's more. I mean, once we begin there are rules. See, should you choose to quit, there will be consequences. Your girlfriend back at the bar, probably by now she's a little stewed and sucking face with Mr. Collier, maybe offering him a blow job in the parking lot. He's a decent guy, all right, but he isn't stupid, and your skank pal seems the type. So, it's like this -- She'll have to suffer a bit should you decide not to play."

"What?" "If you call it quits, your friend takes your place, but I may not be so nice to her. Simple."

"You'll hurt Laurie if I--?"

"See, now you're getting it. That's how this thing works, little Cricket. A newbie sub like yourself requires some motivation, so now it's all up to you. Are you ready to boogie?"

"This is crazy!" The man held some object at his side -- a whip, black and threatening, probably the kind you could purchase in any porn shop, multi-tailed for your pleasure! In the dimness Cricket hadn't seen it, but she certainly knew what it was used for. Maybe it had been near the bed the whole time, maybe it had appeared out of nowhere. She felt too wasted to be certain.

"Roll over! Let me see that ass!" His words sounded rehearsed. He wasn't very good at this, but he wasn't fucking around either.

"My hands are tied together. I can't move--"

"You can! You will!"

Cricket squirmed until she was on her belly, her wrists twisting painfully against the brass post.

The straps came down hard against her bottom -- one time, followed by a long pause, then two times more quickly. Tears welled, and she had to shut her eyes. She feared it would hurt a lot worse, but it hardly hurt at all. Her tears were of terror.

"It's a flogger, Cricket. Deer-skinned straps, for the beginner. Practically like feathers." He whacked his arm as proof, then smacked her ass again. "See?"

"I don't care! I want you to stop. Please, okay?"

He did.

"Safe word?"

She considered the man's threat.

"No."

"In a while, if you're good, I'll free your hands, assuming I can trust you, of course. But for now--"

Again he struck her, this time very hard. It tickled more than hurt, but still she bit her lip.

"Don't you worry, little Cricket. I won't leave a mark. Maybe 'Fifty Shades Of Pink,' is all..."

Liaison, she thought -- but she had to consider Laurie. She forced herself not to scream.

"This isn't the way it's supposed to work, you sadistic prick! You want to play your sick games, I'm supposed to be a willing partner! You've got this Master/Slave bit all wrong!"

"My rules," Freddy said. "Besides, I think in a few more minutes--"

"--I'm not some submissive bimbo you can just--!" Whack!

It wasn't supposed to hurt, although this time it did -- but only for a moment. The flogging thing's wood handle must have struck her.

"Sorry. Bad aim. Didn't mean to -- Any tingling, any numbness? I don't want you to feel uncomfortable, you know." His apology seemed ludicrous.

"I am uncomfortable. I'm very uncomfortable!"

"Safe word, then?"

"No!"

He said nothing, simply untied the ropes and freed Cricket's hands.

"See? Safe, sane, and consensual, as the players of the game say. You don't like being tied -- I get it. But you're not being a very good girl, you know. Roll over again, will you? Let me see your face."

"You're not going to--?"

"No, I won't hurt you. But I want you to do as I say. I want to look at you. And I want to fuck you."

She rolled over, and he stared into her eyes. He kissed her, an awkward but long and very deep kiss. She let him. She could tell he was beginning to sweat, beginning to get himself worked up and excited. Confused as much as frightened, Cricket wasn't sure she should ask, but she took the shot.

"Were you telling the truth about hurting Laurie? She's my best--"

"Not now, Cricket..."

He climbed on top of her, grabbed her face. Whatever was going on inside this man, Cricket hadn't a clue. He blew hot one minute, cold the next; tender for a moment, then suddenly cruel, a poor man's Caligula.

"Bad! Very bad! Now you're going to have to open your legs. Spread them!" He sounded like some kid scolding a naughty pet.

She prepared for another slap, but it didn't come. Instead he reached into his jeans pocket and pulled out something silky and black. Cricket recognized the blindfold and shook her head. In this place, darkness could never be her friend.

"No! Nuh huh! I don't want you to--!"

He spoke softly to her. "Then you put it on yourself, all right?" He handed the blindfold to her.

"See? My hands are in the air. Consensual and safe, remember?"

"I don't give a shit! I said no!" She tossed the blindfold back into his face.

He seemed unsure how to process her disobeying him and stared at the object in his lap. "Okay, fine. Then I'll wear it first. They say if you take away one sense, the others are heightened. I just wanted you to -- well, fuck it."

She couldn't believe her eyes as the man strapped the blindfold on himself. He remained straddling her and set to unzipping his pants. It seemed a fumbling effort, but he kept grinding against her as he did it. Cricket considered pushing him off with every ounce of strength she could muster, but she had no idea where her clothes were, and he probably had locked the door anyway. Worse, any sign of resistance could send the guy into a maniacal rage. If he expected her to be enjoying this, he was dead wrong.

...but, oddly, she felt the moisture of her own increasing excitement.

No fucking way! Cricket couldn't allow this to go any further. The multi-tailed flogger lay on the floor within her reach. Its thick wooden handle had struck her a moment earlier, and she knew it could do serious damage. The man seemed too obsessed with trying to wriggle free of his pants to realize that she was stretching to reach the nearby object. Managing to wrap her fingers around its dark straps, she pulled it to her.

Blindfolded, he slid his hand up her thigh. "You're so warm, little Cricket. I'm glad arousal comes so easily. You're turned on, aren't--?"

"Yeah, I love you too!"

Before he could say more, she smashed the flogger's handle hard against his forehead. He rolled off her, grunting and blindly reaching out. She struck him again, this time sideways across the temple, then brought the hard wood down twice, waited, then three more times swinging wildly until she heard the crack of bone -- his skull. His startled expression turned grotesque, as if his brain had short circuited. Stopping to catch her breath, Cricket hadn't realized she had been screaming her lungs raw. Quieting herself, she listened for the last of his moans. She resumed her battering to be certain, smashing his mouth and seeing chips of his teeth fly. Freckled with blood, she hammered more ferociously at him until he slid off the bed, his face a slab of raw meat wearing a dripping blindfold.

Cricket moved her toes along his bare shoulder and pushed her heal at him, but he was a muscular guy and his body barely shifted. She pulled the blindfold from his face. His eyes remained open, blank orbs staring at nothing, and he wasn't breathing. Freddy, or whatever-his-name was, lay motionless. Sweating heavily, Cricket felt a warm moisture between her legs. The realization struck her hard, the shame harder. Her screams -- she knew what they really were now. They weren't the sounds of her rage.

She'd just had the most intense orgasm of her life.

"Fuck..."

Climbing from the bed, Cricket dropped the flogger and pulled the sheet around her. She couldn't find her skirt, but the thick door to the room wasn't locked. She pushed it open.

Surprise, surprise! She never had left Collier's fancy penthouse apartment! The room she'd been confined inside seemed some kind of crawl space. It was well hidden within a large closet, the room itself maybe a one-time secret panic room behind a false wall, now converted to—

...to what?

Did it matter if it were Christian Grey's Red Room of Pain or the local Chuck E. Cheese? The room was whatever some rich asshole wanted it to be -- an asshole with too much time on his hands and too much money to spend. Cricket stumbled along the hallway past several bedrooms, a pool room and a media room, or whatever other extravagant nonsense the apartment contained. In the nearest bathroom, she washed off the spattered blood. The living room lie ahead, and she hoped her clothes were there. Locating her skirt and panties draped on the couch, she dressed.

The thought haunted her...

She had climaxed while killing a man. What in the name of God was wrong with--?

Cricket heard voices, laughter.

...A man and a woman!

A young couple stood in the darkness outside on the balcony, taking in the night air. Cricket pulled at the sliding door. Startled, the pair turned to her.

"Cricket?"

"Laurie? What are you doing -- here?"

Bruce Collier's arm dropped from the woman's waist. Laurie burst out laughing again. Her lipstick was smeared.

"Having some fun out here like you were having with Mister Freddy in Collier's Joy Room. That's what Bruce tells me he calls it. I'm just learning the ropes myself -- yeah, the ropes! Get it? These two guys are really into that Fifty Shades shit. I never thought I'd be the type to like it so much myself. I hated the book!"

Collier flashed his killer smile. "Sorry for the deception, but Laurie wanted Freddy to show you what the room is about, Cricket. She thought you might--"

"--enjoy it." Laurie added. "You did, didn't you? It takes some getting used to, the Joy Room -- but I've been getting a real kick out of it. Well, more like a whack!" Giggling, she hugged Cricket and kissed her cheek. "So, bestie, you had yourself a good time, didn't you? I know you did! Bondage -- the game anyone can play!" She pulled out a tissue and wiped the smeared lipstick from her friend's face, then did the same for Collier.

"Laurie, this was your idea?"

"Well, originally Bruce here suggested it when we met over drinks a few weeks ago. I figured why the fuck not, for my best friend?"

"Yeah, it was me," Collier said. "See, Freddy -- he's kind of new to all this. Didn't know squat about safe words, even. It was kind of a favor for him too. So, if he seemed a little awkward during tonight's liaison with you --Where is the man, anyway?"

Tonight's liaison with you...with you...with...

(...,With me!)

Cricket shook her head. She leaned over the balcony's rail and watched the city below, traffic still sluggish even at this hour, whatever time it was. She had the urge to laugh like a maniac and bit into her fist so she wouldn't.

"Maybe Freddy should have thought of a safe word for himself," she mumbled.

Then she threw up.

Old Horney

J.J. Smith

Wendi-Lee had some of the most beautiful lips Rimshaw had ever seen. Full and red, she had a sexy little pout that many women sought to acquire with implants and collagen.

So, it was with subdued admiration that he closed the vice grip onto Wendi-Lee's upper lip so that it locked. As he held the tool he thought, *I'd like to believe that Dick would love her lips, but that asshole doesn't give a shit, he wants quantity, not quality.* He then pulled the vice grips forward with his left hand so the lip stretched out from the unconscious woman's mouth. With his right hand, he used the unnaturally sharp scissors—supplied by Dick—to cut the lip from her face. The scissors' blades sliced through her lips with such ease that the cutters made a razor seem like the blunt scissors kindergarten teachers passed out to their students. In addition, it turned out the scissors were more than an instrument to cut with; the tool had other powers such as inducing unconsciousness and

214

applying restraints, both of which he had used on Wendi-Lee, but now, he willed her awake.

Searing pain filled her brain and she would have screamed but for the invisible gag that prevented her from making a sound. However, she was aware of what was happening and she saw the blood-soaked lip Rimshaw held just inches from her face.

"Hey gorgeous, how about a kiss?" he taunted. Pausing for a few seconds he followed up with, "Oh, right, you need both lips for that." He then clamped the vice grip onto her lower lip and said, "The way things are going for you, you won't need this one." He then repeated the procedure. But this time, in one last mean indignity, he put his left foot on Wendi-Lee's chest so he could pick her head up off the ground while ensuring the rest of her remained prone. He did that so when he made the last clip, gravity would take her head and ensure the pain level was increased that much more. As typical with the victims that he did that to, she not only impacted with the ground, but also with shock and, mercifully, unconsciousness.

Rimshaw put her lips into a plastic bag and, his work done, nonchalantly strode from the woods that he lured her into with the promise of a picnic. Because he was aware that the protection provided by the scissors had its limits—it was Rimshaw's employer's way of keeping his agents on a short leash—he moved quickly from the mutilated woman, confident that shock or blood loss would kill her soon enough.

Wendi-Lee was the latest in a considerable line of women who Rimshaw procured lips from for Dick, his boss. Wendi-Lee was just a little more pathetic than most. He met her in substance-abuse rehab—a great way, he discovered, to find wounded birds—and after listening to her drone on and on about her shitty little life, he knew exactly how to approach her. The rehab facility's rule forbade members from socializing outside of the meetings, but Wendi-Lee was a rule breaker, and Rimshaw's faked interest stoked a spark in the woman that he became aware of when he saw her nipples harden at the suggestion they meet at a nearby coffee house. That she was runway model beautiful—even under the battle-scarred body of a drug user—was icing on the cake for Rimshaw. Thus began the three-week courtship that ended in the wooded area of the park.

By the time Rimshaw was driving out of the park, he heard the distant sound of police sirens. They seemed to be coming his way, so he stepped on the accelerator and was off in the opposite direction. *Someone in the park must have found her quicker than I expected, big deal,* he thought. *If she's not a corpse right now, she'll soon be one.*

* * *

Energized by hopelessness, terror and fresh blood, the scissors guided Rimshaw to Dick's latest hangout. However, the trip to where Dick had set up headquarters took longer than expected, with Rimshaw driving 200 miles across the state and eventually stopping at a house in a town he'd never been to before. That wasn't surprising because the old prick moved around a lot, usually only staying in one spot long enough to add a wisp or two to his harem before moving on. To do that took a lot of support, which is why Dick employed—if you could call it that—men like Rimshaw.

As he neared the house, the scissors alerted Dick of Rimshaw's approach, which was standard operating procedure and, as usual, a wisp was waiting for him at the back door. The wisp was nude, intensely beautiful, and as white as marble. Her unnatural whiteness wasn't a matter of a lack of pigment, but it was the substance she was made of that had the marble effect, which included her hair, eyes, nipples, and pubis. Everything except her lips, those were rosy red. Immediately upon entering the house, Rimshaw recognized the wisp's face as that of a woman named Faith, which is likely why Dick sent her to greet him. When Rimshaw found her, Faith had been diagnosed as paranoid schizophrenic, and she had been hospitalized for a time, but she had no health insurance, so she was medicated and sent home where she drifted. Sadly, all she really had to offer the world was a sweet, trusting nature and intense beauty, but in a world that can be heartless, it wasn't enough, because by her late 20s Faith had been divorced twice, and in each divorce the judge declared her to be an unfit mother thereby losing custody of her children. The loneliness of being labeled unfit drove Faith to open her arms and bed to practically any man who smiled in her direction. Rimshaw found that aspect of her so pathetic that he took her lips on their second date. Now, she stood before him, or at least part of her did, as one of Dick's wisps. While following the Faith-wisp, Rimshaw actually took satisfaction in the belief that he helped her find acceptance and a home.

Dick—which wasn't the wizard's name, Rimshaw only called him that for lack of a moniker—had turned the house's basement into a temple. While the room seemed to be under the dwelling, it no longer resembled anything like the basement that originally occupied the space, which was a testament to Dick's power.

As Rimshaw approached the wizard, he held up Wendi-Lee's lips, and Dick, who was hanging about three feet off the floor upside down, lifted his head from his downward hang to look at the trophy. He then turned his lips into an evil smile and said, "Wonderful Rimshaw, you never fail to produce."

Rimshaw knelt and said, "These come from a beautiful basket case, just the type you like." He then handed the lips to Faith.

"Your love waits. Faith will take you to her. Just be sure to attend the ceremony."

"Wouldn't miss it," said Rimshaw who then headed to the upstairs bedrooms where he knew the wisps would be having sex with various locals.

Dick's magical call attracted about 70 of the neighbors who always turned out to be a menagerie of suckers, jackers, lickers, pissers, rimmers, fisters and buggers, to name a few of their predilections. All those acts were available with a wisp, or wisps, in the available rooms, including the bathroom, closet, and attic. If you were a human and you were lured into any of those rooms, whatever you wanted was on the table, or on the bed, on the floor, on the ceiling, or in the dog house if a wisp could swing it. The only catch—there's always a catch—was the effort used for humping, thrusting, squeezing and cuming was sucked right up by the wisps. Pleasure induced by the wisps is the most intense pleasure that a horny rube can experience, but the price is high. The energy siphoned off by the wisps was life energy, and the sex was so good that no one had ever walked away from the wisps. Once they got their lips on someone that was it, he or she would keep going until they dropped, so it would just become a matter of how long they'd last. The record for longevity was set by a female librarian who held on for about 24 hours before expiring. But she died with a smile. The sex energy provided Dick with power, and he used that energy to create his army of wisps, who in turn fucked people to death and stole their life energy. It was a system of perpetual sex motion. So why not just cut the lips off the dead neighbors? For Dick's uses the victim had to be alive—and filled with life energy—at the time of the lipectomy, nullifying the candidacy of the oversexed neighbors.

While Rimshaw was part of Dick's organization, he wasn't allowed to enjoy the pleasures provided by the wisps, for he would die. That is, all but one.

As he moved passed an orgy of wisp and human, Rimshaw eyed an attractive redhead who a wisp had licked into a sexual frenzy. She definitely had Rimshaw's interest, and if she were one of his ladies, he would have her take him orally. *Blowjobs are what separates us from the animals,* he thought smirking. But as enticing as the woman was, that isn't why he was there, so he kept moving. As he passed the redhead, a thunderous orgasm overtook her causing her to moan loudly, a moan that turned out to be the last sound she would make for she then slumped over dead. The wisp pulled back and—like a drone bee servicing the queen, in this, the king—took the woman's life energy to Dick. Rimshaw then saw that the Faith wisp had gotten ahead, and he hurried to catch up, his focus turning to anticipation…anticipation for a meeting with Amanda.

Even before she was a wisp, Amanda was a stunning goddess. She was Aphrodite, Helen of Troy, and Bathsheba, but with the love that filled Juliet. She was marble white, but when Rimshaw looked at her he didn't see the wisp, but the girl he fell in love with. They were both 13 when it happened. They had been in the swimming pool, and they kissed, a kiss that Rimshaw never recovered from. They consummated that night, and it lasted until they turned 17. That's when she said she wouldn't run away with him, and that they couldn't be together ("like that") any longer. It broke his heart.

Rimshaw was in his mid-20s when Dick's call for horny neighbors pulled him to a house that had been taken over. A wisp had cornered Rimshaw, and was beginning the process of stealing his life, when it suddenly stopped, stood, and took his hand. Rimshaw, still in a semi-trance, followed and he was led to Dick. Being partially hypnotized made it easier for Rimshaw to comprehend, yet not freak out over the fact that this person before him was hanging by his penis, which had stretched to about twenty feet.

"Your name is Rimshaw?"

He nodded in the affirmative.

"You ache for someone, someone truly special to you?"

More nodding.

"If you agree to go to work for me, I can help you get her, and keep her forever if you like."

Rimshaw didn't hesitate. "I'll do whatever you say."

Dick then produced the scissors, and thus began their lord and vassal relationship. However, before he could claim Amanda, Rimshaw had to provide Dick with ten new wisps. During that period, he found out he was a natural predator of women, a talent Dick sensed and decided to tap. But with Amanda he didn't need to use those skills, he knew where she lived and he walked up to her door one Tuesday evening just after she arrived home from work. "Hi, what are you...is something wrong?!" she said.

"Nothing's wrong, I just wanted to see you."

"Really, are mom and dad okay?"

"They're fine. I just had to see you."

"Oh...come in," she said holding the door open. He entered her apartment, and she said, "It's been what, seven years?"

"I love you."

"I...know and I'm sorry. I love you too, I really do. I think twins are just really close, but we went too far. You've got to stop obsessing over me. What we did was wrong, the abortion taught me that. I'll do my best to help you stop feeling that way about me...you need to get on with your life."

"I'll never stop loving you," Rimshaw said as he used the scissors to render her unconscious. He carried her to the bed where he then used the scissors to paralyze her. He then stripped her so he could worship her gorgeous human body one last time. As she lay there, he kissed every inch of her before turning to her lips. Like with the others, she had to be alive for this part. Trembling, he cut her lips off as quickly as possible. As he did so he experienced a powerful orgasm. He then spent the rest of the night still worshiping Amanda's body.

As the first rays of morning lit up the room, he wrapped the garrote around her neck. As he strangled her, Rimshaw's body revealed how attacking a woman, even a woman he loved, was natural for him, for as he pulled on the rope his cock became as hard as steel. When he achieved such an erection he called it a "railroad spike," and as he cut the air supply to the only woman he would ever love, he had a second powerful orgasm. When he exited Amanda's apartment, he took her lips straight to Dick.

In a bedroom, the Amanda wisp stood waiting, looking like a Greek statue, she was his again for the night. He removed his clothes and as he approached the wisp he said, "Close your eyes." She did so, and he moved behind her and quickly deployed the garrote. His excitement over took him and a gusher of seamen burst onto the wisp's backside. Soon she was "dead" because that's how Dick had her be. As with the real Amanda, Rimshaw laid the body on the bed, and spent hours tasting her lips. He eventually slept until the Faith wisp woke him for the ceremony. Just before stepping from the room he took a last look at the Amanda wisp safe in the knowledge she would be "alive" for his next visit.

***

Dick was at the center of the receiving chamber, some his wisps played instruments, drums made of human skin, pipes of bones, while others danced in a circle around him. Many of the wisps were still waiting to transfer the life energy that their tricks "traded" to the pimp wizard for a best sex of their lives, but they would have to wait for an opening among the 30 or so other wisps who held Dick suspended by his cock. To Rimshaw the wisps holding Dick up looked like a squad of naked cheerleaders who had formed a hot and sexy pyramid in order to suckle from a sow. However, while the wisps might have resembled piglets feeding, that isn't what they were doing; rather they each had their lips clamped to Dick's incredibly elongated penis and were holding him firmly aloft. The prick at least twenty feet long, and Dick hung as if his cock was clamped to the ceiling with gravity stretching the skin so that his head—the one with eyes, nose and a mouth—was the closest part of his body to the floor. But elevating Dick wasn't all the wisps did, they also licked, kissed, caressed and worshiped the stretched prick, providing the wizard with as much pleasure as their wisp mouths—no hands allowed—could produce. What made it sweeter for the wizard was that the lips doing the pleasuring were all from women who were murdered in Dick's name, and who then joined his concubines. All that power filled Rimshaw with envy.

Suddenly, the music and dancing stopped, and a wisp held up Wendi-Lee's lips so that all present could see them. The wisp's body assumed a more liquid, creamy state and the creature used that state to move up to the tip of Dick's penis by merging and decoupling with the wisps holding up the painfully stretched cock. Once reaching the top, the wisp placed Wendi-Lee's lips so they covered the tip, and then the wisp joined in pleasuring Dick. Within a few seconds of placing the lips at the tip, the pimp wizard began to orgasm, producing a geyser of jizz. But the spunk didn't just splatter on the ceiling and drip to the floor, it took a form.

At the tip of Dick's penis, a wisp grew into existence like a balloon, or in this case a condom, getting blown up. Rimshaw recognized the face that formed as that of Wendi-Lee's. *Well the bastard's got himself another wisp succubus, and he better share some more of that power*, he thought before being interrupted by a scream that sounded like an animal that had just stepped into a bear trap. But the scream wasn't from anything cute and fuzzy, but from something hairy and ugly. It was Dick who was screaming, and Rimshaw recognized that scream as one of intense pain.

"Ahhhhhhh! This woman's not dead!" Dick screamed. "She's not...Ahhhhh!!!"

Rimshaw looked up and saw the wisp biting into the section of the penis that is right below the head. Blood shot out from the wizard onto the wisp's white face as the same magic that created the unnaturally sharp scissors also created unnaturally sharp teeth, and the wisp used those teeth to bite the head off the prick and swallow it. What the wisp couldn't have known is that when she severed the head, she also cut Dick's wand. With the spell broken, the wisps—from those gripping the elongated cock, to those in the audience—suddenly disintegrated into puddles of jizz. They splashed onto the floor, the fleshy lips of the dead being the only solids in each puddle. With all the wisps liquefied Dick crashed to the floor breaking the larger spell and the wizard's audience chamber turned back into the house's basement recreation room. Fear ran through Rimshaw as he thought of the Amanda wisp.

Rimshaw then heard cries from the upstairs area, clearly not all of the human sex batteries had been drained, and that meant someone would call the police, so Rimshaw had to act before the authorities arrived. He ascended the stairs two at time, the whole way saying, "She has to be OK. She has to be OK." He was going to take her with him. Reaching the room, he quickly opened the door and found only a white puddle, Amanda's lips in the goop. Fighting back tears he seized her lips and ran from the house.

***

Seven months had passed since Dick was destroyed, and Rimshaw lived only for revenge. Just before he died, the wizard had yelled that the woman was alive, which meant Wendi-Lee had somehow survived and Rimshaw made it his mission to correct that mistake.

Rimshaw used all of his skills and resources to track down Wendi-Lee, but even with his extensive stalking experience it proved difficult, for without Dick's protection, evidence from old cases was suddenly being reexamined, and witnesses who couldn't remember what Rimshaw looked like were now starting to recall bits and pieces of their encounters with him. Their recollections were slowly producing a description of the stranger who disappeared from the group, therapy, or rehab they had been involved with at about the same time a female member was found dead. However, the scissors still had enough power to keep investigators from fully identifying Rimshaw, thus enabling him to track Wendi-Lee.

He found what was left of her in a hospital. She was already dead by the time he showed up, but her legacy lived on. What Rimshaw had been unaware of when he last met Wendi-Lee, is that she had been two months pregnant at the time, which explained why she took her last rehab stay much more seriously than previous stints. She was still alive when police and paramedics found her disfigured self, and the first-aid they provided, combined with her will to live, managed to get her to the hospital where she fought for her life for 106 more hours. During that time her pregnancy was revealed, and the decision was made to save the baby at all costs, even if that meant a slow death for the mother. Wendi-Lee fell into a coma and would have outright died, but she was kept alive on ventilators and feeding tubes so that the baby inside her could grow. Under nearly constant care, the fetus reached term, and eventually Wendell Lee Englehart was brought into the world.

Once Rimshaw was aware of this, he formulated a plan for revenge. Waiting outside the hospital, he picked a male nurse and followed him home where the unsuspecting nurse was strangled for his scrubs, stethoscope, and ID badge, which Rimshaw made useful by gluing his photo over the nurse's photo. That disguise combined with the scissors' remaining power was enough for him to enter the hospital mostly unnoticed. More importantly, it enabled him to gain access to the maternity ward, specifically the nursery. Normally, a healthy newborn like Wendell would have been discharged two or three days following birth, but the problems associated with the death of the mother and lack of a father placed the baby in the care of the state. Documents had to be completed, and that took time, even when the officials knew what the outcome would be. This worked in Rimshaw's favor, he had come to depend on bureaucratic entanglements to stay ahead of the authorities, and in this case, it made it possible for him to gain access to baby Wendell.

Wearing a surgical mask, he entered the nursery and quickly found the infant asleep in a hospital bassinet. He just pushed the bassinet into the hall, which attracted the attention of a nurse. He held up some official looking forms and said the baby had an appointment in the blood-work lab. The nurse nodded and went back to looking after other newborns. He pushed the bassinet onto an elevator, and alone in the elevator the scissors had enough power to induce sleep in Wendell, who was then placed into a backpack Rimshaw carried with him. Once on the hospital's main floor, he pushed the bassinet into the hall because if he just abandoned it on the elevator it would quickly attract attention. All of those he passed in the corridor were involved in their own business, and he soon found a quiet corner to park the bassinet. Lifting the backpack, and with practiced nonchalance, he headed for the exit. However, just as Rimshaw stepped through the revolving door, alarms went off. It was dark and he took off running through the parking lot to a small wooded area, where he planned to extract revenge.

Once in the wooded area, Rimshaw found a clearing and quickly removed Wendell from the backpack and placed him on the ground. He then set the scissors on the ground to his right so he could retrieve from the pack a pair of pliers that he needed to do the sadistic deed. With his left hand, he clamped the pliers onto Wendell's upper lip and pulled, which caused the baby to cry loudly, cries that filled Rimshaw with the needed resolve to get it over with quickly, so he reached for the scissors, but found none. He turned his head to look for the cutters, and that's when the wisp returned them.

The Wendi-Lee wisp plunged the scissors deep into Rimshaw's neck, but immediately before stabbing him, the creature opened the cutters so its two points entered in such a way as to provide the wisp with the ability to snip his carotid artery. It did just that, and blood squirted out from the wound signaling that Rimshaw had about 100 seconds of life. The baby's cries and Rimshaw's gurgling attracted the security guards who had entered the hospital's parking lot to search for Wendell. The wisp knew it had to act. It then attempted to lift Wendell using its hands, but stabbing Rimshaw had required most of the energy that had kept it together, so its hands, arms, and the rest of its body now had the consistency of putty with very little strength, so no matter how much it tried, it couldn't lift the baby.

The wisp was aware there was only one part of its body that was actual flesh, and, in an act of desperation, it bent forward so that the flesh of its mouth was able to engulf the newborn's tiny penis and scrotum. Once it locked the dead mother's lips tightly around the organs, Dick's penis head rose through the wisp's body to connect with the infant and anchor the child to the wisp, who then lifted the baby off the ground. Despite being lifted by his immature sex organs, Wendell Lee did not cry, or fuss for he felt no pain. Rather, he actually seemed content, the way a baby is when held by its mother. The two then became invisible to the security guards who were nearing Rimshaw's body. However, the guards only found a dead man, and no kidnapped baby, so some of the guards stayed with Rimshaw's body while others continued the search.

While waiting for the guards to disperse, the wisp suddenly felt a surge of energy, and the surge was not only within the wisp for the scissors were also energized, and it kept them hidden as the searchers passed by. The most surprising thing was that Wendell's penis suddenly grew a foot in length, and with the new vitality, the wisp—resembling a lioness carrying a cub by the scruff of its neck—ran off into the night looking for a house to invade and turn into a home for her son, the new Dick.

The Night Stair

Stanley B. Webb

Sister Faith paused in her hoeing, and said, "The sun is fierce, let's strip naked."

"Remember our vow of modesty," said Sister Gloria.

"You sound like Matron. We're twenty-five, yet she guards us like children."

"Matron protects us."

"I don't *want* protection."

The sisters' convent, The Order of the Chaste, stood below Harpy's Mount. The abode of the Taken Sisters lay on the summit.

Faith whispered, "I've offered myself to the Harpies."

Gloria felt horrified. "You've not! We're locked in at night."

"I've found an exit, in the Night Stair. I've stood naked on the roof, and prayed to be taken."

"You're joking, or mad."

Travelers appeared on the road.

"Look, Priests!" Faith lowered her veil, lifted her skirts, and hurried toward the newcomers.

Gloria cried, "We're forbidden to accost them!"

Faith laughed.

Gloria followed, and caught Faith at the roadside.

There were six Priests: four novices, harnessed to the armory wagon. A muscular, gray-haired Father led them, accompanied by a hunchback with a steel crossbow.

Faith said, "Good afternoon, Fathers."

The hunchback scowled. The novices gaped.

"Good afternoon," said the leader. "I'm Father Ben."

"Are you hunting?" Faith asked

The hunchback spat, "Bold female!"

"Be civil, Father Art," said Ben. "We *do* hunt. Two of the Taken Sisters are ill, and unable to perform their duties."

"What *are* the Taken Sisters' duties?" Faith asked.

"Brazen female," said Father Art. "What is your name?"

"Sister Gloria," said Sister Faith.

Gloria tried to protest, but outrage tangled her words.

Art frowned at her stammering, then replied to Faith.

"Sister Gloria, pray that you never know the duties of a Taken Sister."

"Yes, Father," said Faith.

The Priests moved on.

"They'll occupy the convent's guest house," said Faith.

Gloria finally said, "That wasn't funny!"

"You should have seen your face!"

"He'll tell Matron, and *I'll* be punished."

"You secretly enjoy the misericord."

"I do not!"

Faith laughed.

***

At dusk, the nuns returned to the convent. Matron, a huge and severe woman, awaited Gloria.

"It was not I, but Sister Faith."

"Do not blame the innocent for your mischief!"

Matron seized her ear, and took her to the misericord, a stone chamber furnished with a rough wooden table.

"Prepare yourself."

Gloria removed her coif, habit, and underskirts, then bent over the table. Her nipples hardened against the planks. Matron leaned on Gloria's back, and spanked her. Gloria yelped at every blow. Matron's breathing quickened. The punishment continued until Matron suddenly gasped, and clutched Gloria's rump. Gloria looked over her shoulder. Matron smiled.

"You may go."

Gloria dressed, and went to her dormitory cubicle. She changed into her night clothes, knelt in prayer, then lay belly-down on her straw pallet.

The full moon watched through the slot window.

***

She roused when someone entered the Night Stair. Gloria wondered who had gone to night worship. She dozed once more, then heard a sudden wind. A woman's shriek rose skyward. Faith had tempted the Harpies, and been taken.

232

Gloria rushed from her cubicle, crying out for help. She climbed the twisting Night Stair, and discovered a window with loosened bars. She hesitated on the sill, until Faith screamed above. Gloria could not ignore the cries. She stepped onto the tiled roof, and made her way across the peaks and valleys. She found a ladder, where mason sisters had worked, and descended to the ground. Gloria lifted her night skirts, and ran into the fields, her eyes on the clear sky.

Faith cried out again, her voice muffled by something in her mouth.

Warm liquid splashed Gloria's face. She licked her lips. This was not rain, but something thick and sweet, which warmed her throat all the way to her stomach. Her secret place moistened.

Suddenly, the Priests appeared, armed with crossbows.

Father Art demanded, "Why are you outside?"

"It has my friend!"

"Stay close to us, Sister" said Father Ben. "There are two Harpies above. Have you felt warm precipitation?"

Shamed by her inexplicable arousal, she lied.

"No, Father."

Faith moaned.

Father Art raised his crossbow.

"No," said Father Ben. "Kill it, and the sister falls to her death."

"But, it's having its way with her!"

"It will land when it's finished."

For a quarter of an hour, Faith moaned and cried above them. She finished with a series of grunts, a scream, and a whimper.

Gloria's secret place became dripping wet.

"It's finished," said Father Ben. "Listen for its landing."

Gloria heard a thump in the bean field.

"There!"

She went eagerly ahead of the Priests, ignoring their warning cries, and found Sister Faith spread-eagle in the Harpy's shadow, her naked body slick with clotted liquid, her nipples engorged like strawberries. Faith rubbed her secret place, as liquid flowed out through her fingers.

"You can't imagine it, Gloria."

The Harpy came forward on giant bird feet, its membranous wings spread for balance. The creature arched its long neck, its face an owl-eyed madwoman's, its tongue an eel. Enormous, dripping breasts swayed on its chest. Hairy testicles hung beneath its tail, with a huge, segmented worm between them. The worm swelled, and spat liquid.

Gloria stepped forward, repelled, but fascinated.

A strong hand pulled her back. The Priests fired their bolts. The Harpy screamed, and fell.

Father Art shouted, "Foul thing!"

Faith wept, and crawled to the dying Harpy.

Gloria felt compelled to touch them.

"Don't!" Father Ben again dragged her back. "The Harpy is aphrodisiac. If you touch its fluid, you'll be lost."

"What of Faith?"

"God can still use her."

"Did God make the Harpies?"

"No, they were created for *The Night Stair*, a fantasy game whose players subsumed themselves into characters of perversion."

Leathery wings flapped across the sky.

"Back to the convent!"

The Priests surrounded her. She smelled their male sweat, and felt the heat of their strong bodies. Her secret place throbbed. Panting with lust, Gloria reached out, and touched Father Ben's neck.

He misunderstood her emotions. "Don't fear, we'll protect you."

Matron awaited her in wrath.

"The Harpy took Sister Faith," Father Ben explained. "Sister Gloria went outside in concern for her friend."

Matron glared. "How did you leave the convent?"

"There is a way in the Night Stair; Sister Faith told me of it."

"You blame poor Sister Faith for everything!"

Matron dragged her away.

Father Ben called, "Don't be hard on her, she meant well."

Gloria disrobed without awaiting Matron's command, and laid herself over the table. She moaned at Matron's touch.

"You are wicked," said Matron, and struck the first blow.

Gloria's breath caught, as a wave of pleasure jolted through her body. She lifted her rump to meet each slap. Matron struck harder and faster than ever before. Her rapid breathing turned into sobs. Her nails raked Gloria's shoulder. Suddenly, she desisted. Gloria looked back. Matron stood near the door, her body shaking, and her expression bemused. Matron's hair drooped loose from her coif, hanging sweaty tendrils on her face.

"You may go," said Matron.

Gloria looked into Matron's eyes, clutched her buttocks, and spread herself.

Matron gasped, came as if drawn, and caressed Gloria's rump. Gloria moaned, as Matron's finger slipped toward her secret place. Then, Matron whimpered, and retreated.

"Please," said Gloria.

"No, you foul thing!"

Gloria returned naked to the dormitory. She saw no one, but heard sounds from the Night Stair, where mason sisters worked. Gloria lay on her pallet, a-sweat with needs that she had never before known, needs which neither the Priests nor Matron would answer. Gloria fumbled in her secret place, but that proved too small a pleasure.

There came the sound of wings.

She leaped to the slot window, but saw nothing as the Harpy flew nearer. She turned, ran from her cubicle, and up the Night Stair. The masons fled screaming. Gloria pushed at the window bars, and found the repair firm. She grabbed a hammer from the mason's bucket, and pounded until the bars fell free. She went out onto the roof, straddled a peak, and reached skyward.

Gloria shouted, "Here I am!"

The Harpy approached.

Father Art shouted from below, "Who's that?"

Father Ben responded, "There's another woman out!"

"I see a ladder!"

The Harpy circled above her.

Gloria cried, "Here I am!"

The Priests mounted the roof.

The Harpy's wings went silent.

Gloria screamed, "Here I am!"

The Priests stumbled toward her across the tiles, while she strained toward the heavens. Suddenly, the men halted. Father Art aimed his crossbow at her. Father Ben struck the weapon down.

A whirlwind engulfed her. The Harpy grasped her hips with its feet, and yanked her up, forcing the breath from her lungs. As she gasped, the ground spiraled away below. Terror overcame her lust. When she regained her lungs, the convent looked as small as a doll's house.

Gloria screamed.

She hung buttocks-up under the Harpy, her legs sprawled, her breasts pendulous, and her hair flapping. The Harpy's udders lay about her ears.

The worm touched her secret place.

Gloria's terror became exhilaration. She pressed her head between the creature's breasts.

The Harpy stretched its wings to glide, and twisted its neck down, bringing its face to hers. Then, it smiled, extended its swollen tongue, and licked a trail of liquid across her lips. Gloria caught the tongue in her mouth, and sucked greedily.

From behind, the worm's tip pushed at her secret place, but her virgin opening proved too narrow. The worm sprayed her crotch with hot liquid, then penetrated, stretching her lubricated hole. Gloria cried out, her voice muffled by the Harpy's tongue. The worm paused just within her, spurted more fluid, and pushed deeper. She trembled, her secret place squeezing. The worm pulled out, then pushed deep again.

As its worm pumped inside her, the Harpy's tongue slid down her throat. She gagged for a moment.

The tongue thrust up and down in her throat, then pulled out of her mouth. Gloria seized it, and fed it back in.

She grunted, rocking her hips, striving to take the worm deeper. Gloria climaxed with a scream, letting the Harpy's tongue fall, and its fluid pour down her chin.

The Harpy shuddered. A pulsation traveled down its worm, into Gloria. She felt suddenly overfilled with liquid. The excess spurted out on her thighs. The worm shriveled, and slipped out.

She hung limp and satisfied in the Harpy's grasp. They had glided down, to just above the bean field. The Harpy hovered, and gently laid her on the warm soil. She felt liquid flowing out from her. Her secret place contracted, sending pleasant jolts through her.

The Harpy nuzzled her.

"I love you," said Gloria.

She drew it close, and kissed its mouth.

Father Art cried, "Over there!"

Gloria warned the Harpy, "Fly, or they'll kill you!"

The Harpy leaped off the ground, and flapped into the sky.

The Priests arrived. Father Art raised his crossbow, fired, and missed.

"Curse it!"

Father Ben came to her.

"You're a mess, Sister Gloria."

She said, "Put your worm in me."

"I cannot, I've taken a vow to penetrate only other Priests. However, God can still use you. You are a Taken Sister now, and every night henceforth, you will fuck a Harpy, to keep its lust from the decent world."

A Dusty Exhausting Trail

Sergio "ente per ente" Palumbo

"What makes the desert beautiful

is that somewhere it hides a well."

Quote by Antoine de Saint-Exupery

It is said that in the desert of life the wise travel in groups, while the fool prefers to travel alone, the woman considered in silence. Actually, she didn't really repute herself to be a fool, but she was undoubtedly and completely alone now. The desolation of the surroundings appeared to be in perfect harmony with the horrendous dry desert climate, and the preponderance of clear skies made it obvious that rain wouldn't be falling any time in the near future. Even though it wasn't one of the hottest summer months, the daytime temperatures were already exceeding her considerable forbearance, which simply meant that she was already exhausted. Actually, it wasn't frequently that Rose found herself in such a truly hopeless condition. The young woman wore a light gray, tight chamois vest, endowed with a peculiar stand-up collar, with attached yellowish and white sleeves, and gold button details running down the front of the dress all the way to her ankles. She also wore a large leather hat which covered part of her long auburn curls, and had a flashy belt with gemstone buckles at the front and back, and two guns in twin holsters. A violet necktie worn under her chin, two wide bluish detailed chaps covering the dark trousers, and a pair of strong leather-lined boots completed her outfit.

The area of Ojito she was presently riding across was one of New Mexico's lesser known wilderness regions, lying right at the end of the Colorado Plateau. That isolated high desert featured many layered sandstone formations of different shades – depending on how color-conscious you were, of course - and unusual forms, varied cliffs, ancient ruins, fossils, and occasional petroglyphs. As a matter of fact, at first sight it looked more overgrown and less remarkable than other zones she had seen so far. However, the really interesting locations were generally small and took many attempts to find. Most of the region was a mixture of bushy flats, twisting ravines and low mesas, not much different than the land on either side, which appeared to be exactly the same for several miles or more in every direction. She was riding about 50 miles north of Albuquerque and, as far as the woman had previously seen, there were only a few farms in the vicinity that were still in operation.

The trail she had been following that morning had passed by an old site where, probably, a settlement had tried to survive before being abandoned forever. She had turned south and later west, briefly entering a drier area before reaching a worn-out sign full of wind-drawn patterns that the ever-present sand had continuously scratched at for who knows how long, announcing another small village whose remains were only still partly visible today. After another 5 miles across the wide open plain, she had gotten to a scene made up of greatly contrasting colors including red, greenish, yellowish, and, most strikingly, white. There was a narrower path climbing steeply to the top, at the end of a small plateau that linked-up with one of the adjacent trails. The higher points probably had great views eastwards, over the desert beyond to the distant mountains, but she hadn't come here to sightsee, of course. Actually, being a little tired, perhaps even exhausted, the female rider was wondering why she had chosen this side of the area to explore instead of another zone. But she was here now, and she had to follow the stretch of land that lay ahead of her, hoping that it wouldn't be too long before she arrived at a safer, colder point where she could have some rest in the shadow of a large rock perhaps.

There weren't any streams dropping over waterfalls around here, nor was there sagebrush that was close to ice-cold ponds like the ones she had found up north, in Wyoming. Haying on the arid plain didn't appear to be a quiet, restful activity, as the peasants and farmers had to continuously fight to take out of the soil what they needed to make a living. All of this was really a pity as she had always found the constant flow of sparkling water across pastureland very reassuring, the same as she thought it was satisfying to stand at a spot high enough to look into the distance, listening to the motion of a river.

She turned to another path that looked like it had been long deserted, going up to a steep-sided escarpment overlooking a main weathered rock feature at the center of the wilderness. This was not an especially interesting scene, though it did appear to be huge. The land below here started at a small area on the north side of the path, and then there was an open, shrub-covered zone running beneath the east face of the mesa, gaining height gradually and ending at a noteworthy viewpoint on the north side, which also looked out over the wash to the desert beyond.

En route she spotted a number of localized but attractive erosion features, the most striking being a beautiful outcrop of yellowish sandstone, crossed by thin, delicate pinkish-reddish layers. The U-shaped passage in the vicinity reminded her of another place she had seen but was unsure where was located exactly, as there were many and many similar points she had previously seen during her rides across that apparently unending country. Bands of multi-colored shale and limestone kept drawing her attention to cliff sides where some wildflowers and the leaves of those tufted herbs called Knight's Milkvetch stood. Then, slightly west, not far beyond a group of flat-topped structures mixed with large pine trees - some rocks in the cliffs stood higher up, having enchanting colors, fantastic shapes and forms. But that beautiful view couldn't appease the need she felt for a rest. Notwithstanding all of her best hopes, it took other 6 hours before she got down the side of the escarpment and across to the top of the mesa itself, riding south along the second trail then back to the main plane.

At that moment, the woman wondered once more why she had decided to cross that dangerous desert alone - though she already knew the answer to that question in her own mind, of course. There were box canyons and deep meandering trails dotted throughout the wilderness with a few small plants hidden in shady recesses, where conditions might change from bad to worse at any time.

Her present situation was all due to what she was escaping, and the place she had come from, and also to the final thing she was presently searching for. Being cautious wasn't enough in that place, as there were almost no water sources around, and only the many circling birds of prey, shy reptiles, and other deadly wildlife species that called it home freely moved across the area. The lizards, especially, seemed to have gotten used to the desert long ago, and they had the better chance to thrive in such a climate.

In fact, historically, not many humans had tried to carve a living from Ojito's resources. Indeed, there were several types of ancient ruins within the area, including those of the prehistoric cultures, though few records existed nowadays about their lives here. The persistent drought-like conditions must have made their daily existence very difficult, and she was sure that what was left of the house-like structures those ancient residents once built were the clues that some academicians would certainly use one day to tell the story of their presence in this area.

In reality, the woman herself would be very interested in studying such sites, but she didn't have time to do that now. As always, the urge to save her life was a much more important goal, for sure. So, those buildings would be left undisturbed for now, leaving them as she found them along the way so that future explorers might reveal their secrets, who knows. Maybe, or maybe not... After all, the erosion process had exposed large segments of the ground where there were also considerable fossil remains of huge creatures that had probably once walked that terrain, along with other extinct plants and trees. Those stones, too, might prove to be useful and very valuable if only she had the time to turn her full attention to them. But that wasn't an option today. About tomorrow, who knew - but today she had still to be certain she would live to see another sunrise, and that was enough.

Her azure eyes were always ready for whatever came along, always on the lookout as she rode across unknown territories, and this place seemed to require more attention than usual, certainly. It was along one of the few curving strips of fertile land stretching into the nearby hillsides, creating a scene where man-like structures seemed to fit more into the common order of the world, that the woman noticed the typical features of a farm.

It was a lovely sight certainly, after riding through the almost unending nothingness, wasn't it? Her tired mount slowly approached the place, quietly resting in the vicinity, about a mile from where the farm stood. Colorful flowers and verdant brushes seemed to abound the closer she came. She noticed a six-foot-high boulder standing next to some broken wagon wheels. The enormous stone looked like a bizarre wind-and-water sculpture decorated with drawings which had been painted on, probably remembering the hardships and dreams of the first emigrants. There were shadows coming from the few treetops around that homestead, and these covered part of the sturdy facade of the small rural house. Certainly, that hut didn't look like much, and it wasn't a modern structure, but it still maintained a kind of peculiar handsomeness and appeared to be functional and in acceptable condition.

Maybe its roof just needed some repair, and the walls might also require renovation, but it was clear that such work was not something a single woman might easily do, even though Rose was certain the owner of the house had probably tried, given details she had spotted here and there. But she was also certain that the young woman presently working in the open courtyard was a lone resident, as there were many clues pointed to that conclusion given Rose's experience.

As her horse stood before the female farmer's eyes, that one simply remained amazed and raised her face towards the newcomer. She had probably been accustomed to seeing men of all description in the surroundings - be they either outlaws or average citizens - but spotting a woman donning men's clothing with pistols, and dressed like a gunslinger, was something very rare for her.

Truth be told, a female gunfighter on horseback was a very unusual sight across the entire country in 1872 - not that women didn't dress like men when they had to or didn't use guns and pistols for defending themselves or even to go hunting in such wild territories, but this was done only if necessary and if there was no man they could rely on who could do it for them. However, spotting a female rider that had the true look and the bearing of an experienced gunslinger didn't happen every day. One main difference in Rose's outfit was that it displayed a lot of cleavage, as the top of it was specifically cut to reveal a wide portion of the wearer's breasts - which was something you didn't see in a common rider's clothes. Other than that, she never wore a bra underneath, at least she hadn't up to today.

"Hi, stranger. How may I help you?" the kind voice of the female farmer greeted Rose as her horse stopped before the fence. The fact that she hadn't entered the open gate at once, staying outside and waiting for the homeowner's invitation, appeared to be a sign of a certain respect for her, which was something that couldn't be taken for granted given the circumstances and the times.

"My name is Rose and I have no intention of harming you, lady," the rider replied, in her low though convincing tone. Her lips were still full of dusty particles, the same as were on her face, and the woman unintentionally sputtered some sand around as she spoke.

"I'm glad to her this, madam," the other nodded, while sitting the heavy bucket she had in her hands on the ground. "I imagine you'd like something cool to drink, wouldn't you? Allow me to offer you some water."

"That's the best offer I've had in a long time," Rose smiled, eyeing her with a knowing look. "Accepted, of course. Also my horse would be pleased to quench its thirst, if that's okay. I'd also like to wash up in that manger down there…Lot of dust on my skin and my clothes."

"No need to use it, I have a more comfortable tub inside my stable, if you like."

"Even better," the rider conceded, widening her smile. "Nobody can say people aren't kind and hospitable here."

"Not all the people are kind here, not everyone is hospitable…" the other woman pointed out while staring at her in a resolved though dour expression. "I am, and that is good for you, madam. These are some wild lands and this is a very dangerous part of the state. There are very bad individuals hanging around these parts. You were lucky that you didn't stumble in one of those, madam."

"Just call me Rose, lady, I prefer it. And what's your name?" she asked her as she was dismounting and tying her horse to the rope he found along the fence.

"Makayla, madam Rose," the woman said.

"Rose is enough - madam is not a title that fits me, as a matter of fact…" She had made her point clearly, using a reassuring voice. "And your name is really beautiful. Not too common, I admit, but it sounds very nice…"

"Thanks, mada… I mean, Rose," the other replied, correcting herself before ending her phrase. "Please, follow me to the stable, and I'll bring you some clean towels in a minute."

As Rose moved along following the other, her azure eyes lingered in silence on Makayla's back and her overall figure, considering her dress: a long bluish frock with lace ruffles at the bodice and sleeves, that perfectly displayed her noteworthy curved hips even if it was a bit loose, certainly unlined for cool comfort on those sunny sky days on the dry plains. She also noticed that her bearing was that of a woman who was used to working hard for many hours, though her traits, especially her face and her overall appearance was really alluring, the same as her tanned skin tone.

The moment Rose got to the entrance of the small side building that served as a shelter for the very few animals on the farm, she immediately spotted the metallic tub in the middle of the room, and a smirk of satisfaction appeared on her mouth. She had been in many small hotel rooms in the bigger cities on the east Coast, and even in a few disreputable houses in the West which still had some good bathrooms anyway, and that tub couldn't compare to any of those. On the other hand, it also looked like the most pleasing means of refreshment she had seen in a very long time, and that was all she wanted. As soon as Makayla left the out-building and before she was back with the towels, Rose had already completely undressed, leaving her dirty clothes on the ground, along with her pistols and her hat. Rose then poured water into the tub and slipped into it, savoring the wondrous touch of the water and finally giving in to a long, joyful bath, whole heartedly.

∗∗∗

After the comfortable bath, when she had redressed and tidied her hair again, the homeowner let Rose in and said she would prepare something for her to eat, if she liked. Of course, Rose didn't say no, how might she ever refuse such a pleasing offer?

While inside the house, her eyes studied the movements of the female farmer who was putting something into the fireplace and was bringing wooden branches to the opposite wall. Then, she adjusted her shirt on purpose to show some more cleavage, obviously curious to discover if her actions would have any effect on the other woman, of course. Rose had noticed the hesitating look the farmer had given her an hour before, when she had come back to the stable with the towels and had seen her nude body under the water. The woman thought she knew well that sort of curious glance, the same she had noticed before on many lustful men looking at her slender unmasked figure lying in a bed or in a meadow. It was only that Makayla was a little shyer or more cautious, given the delicate matter, which still had to be seen… Rose believed she wouldn't end-up disappointed, anyway, as the interested though a bit secretive behavior told her that, maybe, she could get something extra from that unexpected encounter, much more than some water, food and rest.

Makayla had irises the color of the dark night, the same as her long hair. She was still an attractive woman, even though she was probably over 30. Despite the fact that she preferred to remain alone in that place, running that small farm and looking after her poor cattle, she was in good shape. Rose didn't know why she didn't try to find a man to live with, who could give her protection and work hard in the field. Maybe there was something else and, given the hints and details she had glimpsed so far, she thought she knew what was behind her lack of a husband, who knows.

"You really look like a perfect head of the house," she started speaking, in a plain tone. "No husband, and no lover for you?"

"My husband died some years ago," the other replied. "He left me this farm. Since then I have been running this place, alone."

"Sorry about that," Rose said. "But you're really in your best years, and you're absolutely stunning, so I don't think you'd have any difficulty in catching the eye of any man living within 100 miles of here. Do you?"

Makayla kept on with what she was doing and responded in a hurried voice, without turning towards the guest. "There are fewer men than you might imagine in the vicinity, and the few ones that live here around are disreputable individuals, I can assure you. Or maybe it's only that a real opportunity hasn't shown up yet."

"Did you love your husband? Do you miss him?" the newcomer insisted.

"Yes, of course I miss him. The illness took him away too early." The farmer added in a peculiar tone: "You know how these things go…when men leave, it's only up to us eke out a living, using our strength and the few resources we have."

"Yes, I know exactly what you mean," Rose admitted. And the homeowner's previous statement, along with the way she had articulated those words, made her think she had probably seen it right. She usually did, given her very long experience with desire and love.

"This house was remodeled three years before my husband died," the woman said. "His failing condition during the last months he lived prevented him from completing any more than half of the work he had planned."

The guest looked at her in silence.

"Actually, the first renovation occurred in 1850, under the ownership of the previous residents who subsequently sold the property to my husband, before finally leaving to settle in California. Really, I couldn't tell you if they finally reached the coast or not, but at least that was their purpose," Makayla continued.

"Many try to go West nowadays," agreed Rose. "Not all of them get there, however. It's a very dangerous journey, and when you finally reach the coast things aren't always the way you hoped they would be."

"Have you been there before?" the farmer asked her.

"Only once, but I didn't stay for long. I had other urgent business at that moment. Certainly it's a very beautiful place, and there are many great opportunities waiting for people there, you know."

"Some travelers who have been through here say that the climate and the scenery is much better in that part of the country than it is here. Do you agree? Is that true?" Makayla inquired.

"Indeed, the climate is good, and the surroundings are beautiful. But they have outlaws, problems and fighting, too," Rose pointed out.

"We have some of the same drawbacks here, unfortunately. And the outlaws can be cruel at times..." said the other while making a face. "Anyway, don't talk about it now, just help yourself to some lunch. It's ready now."

"What do I see? Beans, vegetables and sourdough bread! Oh my, after so long...you can't imagine how many days I've been riding across that nearby desert."

"It will be easy to find out if you really like it. If you eat all of it, well, I'll know you really needed to fill your stomach and that you liked what I prepared."

"Don't doubt it for a second, Makayla!" Rose smiled, eyeing the main course served on the table. "You'll be deeply satisfied both because of my hunger and my appreciation, indeed..."

***

The rest of the day went by very slowly, as Rose let her horse rest for a few more hours and she herself had an opportunity to take a nap in the open of the courtyard after the very good lunch, calmly digesting her food under one of the few trees that stood in the front yard. The other woman didn't stop doing her housework and moving buckets and branches here and there in the stable and along the walls. At times she eyed Makayla, considering her slender figure as she walked unceasingly backwards and forwards as industrious as an insect that never seemed to rest.

Of course, as a guest, she had offered her help but the homeowner had plainly refused. Makayla had said she didn't want to bother her, but Rose had thought that maybe she didn't want someone else to interfere with her daily work; or maybe the woman simply didn't trust her, and really how could Rose blame her? That woman didn't know her, and her pistols and overall appearance weren't incentive to tell a stranger anything more about herself or about what her routine was around the small farm.

It was, anyway, almost sunset when Rose heard a metallic bucket full of water falling to the ground. The noise woke her up suddenly - oh my, she was really tired if she had fallen into such a pleasing long sleep so easily ... - and her eyes opened wide just in time to see some liquid spreading across the ground. Makayla was standing next to it, apparently being incapable of speaking, as if something had happened that had stopped her in her tracks. What was going on, the gunslinger asked herself. Then, her pupils turned to the other woman's face and what she noticed attracted her attention at once. Makayla seemed to be staring at something in the distance and a clear sense of desperation was visible on her face. Then she raised a finger and pointed at something. There was a small dust cloud afar off eastwards. Rose decided that it was time to stand up and sped over to the homeowner.

"It's them, those damn outlaws..." the farmer woman finally cried out as she definitely saw who was causing the cloud of dust moving in their direction. It was as if her worst fears had come to pass. "They're coming up the short hill as mad as wild beasts."

Squinting ahead and focusing for a while, in the middle of that small cloud that was rising to the sky, Rose could finally see the two riders in the distance headed up a dirt path towards the farm that Makayla owned. Their horses were completely surrounded by dust and at times their figures shortly disappeared into the dense particles being lifted sideways and behind them. The first question that came to her mind was why would two men have travelled this far? There weren't many explanations available, of course, but the most likely ones were that those people who were searching for something, or someone. But were they coming for her or for Makayla? Hard to say at that point...

Perhaps they were just two ordinary outlaws, something that she could easily deal with on her own. On the other hand, after crossing that desert, after a long dusty trail, what could possibly be better than to find some water and food and possibly even rob a house that was not well defended, and that they already knew?

"Do you mean 'trouble' now?" Rose asked, turning to her. An uncertain Makayla stepped back, without replying. As Rose saw the worried expression on the other's eyes she tried to calm her. "I'll save the pistols for when they get close up. They won't do much good at this distance anyways."

"They're robbers, damn violent raiders! They come and go whenever they like, and it's not only water and food they usually come for. After they feed themselves, they turn their attention to the rest. Then they go away, until the next time. For people like me, we are just free fodder they can make full use of every time they wish to do so. I have never been able to stop them!" the other woman stated in a painful tone.

A few minutes of silence followed after her words, while Rose started readying herself for what was likely to happen soon. Apparently, Makayla looked like she would feel safer if the gunslinger stood with her weapon in her hand. This meant that she was really afraid of those two riders, since she had immediately recognized their horses from afar. They had obviously paid her painful visits before. Had they forced themselves on Makayla before, or were they just cruel plunderers with no respect for any farmer living in the area? She couldn't be sure, of course. Whatever the case might be, and Rose had a lot of thoughts on the matter, the terrified Makayla didn't seem eager to concede to the more experienced woman's wisdom at the moment.

"When the time comes," Rose told her from behind, "Keep as low as possible, if you know what I mean…"

The homeowner nodded in silence, her eyes displaying fear, clearly. But she didn't need to be worried, as Rose was with her today. And that was all that mattered now…

Once the two got nearer and their horses reached the fence, the first one dismounted and stepped forward followed by his friend. In her mind, Rose knew that it wouldn't take very long before things were settled in that place and so the confrontation started almost immediately. It became obvious that this fight would decide who would win and remain alive today, and who might get to plunder in the end, be it food, riches or even persons, like the women.

"Two women for the price of one…" the first outlaw said, with a grin on his dirty face while his dusty footwear stood on the homestead's front yard. Blond hair dangled down to the worn-out collar around his neck and his clothes were made of a mediocre shirt, some black brushed trousers, an old slouch hat and a showy gun belt and holster displaying a six-shot percussion revolver. Rose recognized the gun – a New Army Model of 1860, if she remembered correctly - ready to be used. The other man who stood next to him had a beard and wasn't dressed any better, but his weapon seemed to be a pocket pistol that was 'double-action' and perhaps even newer than the gun his friend had.

"What price are you talking about? There's no one to pay, and it will be us who'll get the money also this time. It's easy money as far as I see, and something else even more appreciable, of course…" the second guy uttered in a repulsive voice.

"Do you see how beautiful they are? I mean both of them…And the new one has also two pistols that will be a splendid addition to my collection once she drops them. Don't you think so?" the blond-haired smirked.

"Yeah, you're right. Quite right…"

As the two were making a spectacle of their worst manners, the female gunslinger didn't move but simply stood and stared at them. Then she spoke. "There's no reason for there to be any trouble here. If you have come for a drink of water before going back to your trail, wherever it takes you, I don't think there will be any problem. This kind lady will be glad to offer you some water. But differently from what you might be thinking, you have not found an easy prey today, I can assure you of this."

"Oh, the woman with the pistols can talk…" the bearded outlaw said with a funny expression, his fingers already stroking his weapon.

"Let them mock us for the moment. We'll have the best part, and all the rest..." the first one added soon after, and moved for his precision revolver at once.

As pistols were drawn by both sides - the ones Rose had at her disposal were drawn a bit later than the outlaws', truth to be said - things began to happen very quickly, as a matter of fact. And a deafening gunfight followed.

Whatever the first shooter on the left was aiming at, a moment later it was clearly behind him as the magical blow hit his body, completely unexpected and unseen. There was a wild scream from the short distance, like a sudden high cry to the heavens. If the man was still alive when Rose's attack by sorcery reached him, it wouldn't have surprised if he had displayed an awkward stupid look on his face, as he saw a cold smile on her lips. He was done, and he didn't even know how, which wasn't important anyhow – as the bandit wasn't supposed to discover how she had killed him, anyway.

Then it was the other man's turn – the one who was standing on the right, just a few steps away from the first one who was now quickly falling to the ground, dead.

Once the two outlaws had been properly dealt with, under the incredulous look of the female farmer who was nearby, Rose thought about what she happened to turn her attention to when the gunfight occurred. She had never been very accurate at shooting, but she had never forced herself to improve that ability either, because of her superior skills using sorcery, certainly. That was why she had two gun holsters on her belt, as she always preferred her adversaries to focus on her pistols while the fingers of both of her hands were left free to make the small, slow gestures she needed to unleash her magical attacks. Who knew where the shots she had fired had ended up! Their casings probably lay somewhere around that dry ground, having hit nothing in their random course. Not that the female farmer would ever figure out what had really occurred in there, for sure... Such magical blows were usually too fast to be spotted, commonly occurring out of sight.

"They will never harm you again. This problem of yours is solved forever," the gunslinger told Makayla who still couldn't come to terms with what had just happened before her own eyes.

"What...how did you?" were her surprised words. "You're incredible, where did you learn to shoot that way, and how can you be so good at it?"

"Am I too good at killing outlaws for a woman? Is that what you mean?" Rose asked the other, making a funny face.

"That's not...it's not what I wanted to say...no offense...it's just that I am really bewildered..."

"No offense taken, my darling," the gunslinger simply said. "It's not the first time I have had to fight bad men in my life, so I have gained some experience at doing such things over time, you know. It's a cruel wide world, and you have to learn how to properly defend yourself, the sooner the better, or you won't get very far."

"Yes, yes..." Makayla conceded. "As you say...after all, you saved my farm and me as well today. I owe you much!"

"Nothing that a good dinner can't repay…and I noticed you are very good in the kitchen, aren't you? After all, I thought I might stay overnight. This is a place that seems so pleasant, and the hospitality is very appreciable. Would that be okay?"

"Yes, of course…" the homeowner hurried herself in replying at once. "You can stay here as long as you want. I'll prepare my best dinner for you and I can also clean your horse, if you like, and give you whatever provisions you want and…"

"A good dinner will be enough for today. We'll see about the rest. Who knows what tomorrow may bring – don't you agree?"

"Indeed! As you like…"

"Now let's get inside…" Rose made a wide gesture, inviting Makayla to lead the way. "I really think I sweated too much while I was sleeping in the courtyard, so I probably need another refreshing bath."

"You can't even imagine how much I sweated until a moment ago, when I saw those outlaws drawing their pistols and aiming at you…" the other confessed in a trembling voice. Then the two young women went to the stable that stood next to the main building, as the sun was starting to slowly go down at the end of the day.

***

That dry night Rose didn't feel ready to go to bed, at least not yet, and she knew she had to drink something before she could fall asleep. The woman was also sure that something else might happen – which could be interesting - if she behaved in exactly the right way. The house she had taken shelter in might turn out to be much more pleasing than it had first appeared when she had stumbled onto it at the end of a seemingly unending journey through the sun-drenched desert that had ended two days ago.

So, she took the opportunity and entered the living room, choosing a chair where she sat as soon as her eyes saw that also Makayla was also sitting in there, wearing only a short light robe that showed off most of her beautiful skin, on her soft arms and long legs. Probably the homeowner was also unable to go to sleep at that moment, and Rose was certain that it wasn't because of the warm temperatures during the night.

Leaning back in her chair with a knowing look, crossing her legs, Rose helped herself and poured some alcohol from an almost empty bottle that stood on a shelf, next to a vase without a plant in it. After the first drink, she swallowed another shot of whiskey and put the glass back on the wooden table nearby. Then, the woman mumbled and gave Makayla a long look. As usual, the more she drank, the less restraint she had and she was almost ready to let talk freely. "A toast now to your courage, the great decisiveness that allowed you to remain here and fight for your farm, despite all the problems you faced and your long years of loneliness!"

"My courage?" the other spoke in surprise, her dark pupils widening. "Really, it was you who killed those outlaws, not me. And I'll never stop thanking you for doing that, for saving me…"

"This whiskey is not going to solve your troubles forever," the gunslinger replied, with a smirk that turned her face into a funny expression. "People get nothing from a whiskey bottle."

"But it helps," Makayla smiled back "And it also keeps a person warm, body and mind."

Rose remained silent for some short moments, and then she nodded. "Maybe you're right." The look she had noticed on the homeowner's face made her think she had understood something, after all Rose had already started to give her hints. Now it was finally time to see if her guess was correct, after all. She was rarely mistaken about such things, and she was certain she had hit the mark this time as well.

That was why she had decided to wear a capricious and sexy orange corset she liked so much, one that she had gotten long ago from a beautiful female singer at a saloon along the way, months ago. It would be something special that she was certain the other woman would appreciate too. So, Rose left that full-length duster coat fall to the floor, the one she used to cover her shoulders when it got cold in the wilderness - the one that she had turned to in this case so as to appear not too shameless.

"It's only you and me here now, no outlaws, no witnesses, only the two of us, and the calmness of the night."

"Yes…" the other replied, in a very agreeable tone.

"Does this help this you figure out what might be next? What are you thinking now, my darling?" a more daring Rose said, staring at her with both azure eyes.

Makayla's heart was racing at that moment, and her mouth was too dry to answer the other's question.

After a few moments, when Rose slowly stepped forwards, the other woman looked lost, though deeply enticed and eager to let her make her next move, for sure.

"What if I show you how you can truly thank me for saving you?" And saying that, the gunslinger reached for her, approaching her face softly, kissing her lips slowly. The other woman looked at her, very glad for her lovely gesture. Soon afterwards Makayla lost track of time. She was only aware of the satisfying sensations of the other's mouth and hands. A feeling of regret only came over her when Rose briefly stopped holding her breasts.

Leaning over, she placed one of her hands against Rose's exquisite slender body, straightened up and then moved her hands downwards, with moments of true, deep passion following.

Soon Makayla lost herself in the other's face, eyes, shoulders, legs and arms. This was proving to be the most pleasing outing that she had ever had, she thought, while she continued to stroke Rose's hair and neck in a passionate way.

It didn't take long before they were in the bedroom, laying on its soft sheets and pillows. "Haven't you waited long enough for this, all alone in this farm?" Rose became more and more aroused and gave her a mischievous grin. "Isn't this better than your husband ever gave you? – better than any man ever gave you?"

Makayla nodded and kept kissing her, while clutching her body tighter and tighter. From that moment on, things just sped up. In that place, far away from the all the others who lived in the far recesses of that desert, they could love each other without restraint. And they deeply loved, indeed, for most of the night.

Fingering through the short light robe the clothes of the young lady in her hand, she selected an area of her slim, soft legs she wanted to fondle, then just went on for a while. Makayla, with a pleased glance, seemed to appreciate Rose's gesture and smiled at her in return. Both women started to undress, then with a knowing movement the gunslinger pulled off her sexy corset and kissed the other, shaking the female farmer's long hair, touching her skin and nibbling her neck. So, Makayla felt herself getting very aroused by that slow and soft stroking and with another kiss she turned her body to face her saver and they kissed passionately.

Love among women was very rare, certainly, and was by all means forbidden in that world of men. How could the homeowner imagine that exactly the gunfighter she liked and had protected her farm was really in love with her, too? How could she ever think that such a great opportunity would happen this way, so unexpectedly?

"I have a little trick here I'm sure you'll just beg me to repeat," Rose said with a mischievous grin soon after. Makayla wasn't quite sure what the other woman meant by that, but the activities of the gunslinger at her very extra sensitive sex organ that was part of her female genital tract had her feeling quite warm. The witch gently inserted two fingers deep in her partner, while other two of her second hand kept massaging and stroking Makayla's erogenous zone until what was the primary anatomical source of her sexual pleasure completely emerged from under its hood and stood rigid. Immediately the younger lady was twisting and turning in response to Rose's ministrations. "Please, I need your mouth, darling. I want to feel your tongue deep inside me," she begged in the end.

Simply and knowingly doubling the efforts of her fingers, buried deep in Makayla's cunt, a more and more daring Rose pushed her other hand beneath her partner's quivering buttocks, and pushed them upward. The other moved her own hands beneath herself and lifted her hips high to better offer her to the gunfighter's mouth.

"Please Rose, don't make me beg. Kiss me there."

The witch still kept her eyes locked on the other's. As Makayla held herself up, she brought her hand back between her opened thighs. Lightly at first, and then more and more convincingly, she scraped her fingernails along the soft insides of her partner's thighs. Seeing the younger woman was about to open her mouth again, Rose slowly lowered her face to the hairy spot below. Makayla tensed before the time, and then nearly went into shock at the first touch. She screamed in pain, and she also tried to shake the gunslinger's mouth from her.

Rose went on and made her way through her partner's womanliness, as a consequence the other moaned and softly yelped as the witch rammed her tongue in and out of her. Within minutes of this continuous tongue stimulation, the younger lady neared an orgasm, her soft moans developing into screams of pleasure as the other's expert tongue lashed in and out of her. There was only a brief pause, then

Rose's tongue renewed its attack on her. Makayla's breathing kept increasing, she rocked her head from side to side, her moans rising... Looking down between her legs, she saw the witch leering at her.

"Well now, was that good enough for you? And if you liked this little trick, I have a whole bag full of them." Rose lowered her head and gave the other a big, wet, loud kiss. Makayla moaned again at the touch and reached out for the beautiful gunfighter. Lowering into her partner's arms, Rose pressed her lips to the other woman's. She opened her lips, and her tongue entered the gunslinger's warm mouth.

The two kissed again, they looked at each other and then smiled in a sign of agreement, finally.

That first night was very memorable, pleasing and full of good moments. They made love with all of their passion, searching for each other in the darkness, as a thirsty traveler who hadn't been able to drink for a very long time who finally had reached the desired well. Finally, they were now allowed to enjoy their time and satisfy their senses, as if they had been on a very long walk made all alone around a seemingly endless stretch of land.

When everything was finally over, quickly becoming only a splendid memory in their minds, standing against an early morning sky, with a new day's sun behind them, the two women remained together for a while just holding each other. Sadly, the moment came for both of them to finally go back to the daily duties that were waiting.

When they had been together, Makayla had told Rose all about her very difficult life, the many terrifying moments she had been forced to face since the death of her husband, some years ago. Not that she had really been in love with that man, but he had proven to be a decent partner who had fallen in love with her and treated her well during the time they had spent together, anyway. On the other hand, Makayla had always been a lesbian at heart, and that marriage had only been a false pretense, nothing more than a fictitious behavior that she had displayed for so long not to be recognized for what she really was. Really it wasn't that different from the flashy clothes and the precious jewelry the old women adorned themselves with in order to avert passers-by from the deep signs of their true age, the unstoppable passing of the years.

It had also been a method she had to undergo so she could move away from her family and be free, at least freer than she had ever felt before. After all, other women she knew had been less lucky than her, having married violent, disreputable men that didn't care for their wives much more than they did for their cattle, as a matter of fact. Makayla had also explained to Rose how bad some villagers of the small outposts nearby had treated her after the passing of her husband, giving her the money - and not much, in reality. She had been forced to run her farm under the worst of circumstances, though her distant neighbors asked for much more from her to appease their deepest, most cruel desires. And there had been only one way she could pay, which was exactly what those evil individuals wanted…

Concerning the outlaws, well, Rose already knew about them, and Makayla repeated again, how very thankful she was for the help she had been given that evening. How many times had they previously come to her house, and had oppressed her lonely life, stealing, damaging her property, while also abusing her! The only reason they had decided not to take her along with them was for their own interest: why deprive themselves of a comfortable and lively shelter at the end of that dry desert, a pleasing fireplace where they could go whenever they wanted, and find a woman who had to work to satisfy their needs, giving them food, water and all the rest? She had been treated like an animal: those men using her however and whenever they pleased. In their eyes, she really was an animal that wasn't ever meant to be killed or removed from that farm, because this way they could get provisions, service and forced sex every single time. In their minds, this arrangement was much better than taking those things only once and then losing them forever.

So, she had been allowed to stay there, live there and attend to her farm as long as they were certain they could find her in that exact place every time, and would have her at their disposal. Makayla simply didn't know where else she could go, or how she might escape. She also didn't have anyone who might defend her, or finally face those outlaws, getting rid of them on her behalf forever. That was how the woman had lived her life for a long time...until Rose had appeared that morning in the desert and had come to her house. Rose was a ray of light that was deeply welcomed, despite the fact that Makayla lived next to a sun-drenched desert. She was a sign of hope the young woman thought she had seen the last of, but finally there was a chance to be optimistic again.

***

A week had passed since Rose had stopped at the farm, and many other passionate nights of love had followed. Now, the gunslinger, who was in reality only a witch, was in trouble because she knew she wanted to remain there, living that pleasing lifestyle as long as possible. But doing that wouldn't be good for her, and it wouldn't be considerate of her partner. There were always those last things to do, and time was running out... This wasn't the right place for her to find what she was searching for. Actually, this wasn't the right place where she could get what she needed.

She didn't have much of a head for thinking about what was best at that moment, but she knew what she had to do. The events from weeks ago came back to her mind again, and she remembered the magical fight that had taken place on the East Coast. She had been caught by surprise, as she didn't imagine that a which-hunter might reside in the small village she had stopped in for a couple of nights. But he did, and he also discovered who she really was and her powers. Actually, the woman didn't know how he had found out about her: maybe she had let her guard down, or maybe the witch-hunter had been lucky, spotting her doing something magical somewhere. Be it as you please, in the end Rose had been wounded by that very capable witch-hunter and, once she had escaped his continuous pursuit, it had taken her a very long time to recover. The poison of the hunter's last blow had sunk deep into her body, which was not something a common sorcerer could remove nor heal easily.

Although she had gotten rid of that old man in the end, what he had thrown against her during their first battle had really left behind its effects that still lasted nowadays.

Actually, by chance, this huge country that was still greatly unexplored so far, being full of outlaws, gold diggers, poor farmers and new colonists, didn't have too many people who believed in sorcery anymore or that were capable of stopping or opposing her power and her rituals. It had just been bad luck when she had stumbled into that witch-hunter in New England who recognized her and tried to kill her by any means.

But around these parts, across those seemingly endless plains, there was no one who appeared to think that a witch could be a real person or that she might live in the surroundings, certainly. Those wild men and strong-willed women who lived in this part of the world were practical individuals and they didn't really know anything about the wars that had been secretly fought in old Europe against her kind. In those old countries, people had tried to wipe out completely all the female practitioners of the bloody rites from the past: there had been so much evil unleashed during those battles, causing so many to die in both the factions that had kept confronting each other for centuries, undoubtedly.

Rose still remembered how she had started learning the rituals of sorcery from her family, when she still was a child, in a little village that stood on the other side of that huge ocean they had eventually crossed long ago to resettle. The image of her teasing in the sing-song manner of her age as she tried to repeat the difficult words and elaborate chants her mother and her father emitted while performing their dark duties in the stable were engraved on her mind. Even though those chants might seem today to be stupid, useless gestures, they didn't seem to be so in her eyes at that time, of course.

Turning to her present situation, the thoughtful Rose considered that the first time she had seen Makayla standing next to the walls of the house, she had immediately noticed she was very attractive, as her appearance had been her most striking feature, and had also gotten her attention at once. Though, with the passing of the days, she had become certain that there was something deeper inside her mind, something that had made Rose eventually fall in love with that young, dark-haired womanly farmer. Anyway, she also knew that such an affair couldn't last for long, as it simply wasn't meant to: sooner or later it had to end, and it would be the best thing for the unknowing Makayla herself.

It was a real pity that now that Rose had found love, a genuine love, a person she never wanted to depart from, she was forced to do so. But that was what the ritual required, or else she would simply die in a matter of weeks. By looking at that beautiful homeowner who had proven to be so strong, so resistant and so capable of running her small farm in that dry soil, fighting all alone against outlaws, evil villagers and other people that had tried to get all they could out of her, Rose couldn't be prouder of her. There had been only a few people who had given her the money she deserved and the provisions she needed in order to survive until the time of harvest had come, but it hadn't been an easy life, for sure. So, the witch wasn't surprised that she could be so fond of her.

However, what she had been looking for - the last ingredients she had to find so as to complete the preparation necessary to heal her body from the magical wounds that damn witch-hunter had inflicted - was a portion of her hair and some fresh tears, which had to be taken from a lover who truly, deep-heartedly was bound to her... and then that person had to be killed immediately after those things had been taken from her. That was all. The magical beverage the witch would get from it was meant to make her recover from those last consequences that she was still affected with today.

The problem was that the target had to be a true partner who really, deeply loved her. And another problem was that Rose was truly in love with her in return...which was a complication she had never even dreamed about. And she didn't want to kill that lovely female farmer. By no means!

Indeed, there were other things that might be taken from a faithful partner like that one: her eyes, her nose or even all of her internal organs, and those things were incredibly powerful ingredients that could be used in a few great remedies and other evil poisonous preparations, Rose knew that all too well. But it also required, again, the life of the target of such sorcery, and it usually caused great suffering to the victim before the final passing.

In a way, she hadn't experienced true discomfort when she had cruelly removed the heart from a cowboy she had spent a night with in a town some weeks before. Frank was his name, and he was still asleep when she had killed him before opening his chest using a mystical ritual that had spread blood everywhere on the bed and across the bedroom they had shared so they could be alone. But his heart had been just the first of many ingredients Rose needed for recovering her full strength. After Frank, it had been time for an old veteran to add his contribution: he had lost his hands after Rose abruptly cut them off so she could add them to her magical beverage. And, finally, there had been a young and stupid trader who believed that Rose was an easy prey: he had ended up being the real prey, and his dead body was now buried in the ground in the forest, lying there without many of his internal organs that she had extracted before getting rid of his corpse.

In a way, moving across those Western states she had met many strong men, and she had done away with a lot of them. After all, finding a tall and beautiful woman who also appeared to be very eager to have sporting sex with strangers wasn't common in those days, unless you were searching for prostitutes of course. Even those easy women weren't very frequent in dirty saloons in little towns that were springing up everywhere because of the gold rush.

By reminding herself of the last man she had been with, the trader - was he named Harry or George?- she considered how loving and passionate he had been. Their sex had been wild, like some beasts, not allowing time for good manners and kind gestures, but it had resulted to be exactly what she needed for her senses and what had pleased both of them in the end. Probably, the man had enjoyed the sex more than she did, as a matter of fact. Anyway, if she compared her last lover's muscles, height and size, where it mattered most, well, you know, he wasn't as wondrous and attractive as the previous cowboy she had bedded the week before, but what could you do about that? She had to take whatever came around, sure thing, and the right person to make the right ingredients was so rare.

Now, after that long journey, she seemed to have found the last thing she had been long searching for. They were on that bed, where young Makayla lay asleep, never suspecting Rose's true motivations and goals. But Rose couldn't go on with it; she didn't want to treat her that way. So, by lovingly staring at her, in silence, she finished dressing, put her hat on and headed for the front door, unnoticed. Then she got to the stable, readied her horse and left the farm.

In the first light of that new day, as Rose looked at the house of her lover for the last time, the woman knew that it was better if it went that way. It was much better to abandon that place, leaving Makayla behind her and trying to forget her warm strokes, her beautiful eyes and the pleasing sensations she had felt while being with her. She knew she could never come back here. That was the way she wanted her lover to remain - alive, safe and sound, putting aside the desire that might be soon growing in her to try to use that body in order to get what she needed to increase her power and strength at the expense of the other's existence.

Makayla would be hating her for her gesture, for having suddenly left her that way, but she didn't know the truth. That was what was really better for her, who Rose wanted to remain alive.

Perhaps it was simply because she had become faint-hearted after everything she had gone through to get here, or maybe she was just tired of so many murders, as a matter of fact. So, she turned her mount around and silently looked at the plains that stretched ahead of her now, being for most part a desert with only a few leaves spurting out of the scrub-brush. It was a dusty, exhausting trail that was expecting her and she was going to face it all without any cheerful company or lovely comfort, but at least Makayla would live. That was enough to make Rose rejoice for now.

After all, wasn't the memory of your dearest ones being safe, though living elsewhere and being very far from you, what made you think that all was going well even when times seemed bad?

Rose only needed to find another female partner who would fall in love with her, somebody who could really adore her, and someone who Rose wouldn't truly love in return. That woman could be sacrificed, without regret - but not Makayla, no, not her. The gunslinger looked ahead, without speaking, and thought that she would find the right target for her ingredients, sooner or later, along the way. Certainly, she would get the things she needed, some day or another.

Demon Lover

G. H. Finn

Halloween. Tonight would be the night. If it happened at all, it would happen at midnight. But not here. Not in this world...

She lit the scarlet candles, then drew the signs upon the wall. Old symbols. Ancient designs. Magic from before the modern age.

The chalk glowed gently in the moonlight streaming through the bedroom window, as eldritch shadows skittered across the wall, cast by the flickering candlelight that dimly illumined her darkened room.

She said the words, urgently, breathlessly. The chalk glowed brighter. The design became a doorway. A route to... *beyond*.

Nervously, she edged toward the door, her bare feet pattering on the smooth wooden floorboards. She shivered, from excitement mingled with apprehension rather than cold, but it made her pause to think. She wore only a nightdress... Should she stop and find some other clothes?

But the doorway was beckoning her... she could feel it pulling at her senses. At her heartstrings...

Darkling butterflies beat their wings inside her as she stepped forward – and through – into the world beyond.

She walked forward into a place... that was not a place... In a time... that was not a time... Into a world beyond... beyond...

It was a forest. Primordial. From before the time of humans. From before time.

The aeons-old trees towered above her, their branches reaching to the ebon-dark sky above. Their trunks were huge, vast, dwarfing her completely. She felt tiny beside them. Very small and vulnerable in this strange place. She felt like a faery taking her first walk through the woods.

That was when she heard the sound. And felt... something... *familiar.*

Her pulse quickened. *He* was here.

She took a breath, almost panting...

He was close... and it made her feel... strange... it made her *feel...*

The shadows seemed to darken around her. He was coming closer. He was almost here...

Her man of shadows...

Her demon lover.

She wasn't sure he was real at first... wondering if he were but a thing of dreams and fancies... stitched together from secret hopes and fears and longings... And yet...

The shadows deepened. Becoming solid. A shape formed within them. A man... of sorts. Her man. At least from the waist upward... below... she shuddered at the thought of his short, stubby tail, and his hooves...

She tried to swallow...

As the shadows touched her.

Arms, far more solid than she had dared to imagine, wrapped themselves around her. Hugging her close. Holding her, wrapped in shadow, embraced tightly, helpless in his grasp.

She realised she could not escape – not now... and she sighed with relief as she realised that she didn't want to... Lips found hers in the darkness. Pressing gently against her face. Kissing, softly – firm but gentle. A hand traced a sigil upon her back, the fingers almost tickling through the thin fabric of her nightdress...

Her mouth opened as she kissed him, the tip of his forked tongue brushing her lips, and gently entering her mouth as he kissed her.

She gasped a little as his hand slid down her spine to rest on her bottom, strong fingers squeezing playfully, pulling her close against him.

She gasped again as she felt him pressing into her through the soft material of her nightdress, he was already hard, bulging with his want for her. Inhumanly huge. She wrapped her arms around his, and he almost crushed her in his embrace. She kissed him again as his hand gently kneaded the cheek of her bottom. Her own hand, almost of its own volition, slid down to find him... ready for her. Her fingers closed around his short and curly-furred member and she felt him tremble with pleasure. His face pressed against hers, whispering, softly into her ear, "My lady – I will make you mine."

She knew what he meant, her knees quivered slightly at the thought, then nearly gave way as his hand touched the inside of her thigh. The fabric of her nightdress hardly seemed a barrier as his hand slid upward, searching. Unconsciously she opened her legs slightly – and his clawed hand found her through the material.

Touching...

Exploring...

Pressing gently...

And moving...

She moaned slightly but the sound was cut short by his demonic, serpentine kisses.

He held her tightly to him, enfolding her with one arm – as his other taloned hand moved relentlessly against the wetness of her nightdress...

Rubbing...

Circling...

Spreading a feeling of fiery lightning through her...

And then a slight pause... as he took her by the hand and lead her to lean against a tree.

For a moment she was confused, wondering, and then with her back pressed against the ancient trunk, he knelt before her. Lifting her nightdress. Exposing her.

She took a rapid breath – and then he was upon her. Kissing her... He pushed at her with his snakelike tongue, its twin forks pressing her back against the tree as he kissed her.

Lapping...

Licking...

Loving her...

Tasting her...

His face wet from her.

Her scent upon him and he ground his horned head against her until she felt she could no longer stand. She reached and touched his goatlike head, gripping, half wanting to push him away... Half pulling him closer still. But her legs were weak... She didn't think she could stand this much longer... She didn't think she could stand at all.

And that was when he stood and lightly lifted her. Cradling her in his arms. Carrying her, to lay her on a bed made of moss and petals. Taking her to a lover's bed hidden in the heart of the deep, dark wood between the worlds.

She lay there, breathless, wanting him. He reached out to her, standing over her, bending to undo the buttons on her nightgown while she touched him, stroked him... eagerly, feeling his deep scarlet flesh stiffen more as her fingers moved around him, responding to her in a way that left her tingling.

He pulled away her nightdress, leaving her naked. Revealing the crimson pentacle painted on her chest, the indigo symbols drawn around her nipples, and the vermillion inked sigils that swirled between her legs.

She lay back, shyly on the moss, feeling it against her skin, catching the delicate aroma of the flower-petals that formed her mattress.

He knelt next to her, reaching out to delicately run a long claw gently across her breast. Teasingly. A barbed fingertip circling her areola, spiralling, moving inward to brush against her stiffened nipple. She felt it harden beneath his touch. His hand cupped her breast, his other hand tracing along her thigh. His crimson mouth suddenly engulfed her teat, sucking eagerly at her soft flesh, while his other hand pushed apart her legs and found her... already wet... waiting... ready...

his bestial fingers teasingly eased their way into her, moving back and forth as he kissed her bosom, cupping her in his large hands and sucking gently. His twisting fingers slid, softly, back and forth within her. His thumb parted her labia... and began to circle. Fingers moving, thumb circling, hand pressing against her. He moved from her breast, his fingers still teasing her nipple as his lips kissed her forehead, then her eyes, and her blushing cheeks and at last, finally, inevitably, her mouth, which opened as he kissed her deeply, with a passion that left her weak once more.

Her hips rose and fell, moving in time to the movement of his fingers. She pushed herself upward, against the gentle pressure of his spiralling thumb. He held her, helpless, covering her with his half-fur covered body, holding her close to him as she moaned, moving against his hand. He kissed her again and moved forward, forcing himself between her legs, pushing her knees apart to open her. He moved in toward her, brushing against her, her soft wetness yielding against his hard, unrelenting, heat. He pressed further forward, sliding, squeezing as he entered her. His movement felt barely contained, full of a wild animal lust – a desire – a wanting – a need for her he could barely hold in check. He kissed her again, moving inside her... pressing her into the moss and petals of midnight – alone together in the wild, wild wood.

They lay there. Together. Thrusting, sliding, heartbeats sounding like tribal drums. Moving as one... Wild in the night.

Like a stag and a hind, rutting in the woods
Like a fox and a vixen, coupled beneath the trees.
Like wolves howling with dark delight.

Bodies entwined, all thoughts lost in rhythm and desire and a hunger – a craving – their limbs wrapped tightly against each other – no longer two bodies – now one flesh, one soul, one desire, one craving....

And one release.

Together.... Long-lasting– shuddering – his back arching, his muscles tightening as he filled her. Her legs wrapped around him, her hands clenching, gripping his red flesh tightly, flooding with delight... The ripples of pleasure washing over each other. Feasting on each other's passion.

A need at last satiated, as they slowed their movement and kissed once more... slowly... no urgency now... lingering... lovingly... folded in each other's arms.

The witch and her demon lover. Together at midnight in the deep, dark wood between the worlds.

Small Town Vampire

Brandon Cracraft

The vampire painted his face with dollar store makeup and dabbed fake blood on the sides of his mouth. He never wore fake fangs: they reminded him too much of when he was human and had to wear a painful retainer at night. The tuxedo was new. Well, new to him. He purchased it from a thrift store in Dallas a couple of days after last Halloween. The satin cape he made himself.

"Happy Halloween," the vampire said, pleased that it was a myth that vampires couldn't see their reflection in a mirror. Like most of the legends, it had a kernel of truth, one that got distorted over the centuries. Vampires didn't cast a reflection in water.

"Dracula again?!" Joey Tyler said, putting his hands on his hips. The vampire wondered how long it would be before the fourteen-year-old realized that he was gay. He was stretched out, already taller than the vampire, oversized hands and feet that prophesized another half feet of growth before the teenager finally crested the other side of puberty. He was dressed as an airborne ranger, complete with his father's helmet and goggles, zits artfully hidden under camouflage makeup. The vampire couldn't help but notice how tight the helmet was. Within a month, the boy would be taller than his father.

The vampire winked. "Can't go wrong with the classics, my boy." He enjoyed hanging out with the kids. Their blood wasn't ripe, so he didn't have to worry about the hunger scratching at the lining of his stomach. The sweetest blood belonged to the old and infirm, at least until he got hold of it. Despite only needing to feed once a year, the vampire felt the hunger constantly.

"How old were you when you died?" seven-year-old Kevin Pierce asked. He was wearing ripped jeans, and no makeup. His mother probably spent the money for his Incredible Hulk costume on her parties.

"Nineteen," the vampire said. He was used to that question, since he only stood five-foot-three. He was half Japanese but naturally blond haired. His eyes changed from brown to vermillion after he died. "I died in 1982 of a disease they used to call GRID."

"It's AIDS," Joey said, rolling his eyes. Every year, a kid asked the vampire the same question and he suffered through the long explanation. He was babysitting the Pierce boys this year, and he decided it was long past time to end that tradition.

There was one question that burned in the gangly teenager's gut. He wiped some green makeup of his thick glasses and asked, "Who are you going to feed from?" The teenager never said the word "kill."

"Thornton Miller," the vampire said.

"He's creepy." The tiny voice came from Kevin's younger brother, Dylan. He was wearing his *Teenage Mutant Ninja Turtles* pajamas and a matching plastic mask that was comically too big for him. "All he does is stare and drool and make weird sounds..."

"That's not nice," Joey said. "Mister Miller has Alzheimer's." The teenager didn't say it out loud, but he was glad that the vampire was taking him. He hoped that that his friend would do the same to him before he got as bad as Thornton Miller.

***

"Benimaru?" Mrs. Baker yelled, dressed up as a mad scientist, complete with fake blood and slime dripping off her lab coat. She smiled, pretending like every step wasn't agony. Osteoporosis threatened to shatter her hip.

The vampire smiled back, ignoring the sudden pang of hunger. Very few people still called him by his name.

"I was wondering if you decided who you were going to visit this year?" the old woman asked, hoping that she didn't sound too hopeful. She was forced into retirement at age seventy-five, and boredom was killing her almost as quickly her fragile bones were.

The vampire loved her. She was his ninth-grade Biology teacher, and the only teacher who stood up for him when the PTA thought his blood made him too dangerous to attend school. She slapped Mrs. Falstaff when she whispered that little Benny Yoshiro was being punished for being gay, even though he got AIDS from a blood transfusion.

Benimaru Yoshiro, III died a virgin.

"Thornton Miller," he said, wondering if he should apologize. It was obvious that the old woman was ready to let go. "I will most likely come for you next year." He paused, realizing how ghoulish that sounds.

"I suppose it was only a matter of time," Mrs. Baker said, inhaling a sigh. There were kids around, and she liked to appear invulnerable in front of them. "I suppose you go to all in good time, Benimaru. You certainly are better than the last vampires. They kept the tornadoes away well enough, but you're a local boy."

"Dad says that the last vampire didn't just kill the sick," Joey Tyler said. "They say she killed whoever she wanted."

"That's right," Mrs. Baker said, a shudder running through her. She was too old. A human shouldn't outlive two vampires.

"I have something for you," the vampire said, handing her a glass. She didn't need to be told what it was. His venom had special properties. "It's not a lot. It will only last a few hours."

"Thank you," Mrs. Baker said, walking into her house and shutting the doors. She waved goodbye to the children and then pulled the shades and turned off the porch light. The candy pail was far enough away from the front door that they wouldn't bother her.

The old woman felt naughty, and she enjoyed that feeling. She stripped off all her clothes and drank the vampire's venom. Her heart raced as she leaned back and let out a satisfied moan.

Emmaline Baker felt like a young woman. No, she *was* a young woman. Twenty-two. Blond. Pretty. Wearing nothing but a sundress with no panties. Panties only got in the way. She smelled wildflowers and felt no pain in her gnarled knuckles as she masturbated.

***

The youngest person that Benimaru Yoshiro ever drank was Joey Tyler's mother. Bone cancer. She used to lock herself in her room and played her Chirstina Aguilara and Brittney Spears CDs as loud as possible to mask the sounds of her sobs and screams from her children. The week before Halloween was the worst. The then ten-year-old Joey felt her agony even when she didn't say anything.

When Benny showed up, he was dressed like Edward Cullen from *Twilight,* covered in gold makeup and glitter. Melinda Tyler's favorite character. Little Joey thought the vampire was supposed to be an angel.

Melinda hugged her children, her grip weak, her wig slipping. "Stephanie," she said, "take your brother trick-or-treating. I need you to keep him out for at least half an hour." She glanced from her husband to the vampire. "An hour would be better."

"I love you." Joey was glad that was the last thing that he said to his mother.

Stephanie Tyler kept them out for over two hours, mostly talking to her then-boyfriend, Adam "Smasher" Austin. Joey liked the cocky jock, the only boy with thicker glasses than him, so it didn't surprise him that his older sister broke up with him a couple days later. Stephanie ended up having four children by three different assholes.

When they got back, Joseph Tyler Sr was wearing the robe that Joey bought him for Christmas. His jeans and boxers were ripped and scattered around his parent's messy bedroom.

"Did the vampire hurt you, Daddy?" Joey asked.

Joseph Sr smiled through his tears. "No," he said, taking his youngest child's face in his hand. "It wasn't the vampire."

It wasn't until last year when Bud Cady's wife delivered a baby girl exactly nine months after the vampire drank her husband that Joey Tyler finally realized what happened in the bedroom that night.

***

"Are you sure you don't want me to go with you?" Joey Tyler asked, looking over at the vampire. "Mister Miller is being taken care of by his granddaughter. She's not from town. I don't think she even believes that vampires can control the weather."

The vampire shrugged. "They don't in the movies."

"Daddy tried to explain to her that our town has never had a hurricane since we made a deal with a vampire. Every town in Texas has something. The worst we ever had was a couple of bad thunderstorms. No power outages for more than a few minutes. No floods."

"Don't worry," the vampire said with a wink. "I can handle her."

***

The vampire prepared his best boyish grin before knocking on the door. He gave the kids one last wave. Joey Tyler kept looking back as he led the Pierce boys back to their street.

"You must be Miss Miller," the vampire said, even before the door finished opening. He brushed some dust off his satin cape.

"Ms. Regina Carson," the African-American woman said. She attempted to hide the bags around her eyes with eyeshadow and mascara. She tied her hair into a tight braid and two of her fingernails had recently been broken off.

"Nice to meet you," the vampire said, extending his hand to be shook.

She refused the hand, stepping back and raising an eyebrow. "I hear that there is some kind of agreement between this town and the vampires."

He lowered his hand and stepped in. Thanks to the agreement with the vampires at the town's founding in 1869, there was no place that he wasn't invited. "Yes," he said. "The humans brought a vampire and stated that they would provide a vampire its food in return for protection from the severe elements that kept destroying settlements in Texas back then."

"I want to watch," Regina Carson said, crossing her arms.

"Some people do like to see what my venom does to people," he said. Normally, spouses and lovers who got to experience its aphrodisiac affects first hand. "When it comes time for me to feed..."

"I want to watch," she repeated.

The vampire felt nervous. "I should warn you," he said. "It's not very pleasant."

Ms. Regina Carson's eyes narrowed. "I thought the blood drinking part was supposed to be painless."

"It is." The vampire couldn't hide his nervousness. "It's just not very pleasant to watch. It's not like the movies. My fangs don't just pop out..."

"You either let me watch," she demanded, "or you leave."

The young vampire sighed. "Don't say that I didn't warn you. Any nightmares you have tonight are on you."

***

Regina Carson dressed her father neatly in his favorite suit. He already looked like a corpse. Dark skin turning to gray, eyes glazed over. His behavior was erratic. Some days, he did nothing but scream and tear off his clothes. Other days, the only way that she knew that Thornton Miller was alive was the fresh shit she cleaned off him.

She didn't know why she was clinging to keeping him alive. Duty. Maybe fear. She heard what the previous vampire did to her Aunt Velma.

Thornton Miller ripped open the front of his shirt, revealing a gray tuft of hair on his concave chest. Drool slithered down his mouth and landed in a puddle on his lap. His pants were open and the disposable briefs ripped and revealing his limp manhood. It reminded his granddaughter of a dead fish.

The vampire leaned down and forced the elderly black man to look him in the eyes. "Thornton," he said, his voice shockingly gentle, "it is over."

For the first time in over a month, the old man smiled. Regina Carson saw recognition in his eyes. "It's about time," he mumbled, licking his eternally dry lips. "Why did you let me get this bad."

The vampire handed him a small cup of his venom. "Do you need any help drinking it?" He started to bring it to the old man's lips, but Thornton Miller grabbed it with shaking hands. The old man swallowed as much as he could, but he spilled some all over his hands. He licked it off his fingers.

"He gets an hour," the vampire said, standing up and stepping back. "I hope that you don't blush easy, Ms. Carson."

"I heard that your poison makes people horny." Regina Carson tried to sound more self-assured than she was. She was used to seeing the old man play with himself, had to take him home suddenly when he dropped his pants in the middle of McDonalds.

"It's a lot more than that," the vampire replied, giving her a sheepish grin. "You might want to wait in the living room. I'll call you in when I'm ready to feed... if you still want to see it."

Regina Carson took out her phone and started playing a game. "Don't forget to come get me."

***

The first thing that Thornton Miller noticed was the smell of cigarette smoke. He looked down at his fingers, surprised to see them empty. He hadn't smoked in fifteen years. Quit the day that his wife Joyce was diagnosed with lung cancer. The old man brought his finger to his lips and tasted tobacco, felt his lungs fill up with sweet smoke.

Cologne. At least a half-dozen different colognes and aftershaves, some trying to mask body odor. The smell made his eyes water, as his drool stained lips curled into a smile. "It's my birthday."

July 15, 1952. Private Thornton Miller turned nineteen. Everyone was screaming throwing makeshift confetti, happy to be thinking about something other than the war for a few minutes. He was surrounded by men, most without shirts. A couple were dancing around in their skivvies.

Joyce Jackson Miller was the only person that Thornton ever told his secret to. She needed to know that she was marrying a queer. When he got her pregnant, he didn't have the heart to tell her that he was thinking about Marlon Brando in *A Streetcar Named Desire.* At least, he knew that he could fool himself. Joyce wanted at least one more kid.

Miller felt a kiss on his forehead. Corporal Tommy Strickland. Had a crush on him since high school. One of the few white boys that didn't treat him different just because his skin was darker. Strick was white trash, through and through. Hair so blond it was almost grey, broad shoulders and a sloping forehead that made him seem a lot dumber than he was.

"What are you doing?" Miller said, jumping up. A bunch of the other guys were laughing. It was a joke. Miller sighed. Of course, it was.

"Don't be so uptight Marine," Strick joked. "I won't tell Joyce if you don't tell my wife." Both married. Prom queen Connie Lipton became Connie Strickland right before her boyfriend went off to war. It was the same reason most teenagers were getting married.

The Four Aces were singing "It's No Sin" and Strick began dancing. "Come on, Thorn. Dance with me."

"Everyone is watching," Miller said nervously. It took effort to remain seated. He used to play with himself as soon as he got home from school, the memory of Tommy Strickland soaping himself up in the shower was too much.

"No one cares, Thorn," he said. "It's me. Your old buddy, Strick." He reached out a hand, and Miller accepted it. When he got up, Strick pulled him close. "We're in the middle of a war. We could fuck in front of all these men and all they're going to do is cheer us on."

Miller felt nervous. "What are you talking about?"

Tommy Strickland's face was right up against his. Miller's lips parted as the king of his old high school pressed his lips against his. His tongue danced into the smaller man's mouth. When they parted, the two of them were in their underwear. Strick's jockeys brushed up against Thornton's Miller's boxers. They were both huge in their skivvies. Their cocks were hungry for each other.

Miller started crying. "I've waited for this my entire life."

They were naked, their cocks moving in unnatural ways. Thornton Miller's entire body erupted in gooseflesh and then became as sensitive as his foreskin. Even the slightest touch from Strick made him harder.

"I need to be inside you," Thornton Miller said breathlessly.

Strick came on Thornton Miller's cock. "Use my own juices as lube." He bent over, biting his lip in preparation for absolute pleasure.

***

"My grandfather certainly looks happy," Regina Carson said. The old man was naked and playing with himself despite the puddle of semen on his stomach. He came a second time and kept stroking.

The vampire gave her one last hesitant look. "Can't imagine a better way to die," he said. It was certainly better than the one he was granted, wasting away from a disease and then violently attacked by a hungry vampire.

"Go ahead," Regina Carson said. "Get it over with."

The vampire turned into a swarm of spiders. In a matter of seconds, they engulfed the old man and drained him.

Valentine's Massacre

Joe DeMarco

It might seem like magic when dealing with that crazy not-so-little thing called love. The way unconquerable love can fade may often feel like a spell or incantation. It is not immediate; it happens slowly, carefully, and deliberately, as if it might be mistaken for something else, perhaps a headache or a bad day at work. Then, one day you wake up, and it's slipped through your fingertips again, slipped the noose in the night like a stray dog that refuses to sit. I guess I might have a pejorative opinion of love; we (Maxine and I) hadn't been having exactly a banner year. We were both really busy. We had moved in together, it was year four of the relationship, and all the magic seemed to be fading out. Maxine had just graduated with a law degree and was working full time, and I had just become a detective. Yes, sir, ladies usually smile, giggle, some even make fairly suggestive comments when I show my badge and tell them I'm ironically Detective Love.

"Detective Love, do you wanna frisk me?" or "Officer Love, I have something you can investigate," I've heard them all. I usually didn't share these suggestive comments with Maxine, but I think she knew the ladies gave me lots of attention in the uniform. I hadn't gotten Maxine a Valentine's Day present and she was long gone before I woke. I figured I'd just pick up some roses on the way home. This would be a different kind of V-day, though, and when I think about the events of that day and the investigation, they seem like a dream within a dream. I guess I was distraught over Maxine or maybe reality started to slip through my fingers, but the events that unfolded are as real as I remember them.

I was one of the first to arrive on the scene of what was being called a homicide. It was technically an infanticide, I guess. The scene was reminiscent of a bloodbath, and I honestly couldn't stomach it at 11 AM on Valentine's Day of all days. I guess my hope for a stress-free day at work was already over. The media, those vultures, had already staked out a claim not far from the overpass. There were dozens of reporters and cameras. They flashed pictures and asked, "What do you know so far?" and "Has the baby been identified?" My face was a stone statue as I pushed past the yellow police tape.

Amidst the flashing of blue and red lights, there was still mass confusion about what had happened, and traffic was backed up for miles. People had pulled their cars over to the side, just to get out and look. There had even been a second casualty; a man had died in his car from heart failure, and, because of the traffic, the paramedics couldn't get to him in time. In all the confusion, no one was quite sure what had happened, in what was truly a horrific scene. As far as I could guess, it appeared as if a baby had been thrown or dropped from an overpass onto the freeway. We weren't sure who the culprit was. We weren't even sure who the victim was. After we assumed the baby had been dropped, the rest of the events were pretty standard. The trucker swerved to get out of the way, but he was going too fast. He slammed into the body going about 40-45 mph. The honest-to-God truth was that there wasn't much of a body left. The body had been turned to paste; the truck's force had left only tiny pieces of the body intact.

I had to stop to regurgitate on the side of the freeway; the baby's arm was found approximately 123 feet from the overturned Mack truck. It didn't even look human, more like a gray synthetic fiber from a futuristic mannequin. A severed baby's foot was found several yards from there. There were other scattered parts around the accident. The Mack truck had swerved into a minivan which in turn had slammed into a Prius. After that it was hard to count the accidents in the massive chain reaction. The main concern was the dead baby, of course; we couldn't seem to identify the body, and the odder part was that no parent had called in a report about a missing baby. We checked the local daycares and preschools, and nothing. Strange. I figured someone would say something soon and went about investigating the accident.

There were several other undiscernible body parts: an ear, a foot, a small piece of the spinal cord, but not much else. Several feet from the severed baby's foot I found what appeared to be the wing of a large, white seabird. Too large to be a seagull, too small to be an albatross. Another oddity? Something didn't feel right. I wasn't sure but bagged the white wing as evidence.

There were several witnesses: two older Caucasian ladies in their mid-sixties, a ten-year-old Hispanic girl, a single female Filipino nurse, yet, here was the odd part, all seemed to have seen the truck hit the baby in one form or another, yet none claimed to have seen anyone, a culprit, drop the baby from the overpass.

The ten-year-old Hispanic girl was the most informative and said something rather intriguing that stuck with me: "It didn't drop" (she was referring to the baby).

The Hispanic girl reached her arms up. "It came from the left...." She paused.

"If anything, it was thrown...." She looked nervous.

"What are you saying?" I questioned.

"I'm saying it looked like it was thrown," she said simply.

The words *looked like it was thrown* stuck in my mind.

"From where?" I questioned.

"I don't know...I didn't see...maybe from a moving car," the girl said with a completely straight face. Was she involved? I took her name, Maria Amado, and informed her I'd be in touch.

On my way back to the precinct, I noticed several couples arguing. One of these couples was having an outright altercation, so much so that I had to stop and break it up. As I pulled this woman off her boyfriend, she was maniacal in stating, "HE TOOK SOMETHING FROM ME."

When I asked what, she broke down in tears. Eventually, I left her sobbing somberly on the front porch.

And then something happened that was seemingly inconsequential except that it was so odd. I was walking down the street, when a harp dropped from an apartment building above and smashed and dashed itself on the pavement below, several yards from where I was walking. The harp was fairly heavy; it made a sound when it hit the concrete as if music herself had cried out for help while being crushed with a sledgehammer. I was unharmed but frazzled. As I stopped at the local florist, I was dismayed to find that they were out of red roses.

Out of red roses on Valentine's Day?

The clerk, who I would have normally guessed was on drugs, then went into some bizarre story about how they had had many red roses in the back but they all mysteriously wilted and died around 11AM. Something weird was going on; I could feel it.

In the car, that old Sam Cooke song was playing, *Cupid, please hear my cry, and let your arrow fly,* except somebody had replaced the word *Cupid* with *stupid.* Old Sam Cooke was bizarrely singing, *Stupid, please hear my cry, and let your arrow fly,* and I had to look around as reality seemed suspiciously like some Reality TV show. At the precinct, there were more strange occurrences than one could count.

Something was seriously amiss; the place was a madhouse. It was practically overflowing with perpetrators and witnesses, people complaining for one reason or another; there were dozens of assailants and solicitors waiting to be booked. The phones were ringing off their hooks with what Janice claimed were hundreds of domestic disturbances. Hundreds of domestic disturbances on Valentine's Day? I needed a break. I grabbed a coffee and went upstairs to the forensics laboratory. The rather large wing was first thought to be synthetic. Dr. Yupik was looking at it under a microscope and still seemed somewhat baffled by the white wing.

"I don't know what to make of it. If I didn't know any better, I'd say it was biologically engineered," Dr. Yupik said scratching his beard. "I've never seen anything like it. Did you find the rest of the body?"

I replied that I hadn't.

When I arrived back downstairs, I checked if anybody had reported any missing babies. Still nothing. Again, I pondered. How could that be, what kind of mother doesn't know her baby's missing for what was something like four hours?

"Maybe she's at work," Officer Hogan suggested. It was a distinct possibility.

Officers Hogan and Nunez and I went looking for clues back at the scene of the horrific accident. Traffic had resumed its normal flow. We still didn't even know how the baby had gotten up on the overpass. Theoretically, someone would have had to have dropped him down. The spot where the Mack truck had slammed into the baby was far from where we had found the body and the white wing, so we spent some time searching the scene of the accident.

I wandered around aimlessly as if it were a dream, perplexed by what I was seeing. When I got home, it was odd, but my love Maxine seemed even more distant. She was staring blankly at the TV, a stack of depositions on her lap. She wasn't really there. On the tube, a famous Hollywood couple had separated, hardly headline news. I leaned over to kiss her, but as I moved toward her, she retreated as if I were toxic or had leprosy or some other infectious disease.

I pulled a bouquet of flowers from behind my back. "Happy Valentine's Day."

She inspected the flowers. "Why'd you get lilies?"

"They were out of roses," I explained.

This fact seemed to annoy her. She put her head back down.

"Is something wrong?" I inquired.

She didn't even answer.

"Can you at least answer me?" I raised my voice attackingly.

"Babe, I worked a fourteen-hour day," she said sadly and put her head down.

"Did you hear about the baby getting thrown off the overpass?" I interjected. She gave me a disgruntled look.

"I'm just saying that my day wasn't all puppy dogs and rainbows," I said defensively.

I went into the bathroom trying to make sense of this insane day. Outside the door, I heard the phone ring and Maxine pick up. "You'll never guess," she told the phone, happily chatting away, as if moments ago she had been a completely different person. I wanted to call her out on it, instead I went to bed angry. When she finally did come to bed, we didn't cuddle or spoon; our backs practically touched like two great walls coming together to crush our love.

February 15th

The day's events seemed to play on in my mind long after I had laid my head to rest. *What had I just investigated? Like Dorothy in the Emerald City when she saw the curtain pulled back, I was suspicious that something was not right. I kept thinking about the white wing and what it might mean.* When I awoke, something had shifted in my mind, as if the puzzle pieces that were my beliefs had somehow changed their form. I felt empty and it wasn't just the fact that Maxine was gone, which was extremely unlike her, even considering how cold she had been acting. I checked my voice mail and there were something like ninety-nine messages. In the distance, I could hear sirens and see the red and blue flashing lights of the long arm of the law. I absently fumbled for my keys, but found myself unable to unlock any doors. I felt as if there were literally something wrong with me; it was hard to pinpoint what. Looking out the window I could see the street littered with debris. The thrift store across the street had been looted and vandalized during the night. I felt a slight pain in my chest and had to sit down for a while. I dialed Maxine's number, but she didn't pick up. She was probably at work.

Eventually, as I got in my car and started it, I still felt as if I were in a movie. For example, the radio played "Love Me Do" by the Beatles. The part where John and Paul sing, "So pleeeease...love me do" seemed to ring in my mind, and looking up into the sky I half expected the gods were messing with me.

The civil unrest of the next day was unparalleled, speaking personally as an officer who has worked race riots. The tsunami of anarchy did not abate, and I found myself working till well after midnight. It was just as well. On the fateful day after what I have now so vehemently termed the death of V-Day, I thought little of Maxine and the way she acted cold only toward me, the way her disposition seemed to change when she spoke to me as opposed to her friend on the phone. My first response of the day was a suicide; a man had plunged off a ravine after his wife of twenty years had just up and left him. Up and left him on Valentine's Day? Everybody seemed to be acting extremely irrationally, as if someone had drugged the water, or something even more sinister were afoot. It had all happened rather quickly; it seemed as if the city had erupted with madness overnight. Too many atrocities to list. There were riots, some shootings, some even more bizarre cult deaths like hangings or drawing-and-quarterings, a hostage situation; several larger complexes and skyscrapers were still ablaze with fires. The fire department was understaffed but had been working tirelessly all night. The city was in shambles and it would continue to get worse.

What was going on? Hadn't it all started with the homicide yesterday? The madness clearly started then; my mind kept coming back to the alleged baby who had been dropped from the overpass. What was I missing? Was it even a baby? The mother of the alleged missing baby had never called. In fact, nobody had reported a baby missing. Our second call was a double homicide; a husband had found his wife in bed with her lover, normally an open-and-shut case, except, I thought, what does this case have in common with the others? Looking down the list of incidents, did all of them involve disputes over relationships? There were a few that didn't, but for the most part they were all domestic disputes or altercations, in most cases involving that crazy not-so-little thing called love.

I felt reality slipping by the third call; when we apprehended a man in his twenties for kidnapping his girlfriend who had broken up with him, I had ascertained something very out of the ordinary was happening. The man was a timid, middle-class, blue-collar worker, no prior arrests. It had something to do with the baby dropped from the overpass and something to do with love and relationships.

The accident had long been cleared, but I went to Joy's Auto Yard where the Mack truck that had hit the fallen baby was taken. I was searching for something out of the ordinary, something that might confirm my weird suspicions. The truck had barely been damaged; there were a few dings here and there, one on the bumper, and another in the grill. There were, of course, bloodstains here and there, where the baby had been turned to human pulp. After examining the truck, it was clear we had overlooked something. Near the bloodstains where the baby had been essentially liquidated, it appeared there was something stuck in the grill of the truck. It was small and appeared fairly inconsequential.

As I got closer I couldn't believe what I was seeing. It had to be some kind of joke. I stammered in disbelief, "It couldn't be."

"What is it?" Officer Davis, who had come with me on the investigation, asked.

Wedged into the grill of the truck appeared to be about half an arrow. It was a normal-looking arrow made of wood, but the arrowhead appeared to be sharp and golden. It was rather odd; when I touched it, I felt a tinge of something that resembled regret in the pit of my stomach. It was stuck in there good, but I eventually fished it out. The arrow was strange; on it were Greek letters that I was unable to read.

I handed it to Officer Davis and asked what he made of the latest piece of evidence.

"It's an arrow, sir," he stated.

"But where did it come from?" I questioned.

"It could have been in the grill of that truck for months. It could have come from anywhere," Davis explained.

"What if it came from the accident yesterday?" I challenged Davis.

"What are you saying?" he questioned.

I wasn't even sure.

"I don't know," I informed him. "I might be losing it."

Everybody (including myself) had apparently lost his or her mind, or maybe it was just everybody in a relationship. On the way back to the precinct, the streets were jammed. Someone had detonated an explosive device inside the lobby of a downtown major bank branch, and it had essentially shut the city down. There were reports of several shootings in the street. It was a massacre out there. The death toll was already up to something like sixty-eight and it would get much higher as the fresh fires burned all through the night. Sunday's obituary page would have to be enlarged and would probably take up six to seven pages. By this point I was entirely convinced it all had to do with the baby dropped from the overpass.

When we finally got to the precinct, it was difficult to even make it in the front door. There were people flooding out the entranceway, and the main lobby was packed. The holding center was overcrowded with prisoners, and some people had just been cuffed to the radiator in the lobby. I finally made my way up to forensics with the broken arrow. Dr. Yupik looked dog-tired; his hair was all disheveled and his glasses were askew. He was still running tests on the large, white wing and was intrigued by the arrow.

Dr. Yupik, pondering something, stared off into space. "I'm not sure it's a species of bird that I know of," he said, a bit perplexed, taking off his glasses and rubbing his eyes. "Its DNA is very strange."

I showed him the broken arrow. He read the Greek lettering as if he were reading a spell. "It conquers all and Time it steals, inflicted by the wound that never heals." The words seemed familiar, and Dr. Yupik touched the tip of the arrowhead several times.

"Is that a riddle?" I asked about the Greek lettering.

"I'm not sure, but it's obviously speaking of love." Dr. Yupik touched the tip of the arrowhead again. He tapped on the arrowhead several times with his finger.

"It appears to be giving off some minor vibration," Dr. Yupik explained finally.

"Like a tuning fork," I reasoned.

"Like a tuning fork," he repeated.

He pulled out a small mallet and struck the arrowhead lightly. It gave off a hum that was something akin to *ooohhhmmmmmmmmm*. It was strange, but despite the last two days, the hum made me feel as if everything were going to be all right. I felt the vibration spreading to my heart and my loins.

He hit it again, this time harder. The sound was much louder; everything in the room appeared to quiver, *OOOHHHMMMMMMMMM*. We were both dumbstruck, and I even felt light-headed.

"What the fuck was that?" I questioned.

"I don't know," Dr. Yupik stated shakily.

We both tried to ignore what had just happened as he went about his tests. Most of the results came back inconclusive, but Dr. Yupik could confirm that the arrowhead was made of gold, and after a carbon dating test, that it was very old. How old, was in question. He said that was hard to say. I eventually decided to put forward my very crazy hypothesis to Dr. Yupik.

He looked at me with something that was bordering on contempt. "What makes you say that?"

"Just a hunch." I explained, "I mean, look at the facts: a baby 'dropped' from an overpass, no perpetrator, no witnesses, the large, white wing, the golden arrow."

"That's preposterous," Dr. Yupik voiced.

"I know, but look outside," I stated. He knew what was happening; outside, the streets were wild with insanity, buildings were burning, and civilization itself seemed as if it were crumbling.

I checked to see if anyone had reported a missing baby, a missing child, a kidnapping; still nothing. I called Maria Amado, the witness who claimed the baby had been thrown. Her mother answered and said she was out back. I explained to her that I was an officer of the law and it was imperative that I speak with her daughter.

The streets were like something out of Carnival in Brazil, except the people were not celebrating, they were suffering. The mob marched, not with protest signs but with weapons. A topless woman bleeding profusely from the head screamed as she ran past us. A burning man ran from a blazing building before crashing through a plate-glass window.

Maria's house was a small, dilapidated shack that was clearly in need of serious renovations. Maria was playing out back down by a stream with a group of friends. When I approached, all the laughter and child's play ceased immediately as if it were snuffed out by a monster. The children seemed to sense I was an officer of the law and that trouble was afoot; children can always sense that sort of thing.

Although it was unprofessional, I decided to conduct the interview in front of the group of children. I figured Maria would be more truthful, but I wasn't sure how to start.

"Uh...I wanted to ask you a few more questions about the accident you witnessed yesterday," I stammered. None of the children were breathing; it was as if I had sucked all the air out of the streambed.

"Okay," Maria said calmly.

I searched for what I was trying to say, but stammered, "The baby...if it even was a baby...you said that he was not dropped...he was thrown."

"That's correct," Maria said.

"Could you elaborate?" I insisted.

"Whatta ya mean?" she asked honestly.

I had trouble coming up with the words. "Just - er - go into more detail."

She bit her lip, and I suddenly realized everybody was staring at her. "I don't know, I was walking across the overpass. I was looking down most of the way, but out of the corner of my eye, I saw the baby fly across the bridge." She used her hands to gesture positions. She squinted her eyes. "Like I said, the baby came from the side. He wasn't dropped."

My mind was reeling. *Flying, did she say the baby was flying?*

"So, what, then, somebody threw the baby?" I inquired.

"I didn't see anybody throw the baby," she confessed.

"But you said you were looking down," I stated.

"I have excellent peripheral vision," Maria explained. She had trouble pronouncing the word *peripheral*.

"Really?" I inquired.

"Yeah," Maria said nodding her head, "I can see for miles."

"Did you see anything out of the ordinary?" I queried.

"Like?" Maria questioned.

Like a flying baby with white bird wings, I wanted to yell out, but withheld.

"The whole scene just seems really suspicious. Something's amiss," I admitted.

I made my way to the car not really knowing anything more than I had when I came to interview Maria. I needed a strong drink as I felt this case once again pulling at my sanity.

February 16th

The hours seemed to drag on into grayness. I'm not even sure what time I got home on February 15th; I do know it was well after dark and I was beyond exhausted. I'll admit my sanity was slipping; after all, I half believed I was investigating the death of the winged god of love. Insane thoughts slipped through my mind. *If the baby was Cupid and Cupid is dead, does that mean love is dead? Is that why all these horrible things are happening? It must be. It still felt like a dream.* I just wanted to slip under the covers and cuddle up next to my love, but she was gone.

"Maxine," I called out into the shadows of the bedroom.

"Hello?"

"Maxine?"

There was no answer.

Sometime during the last twelve hours, she had fallen out of love with me and moved all her stuff out. I desperately searched for a note. Nothing; apparently, she had left me.

My day (if you want to call it that) started extra early at about 4 AM; sirens were going off and the building had to be evacuated. There was a structure fire on the first two floors and it had spread to levels four, five and six. With nowhere else to go, I grabbed an extra uniform from out of my car and headed to work. The streets were pandemonium as if it were rush hour on parade day and not 4 o'clock in the morning. I weaved between looters and pedestrians, and tried to ignore the many violations I witnessed just on my way up the block.

Rubbing my eyes, I could not believe the scene unfolding before me. *Was this the Apocalypse?* I drove past several bodies lying dead in street; whatever this was, it seemed to be spreading like some kind of Cupid-bomb and we seemed to be the epicenter. There were now reports on the radio of several other cities experiencing the same sort of citizen chaos. In my neighborhood, crowds were scattered here and there, watching the major landmarks. As my headlights ran along the pavement, they reflected thousands of shards of broken glass from all the windows and streetlights that had been shattered. On my way to the station, the electricity of the entire city seemed to waver, flicker, then shut off completely, and that's when the real chaos began. As soon as the few remaining streetlights shut down and darkness spread across the land, traffic came to a complete standstill. I saw people fleeing from their cars, and several of the empty automobiles, doors still ajar, being ransacked. Hand on my revolver, I opened my vehicle door and ventured out into the dark streets. A mob of people, all excited about the craziness going on, sprinted around a corner and disappeared. The air was filled with acrid smoke and the only light permeating the haze was from the sky, lit by the hundreds of fires that had been set ablaze. I came upon another smaller mob, but upon seeing my revolver they chose to go in another direction.

The air was thick with smoke, and it was getting fairly hard to breathe, when I came upon a donut shop still open for business. It seemed to have many peaceful patrons, and they had set up some candles but were almost out of donuts. Although everybody was calm, it seemed most people were really nervous, as if they thought this was their last night on Earth or the end of society in general.

I found a booth, one of the only empty ones in the whole place, and sat down. There was a quiet hush about most people, as they were quietly discussing the happenings outside and what it might mean. *What was going on? Was this the End of Days? Was this all caused by the god of love getting smashed by a Mack truck?* Well, no one was discussing the third question; still it was on my mind.

Against the ghoulish reflections of candlelight, a meek little waitress came over and took my order. They still had a little hot coffee left and a few donuts, though the donuts seemed kind of stale and may have been more than a few days old. I was sipping my lukewarm coffee and gnawing on my stale donut when a teenage boy, barely a man, entered through the front door. He wore a dark baseball cap backwards and looked as if he might be bleeding beneath the heavy flannel jacket he wore.

I could almost sense something was going to go down; sure enough, after limping a few steps, the boy whipped out a pistol and yelled, "FREEZE, I need everyone to empty your pockets or I'm gonna start blasting."

The customers were worn and had already been broken as they weakly reached their hands into their pockets. My hand was already on my revolver and in the darkness, I knew it would be fairly easy to take him out. The teenage boy was jittery and shaky as he pointed that pistol around the darkened donut shop. "DON'T MOVE," he screamed, his gun shaking in several different directions.

People had started to dig into their pockets and pocketbooks to dish out money, when there was a large explosion outside. I could've shot the boy dead right there, but somehow that didn't sit right with me. I wanted to find the reason for his holding up people at gunpoint. The boy had pulled out a plastic bag and was collecting wallets and watches and some purses. Nobody was putting up a fight; many of them figured they were dead already. As the boy got closer, I noticed his attention wavering. He was focused on getting the hell out of there and didn't expect a confrontation, so when he sauntered up next to me with his plastic bag full of treasures, I drew my revolver as quick as Billy the Kid, put it straight to his head, and asked snidely, "Why do you look so sad and forsaken?"

"Put down the gun," I said calmly.

He did not put down the gun. The boy was clearly in shock; he almost panicked, and I almost had to shoot him dead right there, but then reason seemed to kick in.

He had a sad look in his eye, a look of helplessness and lost faith. "My love is gone," he said simply.

"Where did she go?" I inquired.

"I don't know," he said blankly.

"And that's why you're robbing everybody at gunpoint?" I asked.

"I don't know," he stated, this time looking at me.

I had his attention; I had to act fast. "If I told you what really happened, you'd think I was nuttier than the Son of Sam."

"What's that?" he asked lowering the gun and the bag.

"You'll think I'm nuts," I informed him.

"Try me," he said with a hint of a smile on his lips.

I cleared my throat; I wasn't even sure how to proceed. *Should I be completely honest?* "This all started two days ago when that baby got dropped off that overpass."

313

"Do you remember?" I inquired.

The boy nodded.

"At the scene of the accident, I found a large, white wing and a broken arrow with Greek letters engraved on it that said It conquers all and Time it steals, inflicted by the wound that never heals."

The boy seemed unimpressed.

I continued, "Since that accident, everyone's gone crazy, particularly people in relationships, so much so that you know what I've been thinking?"

"What?" the boy questioned more out of humor than anything else.

"I've been thinking that maybe, just maybe, that baby was Cupid. And if Cupid's dead, does that mean love's dead, too?"

"You are crazy…" the boy said plainly.

But I cut him off. "My love is gone, too," I said loudly. "I feel completely empty, but I'm not using this gun in my hand to go around robbing people."

In the darkness by candlelight, it looked as though the boy had tears in his eyes. "I feel like I can't breathe," he said gasping a little.

"It's all part of love," I said, trying to sound wise.

"Your love seriously left you, too?" he asked.

"She did," I answered, my voice continuing to elevate. "And for a while part of me was convinced it was because of that baby. But part of me thinks that maybe it was just a baby, and it's actually my fault and maybe love doesn't exist."

It all happened so fast, I didn't even really have time to reflect. I do remember thinking, *I thought I'd have more time.* Quickly, he jerked his gun, and, I'll admit, I did not hear it go off, but I could feel the bullet hole in me and the warm life running from my body. The scene was surreal; I clutched my stomach which had grown red and wet. This wasn't happening. The lines of reality continued to blur. I felt weak and tired so I slid to the floor of the donut shop, the boy having run off in fright. I closed my eyes and thought of the accident.

As I lie on the floor dying, I find that when I open my eyes the has scene shifted and I am back at the overpass, except I am still bleeding from the stomach. My mind is trying to process the whole thing. It feels like a bad dream, the overpass, investigating the death of Cupid, my love dying, everybody's love dying, civilization crumbling and falling, and I am beginning to wonder if I wasn't the one who jumped from the overpass. I am looking for my love, Maxine, but she is gone. I look around me unsure of my reality as the life drains out of me.

Desire

Xtina Marie

You are a party favor. A treat. Candy wrapped in cotton and leather, for ubiqutious consumption.

You are a consumable. A property. Durable goods, if damaged. You know they won't notice if you happen to be worse for the wear. A bruised apple, after all, is still tender and juicy underneath it's bitter skin.

We see her, standing outside the door, outside the looming gate, an invited performer, not a guest. She gathers herself, she says, "I ask myself, who is this I? What are these thoughts that are things? What is art? Am I art? Will there be wine or cake? Will we get those Placebo tickets?" Matters of great importance matter greatly.

She drops the butt of her cigarette (a pink colored gold-tipped Sobranie) on the cement, stomps it out with the heel of her boot--after kissing and felatio, it is her most practiced and perfected gesture.

She stops in the doorway, thinks to herself that she is a vase, she is a moon, she is a tree, she is three holes and a pair of tits. She is light.

Escorted from the doorway arch to the overstuffed leather couch, she sits with her legs splayed out in either direction, one foot pointed outward and left, the other outward and right, the broken doll posture. Her hands are tied deftly behind her back, by the gray-haired one. It's a silk cord. It's the candy bar wrapping. She will be displayed and then opened like Christmas. But none of these men are Jesus.

A quick slap lands on her right cheek, and then one on her left. It feels like getting hit with a paintball, it feels like being stung by a honeybee.

Her forehead is licked.

Her eyes are lowered and she knows not to raise them until it is time.

Her knees are gently parted by a hand with laquered nails. She is inspected. She hears pencils on paper and smells paint---she's being rendered, or at least her pussy is. These people like to think they are artists, some of them. They all think they are Georgia O'Keefe or fucking Nan Goldin. But this isn't a salon or a hotel room in New York City. This is a gated estate somewhere in Orange County, and it might just be a circle in hell that Dante neglected to describe.

Something cold and long is inserted into her. It's the night's innaugural fucking, and she thinks she'll be fucked to the verge of coming and left to pant like a dog in heat. Her eyes are closed and she thinks of the pressure inside and the preciscion of the guest who is playing her like an instrument, exploring her like a lost city. It is a male.

Her right cheek is slapped again, and the fucking stops for a second.

"Come, whore!"

It starts again, merciless and fast, a porno fucking, it feels intensely good, it's driving her crazy and she resents it, resents being commanded to come, and so when she does, finally, she bares her teeth to them, growls, shouts "No!".

She is opened, assailed with wet, fat tounges on her nipples, a man stands over her and shoves his cock into her mouth, where she sucks it to a fully hard state. There's a hand rubbing her mound and searching for her clit, she wonders when she'll have to open her eyes. The worst part is opening her eyes. Seeing all of them, these anonymous spectators, these baudy players, who look at her like last season's handbag.

The man fucking her mouth is at least gentle and guides her head so she isn't choked. She feels him stiffen and jerk back a little, coming warm salt waves into her mouth, she shivers and swallows the ocean. He tastes nice and pleasant and earthy, like when she once ate dirt on a dare as a little girl.

There are soft lips grazing her bare shoulder, trying to nudge room underneath her arms. A woman is licking the auburn fuzz there, and teasing the fleshy space with her nose. Her mother was a poet, and when she first saw hair appear under her daughter's arms she exclaimed, "Oh Desiree, you are like a garden! Something new every day." She refused to shave her armpits, and took to perfuming the hair with essential oils or vanilla extract---she always smelled like something good to eat.

The players eased off then, one by one. She felt the cold, stale air, and opened her eyes, raised her chin. The room came into focus---a half-circle crowded 'round---a blonde woman of about forty, a boy of maybe nineteen or twenty, wearing a tank top and ripped jeans, an Asian couple dressed like they had come from dinner---she in a black silk sheath, and he in a suit jacket and wing tipped shoes. A tall, slender woman, wearing violet contacts and no bra beneath her mesh shirt----skin like honey and pink nipples standing erect. A grey-haired man in a polo shirt. A black man she recognized as a former boxer, his face is scarred but his eyes are bright and inquisitive. Drawing pads and tubes of paint were set down on the floor, there were easels in the corners. She saw a few half-empty champagne flutes, she saw the gold-leaf bubbling liquid, and noticed how it caught the light in a certain way, almost like a prism to reflect it back.

The gray-haired man came forward and moved her up onto the couch, told her to get down on her knees and rest her head on her arms. Her ass was pointed up towards the ceiling, and her short skirt was lifted. She had been told not to wear any panties. The man entered her carefully from behind, and because he was vain, and terrified of aging, he watched himself fuck her in the mirror, enjoying the sight of himself tearing into her, enjoying the way her ass looked like a new peach jutting out in front of him, this girl like sweet cream, taking the thrust of his insistent cock, like a good slut, like a well-trained and prosaic little whore.

A leash was placed and buckled around her neck, and she was fucked from behind and pulled forward to suck the brown, tumescent cock of the boxer. One of his large hands held the leash and pulled it with each

319

thrust, out and up a little. If she didn't keep her balance, she'd fall. If that happened she might be beaten, she might not be paid, she might lose her reputation with the clients and have to go sell herself on the sullen, midnight streets, where there'd be no champagne, no lights, no dirty whispered diminutives, just sweaty bills and bad drugs and shame.

She thought of the botany class she took in High School, she thought of root systems, she thought of the small changes in the soil that told the trees when to drop their leaves. She thought of how lucky she was. She thought of how one night at a party could pay her rent for three months. She thought of her father and that time at the horse races, sitting on his shoulders, wearing her mother's big red hat, while she rooted for her favorite, Serendipity. She suddenly remembered that night---the screaming, the fighting, and when her father came in to check on her. She'd felt so guilty, like going with him to the track had caused the fight. It hadn't, he assured her. He rubbed her back and said, "You don't need to be sorry." The furtive fingers wandered, and the guilt was erased and never mentioned. She felt like she was flying when he touched her like that---and she loved him, but hated him a little, too. And she swore she'd never feel sorry or guilty again. That night was when everything changed.

On this night, it was really all the same. She smirked thinking of how these people must see themselves. As mavericks maybe, as iconoclasts. But they were locusts---fat, and greedy, and common. The boxer pulled his cock out of her mouth and shot onto her face. A doberman then walked up to her and casually licked it off. The Asian woman laughed a dry little laugh, said "You're a little bitch, aren't you?" Petting the dog with one hand, tilting her wet face up with the other. "You're going to get fucked until you have puppies." The woman was cruel, but had obviously failed biology. She didn't think anyone had guts enough to make the Doberman fuck her, though people had tried.

She remembered one morning after her friend May had slept over. May asked her what she thought of actual sex with boys. Lena thought for a moment, she wanted to be honest. She looked May in the eyes and said, "I could have done that with a German Shepard." May giggled and ticked her under the arms. That sensation was something she never lost fondness for. She enjoyed being tickled by friends, or even by her father, although he wasn't always so casually affectionate.

She wasn't very old, barely out of High School, and yet it was getting harder to remember the firsts: The first kiss, the first fuck, the first joint, the first line. It all spun around to form a web around her, a web made of cotton candy, and pink things from a time long gone, of a time when she was a person, and not an object like a lamp or a rug or a vase. She was moved to cry.

But still she remained planted like a Willow, the tips of her hair fanning out on the lake of the couch. Her ass was spanked by hands, boards. She was fisted from behind until she yelped. Her ass fucked with a champagne bottle. She noted in horror that she had pissed a little on the couch, she bit her lip and hoped no one would notice.

She couldn't help but think of the time in the mountains at Julian. She'd sucked the cock of one of her father's friends. The man was so guilt-ridden he held her afterward and cried and shook like a junkie "This is what the world does to love! I'm so sorry."

It was sad and pathetic.

Whatever you did, she thought, at least own up to it. Don't suck your guilt like a pacifier, because that won't make it better. Be real. Be a lamp. Be a chair. Be a fucking rolodex---just don't be sorry.

They weren't. And she wasn't.

The party would be over soon, and she'd hear her favorite band play. She'd kiss boys who wore lipstick and called her "love". She would spin around in circles, high on x, wired on cocaine. And if she died, she'd die knowing that she was real after all. She was a princess. She was light. She was golden. She was sullied.

But not sorry.

Black Dress Society

Michael Sutton

It was her fingernails that first grabbed my attention. I'm not even sure why. Perhaps it was their length, long enough to make typing impossible, yet she was still able to hand over the paperwork and sign a copy with ease. Perhaps it was the way they were shaped, curved and pointed at the end like delicate garden spades. Or maybe it was the elaborate design that was painted on them. A detailed dragon that worked its way across her fingers, dancing its body up and down as she tapped her nails on the counter top waiting for me to sign.

Tap tap tap tap

Savannah, her name tag read. You would have thought I would have known her name. I knew she had been making deliveries to this office ever since I started work there. Every Tuesday and Friday. So why couldn't I take my eyes off her today?

Tap tap tap tap

It was her nails, definitely her nails. She had short black hair with a curl that worked its way under her left ear. Black eye liner highlighted her green eyes, and a glossy red covered her lips, which had a piercing on each side.

Tap tap tap tap.

I signed the receiving order and handed her the copy. She smiled, shot me a wink and walked out the door. I didn't know it yet, but from that moment forward, my life would never be the same.

***

I had always wanted what most girls want, growing up. The white picket fence, the blessing of motherhood, an attractive wealthy husband I could cook for, and for the most part I did. Mark was a great father of our two boys, a good provider and a good lover. We had meet in college and were married soon after. Even though it seemed like the cliche suburban lifestyle, I had thought myself satisfied. We still made love at least once a week, although more traditional than I would have sometimes liked, he satisfied me.

August 12, was supposed to be a big day at the office. Some sort of corporate audit that had all the higher ups in a frenzy. Marketing was supposed to be printing off all kinds of material, and of course as it would always go, the lowly secretary was expected to pitch in. More materials meant more supplies, more supplies meant another delivery. The bell on the front door rang at 9:00 that Tuesday morning. What was usually delivered in a single box was now a dolly full of them. Savannah wheeled in her load and leaned on my desk, waiting for me to look up.

Tap tap tap tap

A different design today. An explosive array of colorful flowers decorated her fingertips. I looked up from my desk to catch her smile.

"More than usual today?" Savannah said.

"Some corporate thing." I said smiling.

She handed over the receiving documents for me to sign. I fumbled through the blizzard of papers on my desk looking for a pen.

"Here." She said, reaching into her shirt, retrieving a black pen from her bra. I signed the papers and handed her the copy. She smelled like a coconut drink at happy hour.

"Where do you want 'em?" She asked.

I stood up and opened the side door, allowing her into the office space.

Storage room for now I guess." I said leading her down the hall. The storage door was open and Savannah wheeled her boxes in. Taking each one off separately, setting them down gently in the corner. Her khaki shorts rode high on her thighs as she bent down. She cut her eyes back at me, I blushed and looked away.

Before she wheeled her dolly out the front door she turned around. "Thanks again Mrs..."

"Maria" I said.

She smiled and opened the door. "See you next time."

"Is something wrong?" Mark asked.

"Huh...No, No." I said, gripping the back of his head again, pressing it tighter between my thighs. He had been going down on me for over an hour and I hadn't climaxed once, which was unusual for me. He tried breaking out his fancy moves, twirling his fingers inside me and reaching upward, but my mind was somewhere else. After another twenty minutes he stopped, and I sighed.

"I'm sorry honey." I said.

He crawled up to me and wrapped his arms around me spooning my rear. I knew it was going to be a long night if I didn't help him out. I reached my arm behind me and finished him off in his pants. Not to long after that he was snoring next to me. I rolled back over to my side and stared at the clock, watching the minutes drip by until I was asleep as well.

There was a tension between us the next morning but I tried to ignore it. I got the kids off to school and Mark off to work with his thermos of coffee. I kissed him lightly on the cheek before he left, then headed to work myself. I usually dreaded Fridays, except for this one.

The office seemed to clear out after lunch. Marketing always left early on Fridays, and the office wigs rarely even showed. The janitor was done by 10:00 and the two sales reps wrapped up their day by 2:00. That left me, as usual to close up at 5:00.

At 3:45 the bell rang, and in walked Savannah, carrying one box. Her hair was slicked back, and her lips were more red than before. She placed the box on my desk and handed over the normal paper.

Tap tap tap tap.

No design today, just jet black nails.

Before I could hand her the paper back she was already at the side door, box propped under one arm. Her hand lightly brushed my thigh as I let her in, I

326

could feel my stomach flutter. She followed me back to the storage room and I opened the door. I glanced up at her eyes and blushed as she walked through placing the box in the corner.

"What...What's that tattoo mean?" I asked pointing to a small circle on the inside of her wrists. She stood up and unbuttoned her sleeve pulling it back, revealing a line of half circles that gradually filled out the further along they went.

"It's the moon cycle." She said, taking a step closer to me.

I could feel my heart beat a little faster as my eyes ran along her skin, following her tattoo up her arm disappearing back into her shirt. I glanced back up at her and she took another step closer, I could feel her sweet breath on my face. I breathed it in slowly.

"Do you want to see the rest of it?" Her voice was soft and inching its way closer to me.

I tried to respond but I couldn't. She took my hand and gently placed my fingertips on her tattoo. Her nails dug slightly into my skin. I breathed deeply again.

She brought her face close and opened her mouth, brushing her lips across mine as she scratched my neck slightly. I didn't know what was happening but I didn't ask questions. I took my hand to her back, but she grabbed it, and forced me backward, pinning me against the wall, holding my hand above me against the sheet rock.

Her lips pressed firmly against mine and moaned softly as she bit my bottom lip. I could feel her nails go under my blouse and pull away at my bra, exposing my breasts. I was her prisoner against that wall, and I liked it. Her other hand went down my skirt and scratched the inside of my thigh, the sharp pain opened my eyes and I thrust my mouth onto hers again.

Her nails pinched my nipple hard and I moaned louder into her mouth. A scratching sensation went from my breasts down to my stomach as she dug the nails deeper into my skin. It hurt but I wanted more. Her other hand worked inside my skirt, until I jolted forward soaking my panties.

I breathed heavy into her neck and she grinned, bringing her hand out of my skirt and up to her mouth, licking her fingers. My chest rose and fell as I caught my breath, holding myself against the wall like a drunk regaining their balance.

Savannah leaned in closer and bit my neck, digging one more nail into my arm before she pulled away.

"See you next week." She said, turning around exiting the hallway. Leaving me alone and confused but utterly satisfied.

I came home late that evening. When I pulled into the driveway I put my car in park and stared into the windshield. The aftermath of the day had left me winded and I couldn't hold a thought steady, walking into the house like a wounded zombie. Mark had already begun dinner and the kids were halfway through their homework.

"Long day?" Mark asked, placing down his beer to kiss me.

"A...normal Friday." I said, giving him a light peck on the mouth.

"Dinner's almost ready." He said.

I went up to our bathroom and undressed. My panties were still damp. As I slid them off, I saw the open cut on my thigh. It wasn't big, but the skin was definitely open. I remembered her scratching me and it had felt incredible, but I didn't think it had been that hard. I ran my finger over the cut and shivered thinking about her hands touching me; I started to get wet again. I had no idea what to tell myself. I had always found other women attractive, but never like this. It was as if she had opened a brand-new channel of arousal from inside me, and I wanted more of it. I desperately wanted more of it.

I had to get out of my head. After dinner, I almost finished a bottle of wine. Mark didn't say anything about it, he knew where it would go. When he wouldn't move in on me I attacked him, pushing him against our headboard. Riding him hard, almost violently; trusting myself forward as hard as I could, as fast as I could until he blew his load.

I didn't come that night either.

That next Tuesday I arrived early to work, almost in a rush. I knew the delivery schedule. 9:00 I was to be expecting one. The seconds ticked by sluggishly. At one point, I could have swore that the second hand on the clock stopped moving just to mock me.

When the bell rang on the door I jumped up from my seat, and almost cried out loud in disappointment. Savannah didn't come through the door. Instead it was a large balding man carrying a box addressed to the company. I couldn't help but ask.

"Savannah have the day off?" I asked, taking the box from him.

"Nope, she quit." He said handing me the paperwork.

My heart sunk, and I scribbled my signature on the paper almost tossing him his copy.

I should have just clocked out and went home after that. I didn't get anything else done that day. I was almost mad at her. How in the world could she do that? Give me that kind of experience and then just disappear.

Once everyone had left the office for the day I closed down my computer. I was about to walk out when I tripped over the box left by the fat delivery man. I muttered to myself and hauled it back into the storage room. When I opened the door the memory almost overwhelmed me. I could almost see her bending down in front of me again, in her tight khaki shorts, her round ass taunting me to grab it. That moon tattoo whispering for me to come closer. Out of frustration I threw the box on the ground, popping the lid off. I was about to close the door and walk out when I saw a manila envelope on top of the stack of papers inside, my name written across it.

I fumbled with the fold and opened it, sliding out a piece of paper, my name written in cursive at the top.

"Maria
I didn't know you had it in you.
You have a lot more sexual energy than you give yourself credit for.
Inside this envelope is a card, it's your invitation. Friday night, 11:00
Tell no one, hope to see you there, you dirty little slut.
Savannah
*   P.S- Password is cocktail"*

Below her name was a lipstick kiss.

I turned the envelope upside and a business card fell out into my hand. On the front was a picture of a man and a woman, both in proper dress attire, holding drama masks up to their faces. "The Black Dress Society." It read.

I turned the card over and in bold black letters was an address.

I wasn't sure what to make of it at first. "dirty little slut" I didn't know if I was insulted, flattered, or slightly aroused. Possibly a mixture of all three.

I put the car in park and lit up a cigarette. I hadn't smoked in 15 years., it didn't calm my nerves as I remembered. I had stopped three blocks away from the given address and I started to debate rather or not I even had what it took to open the door. I had told Mark that I was going to a true romance party to support one of my coworkers, and that I would most likely be late getting home. He hadn't asked any questions.

I hated the fact that I was lying to him. Mark and I had been through so much, and I loved him dearly but something had opened up inside of me. Savannah had triggered an explosion, and I felt that I had to see were the rubble was going to land.

I talked myself out of the car and down the sidewalk. The address had put me in the downtown area which made me nervous. I pulled my coat up around my neck, and snugged down my hat hiding my ears, keeping one hand inside of my coat pocket, wrapped tightly around my pepper spray. I took the left on the street and stopped. Cars lined the street, people walked the sidewalk, and light posts flickered, but as far as a building hosting a party, I saw none.

I stopped in front of 4706 and held my breath. No lights were visible and the windows were boarded, it truthfully looked like a repossessed industrial building. I looked at the card again.

4706 E Terrance. I was in the right place. The doors were even boarded up. I had been stupid to even come, maybe this was God's way of telling me that I needed to go home. I turned around prepared to leave when a voice crept from the shadows by the door.

"Looking to come inside?" It asked.

I stumbled backwards slamming into a light post. The man walked into the light. A dirty grey beanie was pulled over his head and a torn green jacket covered him. He held a brown paper bag that held a bottle of something.

"No, I think I'm in the wrong place." I said, slowly pulling my pepper spray towards the top of my pocket.

"Looking for 4706?" He asked.

I eyed the man, afraid to answer.

"Well?"

"Yes."

"Password?" He asked pulling his beanie higher on his face.

"Cocktail."

"Card?" He held his hand out.

I dug in my pocket and handed over the card. He looked over it thoroughly.

"Have fun." He said, walking up to the door, re-moving the large board. The hinges creaked, and the door swung open. I crept by the man not turning my back to him.

"Follow the walkway." He said, pointing a finger behind me.

The hinges creaked again and I was alone.

The darkness was thick, cut only by a path of lit candles that led further into the massive room. I didn't want to continue. Taking this plunge into the unknown was far from my character, and I couldn't believe I had even made it this far. I stood like a lost child for what felt like hours until the door opened again. My heart flew into my throat and I scurried off, hiding in the darkness.

A couple came stumbling in laughing. The women holding a bottle, and the man had an arm wrapped over her kissing her neck while they sloppily made their way down the walkway of candles. The women giggled as the man groped her.

I watched them fall deeper into the room, and when I could no longer see them I heard a door open and the faint sound of music ring through the empty air. The door closed and the music stopped.

I closed my eyes and breathed deeply. I had to

continue. Shrugging my shoulders, I followed their lead down the dimly lit walkway. The candles reached a large door with a lit red sign above it that said enter. I grabbed the handle, shook my head and walked inside.

The vibration of the music shook my arm as I closed the door behind me. I found myself in a vacant small room, a bright light flashing from its open exit leading into a narrow hallway. The light beckoned me forward and I obliged. As soon as I exited the hallway a strobe light nearly blinded me and the techno music blared in my ear.

The room was huge, and packed to the brim with people. I could barely hear my thoughts as I tried to take it all in. A sea of diversity covered the floor. I saw costumes, dress clothes and everything in between. A woman screamed next to me as her partner held her against the wall rubbing her groin area quickly while he pulled her hair backward forcing her head to look at the ceiling.

The woman was shaking hard, wearing only stiletto shoes, bracing herself on the wall so to not fall over. Her moans aroused my inner curiosity. There were multiple stages placed around the room were dancers stood center, some male and some female, all dressed in dark revealing costumes. Crowds gathered around each yelling and hollering. A man wearing black skin tight shorts, a bow tie and a zombie mask danced on the stage closeted to me, his crotch area completely gone. A woman wearing a sadistic cat costume jumped on stage with him, thrusting his exposed area into her mouth shaking her head violently like a dog tearing into a piece of meat. I watched in what I thought was terror until I came to my senses and found my cupping my own breast tightly. I blushed and quickly threw my hand down.

Out of the crowd came a woman painted in dark red, completely naked. Her hair slicked back, and white fangs dropped down from her smiling lips. It was Savannah.

My heart jumped and I almost ran to her. She held her hand up for me to stop, and threw both of her palms hard into my shoulders forcing me back into the wall. The impact almost drove the breath out of me and before I could react her lips were pressed hard against mine, both of her hands pinning my wrists above my head as her tongue went wild in my mouth. I kissed back hesitantly. She felt my hesitation and drew her face back, revealing her fake fangs.

"I'm gonna need you to loosen up!" She yelled over the music.

She ripped at my shirt and tore it open, then lunged at my neck, sucking hard. I finally gave in, and pressed my body back onto hers, running my fingers through her damp hair. She leaned up and pretended she was going to bite me. I smiled then she kissed me softly before backing up.

"I didn't think you were coming!" She yelled

"I didn't either!"

We both looked out over the sea of people devouring their desires upon one another.

"So, what is all this?" I asked

She shrugged "A place where we can all be ourselves!" She pinned me against the wall again, I could feel pressure between my legs as her knee rubbed against me. I looked up at the ceiling and breathed deeply.

She grabbed my hair hard and pulled my face towards hers. "Do you want me to take you to a room?"

Her smile was devious and she licked her lips as though she wanted to tear into me. I smiled and nodded my head. Holding up a hand she signaled me to wait, and she walked over to a nearby table were multiple collars and handcuffs lay.

A moment later she was back, and I had a tight leather collar wrapped around my neck, and my hands bound in front of me. She tugged at the chain that was attached to my neck and I stumbled forward trying not to trip over my feet as she forced me to follow her through the crowd. Everyone parted and she dragged me behind her like a prisoner.

Random people were cheering as we walked through, some high fiving Savannah, some swatting at my rear end. It felt humiliating, but overpoweringly arousing. I almost felt as if she was showing off her catch, and all the others cheered in approval.

She dragged me into a hallway where there was a line of wooden doors, each had their own lit torch and a man in a black suit standing in front. She tugged me a few doors down and nodded to its keeper. He unlocked the door and swung it open. Savannah pulled the chain hard and I almost fell over trying to keep up. The door closed behind us and a heavy lock dropped in place. She pulled one last time harder than before, I stumbled again and fell to the floor skinning my knee. She towered over me, her firm body highlighted in the dim flames that lit the corners.

"What are we-" A quick backhand to my face stopped my sentence. I looked back up, I could taste blood in my mouth. She leaned down and softly held my face. "Tell me if it's too much." She whispered. I nodded my head.

She firmly grabbed my hair and pulled my neck back, forcing me to look at her. She spread her legs forcing my face inches from her body. "Do you want me to continue?"

I cut my eyes at her clean-shaven privates, and nodded. "Good." She whispered, thrusting my face into her, rubbing it back and forth before walking away.

I was strapped to the wall completely naked, both hands extended, both feet bound, my head free to witness everything done to me. An explosive mixture of inward terror and outward excitement crawled over my skin as Savannah slipped on knee high leather boots, twirling a leather strap in her hand.

She approached me slowly, her smooth legs carefully taking each step forward until she stood in front of me. Her short black hair fell across her face as she eyed my skin, a devious smile spreading across her lips. Lunging forward she pressed her bare body against mine. Her soft nipples grazed against my stomach, her nails softly dug into the small of my back and I breathed heavily into the air, wanting more, needing more, my body begging for it.

She thrust the leather strap into my mouth and around my head, holding it taught in one hand. She had complete control of me. She forced me to look downward at my exposed body, her sharp nails trailing up my leg, scratching my inner thigh; the sensation was electrifying. I felt her breath along my skin, her nose tickled my neck and she bit down on my ear. I pulled my arms forward wanting to reach out and grab her, but they wouldn't move. I breathed sharply into the air as she scratched my ribs tenderly and moved her hand down between my legs rubbing me slowly. I had never been so wet in my life, the urge to break from the chains and wrap my arms around her had my body pulsating.

Her lips grabbed mine and her movements intensified, biting my lips harder as her hand moved quickly against me. I moaned into her open mouth and started to shutter, almost on the brink of an orgasm. Before I could cum she drew back, snapping the leather strap from my mouth and wiping it against my open thigh. I screamed with a mixture of pain and intense pleasure.

Her moments didn't stop; she threw herself to her knees and thrust her head between my legs, forcing her head upward, her tongue digging into me wildly. Her nails from both hands grabbed my breasts and she slowly scratched them down my skin into the small of my stomach. Her mouth lashed back and forth and she scratched harder leaving light red marks down my sides. I moaned loudly into the open air and my body started to convulse. Savannah quickly unbound my legs and threw my thighs over her shoulders as she lifted me up, my hands shook in their chains and I arched my back upward as she went wild on my clit. I wrapped myself around her face and screamed into the ceiling jerking my body as I had the most intense orgasm of my life.

I softly whimpered as she placed my feet back on the ground. My hands became free and I collapsed to the floor, breathing heavily. I looked up at her and she smiled back at me.

"Everything you ever wanted?" She asked.

I couldn't talk, I could only let go a quick succession of giggles and I shook my head. She threw my clothes on me. "Get dressed."

We walked out of the wooden door, and the man in the black suit was smiling. I looked down at his pants and he obviously was aroused. I wondered if he had heard everything. The party outside the hallway had not slowed down a bit, in fact it seemed as if it had increased in intensity.

Where single dancers had once held the stage, now was fully occupied of party goes, thrusting themselves onto each other. We walked into the crowd, Savannah slapping random people's behinds, others doing the same to her. The strobe lights suddenly went insane, and everyone cheered as water began spraying from multiple outlets in the ceiling soaking everyone.

The music stopped and a strong pulsating vibration rattled through the speakers. The entire crowd went silent and cleared an opening in the center of the floor. A huge man wearing a black executioner's mask made his way through the back of the crowd. As he got closer to the clearing the crowd began to chant. All strobe lights fired in unison and once he had made it to the center they stopped and a strong spotlight lit up the clearing. The man's body was chiseled with muscles, and my mouth fell open. The crowd went insane as he stood in the falling water, flexing his sculpted body.

"Who is that?" I yelled to Savanna over the deafening crowd.

"Titus!" She yelled back.

The monstrous man walked closer to the edge of the crowd, intensifying their screams. He raised both hands and they went silent. The only sound audible was the steady dropping of water that was still pouring from the ceiling.

He scanned the crowd and looked in our direction. Savanna perked up, standing on her tippy toes. His heavy steps echoed in the large room as he made his way through the crowd, everyone clearing a path, the spotlight following him. He came closer and by the time he stood in front of Savanna I was convinced he was at least 7 feet tall. Savanna bounced up and down, both hands clasped together at her chest. Titus started at her, then pushed her aside, centering on me. Taking two steps forward he stopped, towering over me. My heart stopped beating, and I forgot how to breathe.

I was absolutely terrified. He looked me up and I trembled, shooting a glance to Savanna who shot daggers back at me. I wanted to run. He stood, a silent mountain eyeing me, before he thrust both arms into the air. The crowd erupted in applause. At that moment, a tight metal collar was latched around my neck, and its chain was tossed towards Titus's massive arms. He caught it in midair, and yanked it, toppling me over to the ground. I looked back up at Savanna who had both of her arms crossed, a mean scowl shaped her face and she shook her head.

I climbed back to my feet and ran, catching the end of my chain falling back to the floor. Titus turned around, kneeling down. His eyes peered deep into mine, and every muscle in my body trembled. I didn't want to do this anymore, I had my fun. I wanted to leave, I wanted it to be over. But as he stood back up, whipping the chain tightly behind him, I quickly realized my night had not even begun.

Knife Play

Jaap Boekestein

Fear.

Fear and making love, it is a delicious combination.

I don't mean the Big Fear, the all-consuming, paralyzing kind of fear, although that can be fun too. Seeing that kind of fear in her eyes: He is going to kill me! No, no, please don't!

The Big Fear is so sweet. It is the ultimate Domination. The cherry on top (pun intended, be on top when you do this), the spice of life and so on. For those who are curious: you are on her, in her maybe. That is the making love part. Suddenly you have your hands around her throat, or you raise a fist, or a knife, or a baseball bat. Or you have a hand on her neck with her face inches above a tub full of water, or you pull a see-through plastic bag over her head, or... well, whatever. Of course, that in and of itself is not enough, it's also your body language, your eyes, your voice, everything. At that very moment, you will really have to mean it if you want it to work. You must be willing to kill. The Dark Beast must be controlling your mind.

(Admit to yourself you want it. I know you want to.)

Yes, the payoff is big, but you can't use that kind of spiel very often (Duh, once?). You have to surprise her (him if you are so inclined, not my thing, but be my guest).

As said, the Big Fear is sweet, but use it wisely. Don't overspend it, otherwise you will be left with little in a very short time. Treat it like something special, because it is. How does that song go again? Killing me softly.

Back to fear and making love. The Little Fears. Ah, now those are like sweet raindrops at the end of a hot spell, eating ice-cream in bed, getting out of those office clothes at the end of the day.

The Little Fears go something like this: Is he going to do it? Or not? He surely won't... No, don't go there, please. Yes... please go on.

The Little Fears wake you up, make your heart beat a little bit faster, heat up the blood and cause you to hold your breath. You can stretch the Little Fears, use them as a series, as a built up, going on and on and on. Just like the best orgasms (Yours, ladies. We men are sprinters, you are long distance runners. I applaud you).

There are many ways to initiate the Little Fears.

I use a knife.

Knife play it is called.

Yeah, it's a whole sub-scene. People do knife play, it's a broad field, with lots of variations and degrees.

342

There are forums and there is fan art, and photography. If you know where to look.

Knife play.

And sex.

Now, let your mind wander. What do you think of?

She/you chained up in bed? Blindfold, handcuffs? Helpless, subject to my dubious mercy? And, of course the knife, big and shiny, sharp as whatever. Cutting, stabbing, blood, screaming, manically laughter, lighting and thunder.

Madness and ecstasy.

Okay... You are thinking all that? Fine, it is your mind, your fantasy. I have nothing to do with it. I just mentioned knife play, and sex. You were thinking of all those other things. (Stab, stab, blood spraying. Wahahaha!)

But keep that thought, we may get there. First let's do it my way.

Now I am gonna pretend you are a girl. I only do this with girls. Of course, it would work just as well with a guy and that definitely offers some other opportunities, but now you are a girl. So, fellows, suck it up and get in touch with your feminine side. And be glad I am not doing knife play on you. If you want me, give me a call. I am not shy of a little bit of experimentation.

Good.

You are there, alone with me in a room.

You are naked, it is easier that way. Unless clothes are going to be cut, but that is the kind of messy I am not looking for. And some clothes are surprisingly hard to cut.

Okay, I am naked too. Just as vulnerable. Yeah, sure.

"I am a sadist. A sweet sadist," I have told you a few days before.

Sadists, aren't those people who like to hurt other people?

Yup. And I am one of them.

You were intrigued and now you are alone with me. You are suddenly very aware of that. And butt naked.

Are you afraid?

No.

Not yet.

Maybe a little.

A tiny fear.

Nice, isn't it?

But you trust me. Trust me enough to be alone, naked etc. And I said I was a sweet sadist.

"I only hurt you if you enjoy being hurt." Those are my words. And you gobbled them up like candy.

He is not going to do anything I really don't want to. Won't he?

Hang on to that thought. Hang on with your dear life.

We are both sitting on the bed, me behind you.

By the way, I love your silhouette, the curve of your back and buttocks, your neckline. So erotic! I want to touch all of it, but I restrain myself. Not yet.

"Are you okay?" I ask.

"Yes." Get on with it. You are tiny bit nervous.

"If you want to stop, or it doesn't feel right, just say so."

"Yes." Yesyesyesyes. You have come this far, you don't want to give up now. You want it to start. Now.

I smile, I know how you feel. You are so easy to read. Your body is an open book.

I take the knife.

You hear it, you tense up. It is going to happen.

I am a sadist. So, I lean forward and blow softly over your neck and shoulders.

You shiver, your first impulse is to react, but you don't. No, you want to be strong, to feel, you want to submit, to be good. (Although you are doing this, so actually you are a bit of a bad girl... Never mind.)

I clench the knife in my fist and stab you violently in back, in the left kidney.

You die, in pain. It takes a while.

Smile. No I don't. Do not worry. That does not happen. Shh.

But I bet somewhere, deep down, in the back of your mind, you entertained that fear.

Good. Fear is a survival tool. Don't ignore it. Embrace it.

I have the knife in my hand. I haven't shown it to you. Is it a big knife? You know, those knives serial killers use in the movies? It must be huge!

To tell the truth, no it isn't. I prefer something smaller. It isn't flashy (who cares, there are no witnesses, nobody knows you are here) but it is much easier to use. More precise and a lot lighter. You don't want my hand to tire and start trembling, do you?

The tip of the knife lands very lightly on the base of your neck.

Reflexes, you can't help them. Your muscles contract, your body wants to move away from the foreign object – Threat! Yes, your body knows. It is only a tiny reflex (the perceived threat is tiny), so you suppress all that.

Softly I let the steel tip dance down over your shoulder blades.

Ah, you know I do this with a knife. And it feels like a knife, but you don't turn away, you don't flee. Your body decides it is time for goosebumps. I guess it is some ancient fight reflex. Hairs stand up to look bigger? Something like that.

"Are you all right?" I ask, knowing damned well what you are feeling.

"Uhu," you answer a bit impatiently, maybe a bit annoyed by your body's reactions. You want to be tough, to endure, and your body betrays you at the very first opportunity. Bad body!

Hm, does the body needs to be punished? No. I push away that tempting thought.

I start making a series of loops and S-curves on your skin with the knife tip. Lightly, all over your body. I get to know your body and I check if can reach you everywhere I want. In the meanwhile, your body gets lulled into a sense of safety. Look. Nothing is happening, you are safe, it only tickles a little.

It does, doesn't it?

I know your mind isn't fooled that easily, but hey, I know you are smart. I really like smart ladies. They tend to think more, which actually makes it easier to manipulate them. Me smart too, ugh. Me know how you think.

I got you this far, didn't I?

Ever so slightly I increase the pressure of the knife. It isn't cutting, not by a long way, but it is almost scratching your skin. Just not yet.

Shoulders, arms, the outside and back along the inside. The elbow pits are very sensitive. Fluent, organic lines, smoothly drawing invisible circles. Never be abrupt, don't do corners, do lullabies.

On and on, the knife point skates, on your back, your buttocks, your sides, your neck, which isn't that sensitive, but your skull certainly is, just below your hairline.

I am hypnotizing you, a sort of. It is about rhythm, touching nerve ends.

I put my free hand on your neck, slowly but firmly. The fingers of my other hand flip the knife just a little.

The edge touches the skin of your back, a bit like a razor blade, and lightly I scrap your skin all the way down your spine.

You shiver. Your body suddenly remembers again that I am holding a knife.

It isn't the nicest feeling and when I am down there, at the end of your spine, I lean in and take my hand off your neck. I reach all around you and cup one your breasts.

That is very intimate. I know. Don't worry, I am not going to squeeze.

Instead I gently lift your breast and with the edge of the knife I cut the underside of your breast a little.

I say a little. Just enough to let you feel. Just enough to superficially cut the skin. Two or three layers of cells.

He is cutting my breast! You sharply inhale. You want to escape, but don't (And can't, I have you in my arms. They are big and strong. You can't run, dear. Even if you wanted to).

By now your breathing is quick, just as is the rate of your heart beat. Your body is tense.

God, do I bleed? I don't feel blood. I... No, he is not going to...? No!

Yes I am. I cup your other breast, lift it, cut it. Just a little. I have a deep routed need for symmetry.

I hold up the knife. It is the first time you see it. You see the curve, the weathered steel, the edge without blood.

It is a knife. And: he cut me. My breasts.

While your thoughts are a maelstrom of little fears and doubts, I check something.

I smile. Your nipples start to harden, just as expected.

Little fears are exhilarating. Don't deny it, your body betrays you.

I give you a few seconds to compose yourself and say: "I want you to lay down, on your belly."

I pull up a pillow for your head to rest on.

You lay down, turn your face a little and try to relax. You haven't forgotten the knife.

Good.

The altar of your body is in front of me.

High priests with knives?

Just a thought. Nothing to worry about.

I lick my lips, they are dry. You are so fucking beautiful. The lines, the soft skin... Wee! Some painters hate an empty canvas. I love it.

Again, I put one hand on your neck. Partly to prevent you from moving, but mostly it is symbolic: I dominate you, you are mine. In the animal kingdom, some males bite the neck of the female when they mount them. I suspect we humans still have some lingering traces of that in our brains. Anyway, it works.

Now the knife has less mercy. You have been cut, your skin has been violated. It was just the beginning.

Again, the circles and S-curves, but now the point of the knife scratches, bites. Ley lines, Nazca lines.

You are tense, on your guard, but you allow it. You are though, aren't you? No crying, just bite your lip, groan if you really need to. It isn't as bad as the tattoo needle. No, it isn't, but it is everywhere.

Bastard, bastard, bastard.

Yes, dear?

My one hand leaves your neck, joins the knife point in the dance over your body. Fingers, the palm of my hand, knuckles, sometimes even my elbow. Skin on skin, soft but strong, in contrast to the hard, biting steel.

You want to sink into the bed, your nerves sending all those conflicting signals.

With my fingers, I pull your buttocks apart.

No! You are not going to...

Yes, I am. The knife point slips down, following the valley between those lovely hills.

And...

And turns away, upwards, climbing one of your buttocks.

No, I am not going there. Take it easy. That would be stupid, out of balance, that would disturb the flow. I do Fucking Feng Knife Shui. I am not going to put sharp objects in your ass.

But you felt the Little Fear, didn't you?

Ha ha.

The back of your legs and knees, your calves, your heels, the sole of your feet, your toes.

Very sensitive areas, all of them. Nice to feel the steel down there? Sure.

Play, play. You want to retract your foot, you want to scream or giggle or cry. Every instinct tells you that having something sharp down there is an extremely bad idea. And still you allow it, do you fight your instincts.

It is so sweet to see you struggle. I say nothing, but just continue, sweet and completely innocent. I just move my knife in this way. Oh, that tickles? I am sooooo sorry. Not.

We go on and on, you and I. It is a game, we both know it, and we both know it is not. It is torture, foreplay, seduction. I am all over you, with knife and hand, sometimes my breath and once or twice with my lips and teeth. Hey, I am only human. Do you know how damned sexy you are, squirming, moaning, biting your lips, softly cursing?

Believe me, you are sexy.

Your back is on fire now, from the top of your skull all the way down to the tip of your toes.

"Please turn around."

You do.

Nipples hard. Eyes dilated. You are excited.

Don't worry, so am I. Hell, I sure am.

But no, no. Not yet.

You have to suffer some more.

Because you want to.

And I want to give you want you want. What you need.

Time to be nasty again.

Quickly, as a leaping panther, I move. I lean on one arm, my face is about a foot away from yours.

You see my eyes. They are empty and cold.

> In your mind alarm bells shatter the fuzzy hot sexy cloud eight you were swimming in. (Not yet cloud nine.) What...?

I put the knife on your throat, the tip hard against your flesh. Your skin is almost at breaking point.

You look at me, and see nothing. No emotions.

The knife stays on your chin.

You feel the urge to say something, but you don't know what.

"Open your mouth." My voice is cold.

"More."

"Stick out your tongue."

"Further."

It is not easy with a knife at your throat, but you obey. What choice do you have? You don't want to risk anything. Those eyes are so empty.

The knife leaves your throat.

Relief.

I put the knife down on your tongue. Rather hard.

Nggh!" you say.

I shake my head.

"Nnnnnnnn." You sound desperate. I can't imagine why.

With a sigh, like you have failed a test, I lift the knife. Before you can speak, I turn the blade 90 degrees. Suddenly the thin sharp edge is parallel with your mouth, is on the corners of your mouth, with nothing in between.

Ever seen Ichi The Killer? No? Okay, how about Heath Ledger as the Joker? You know, where the corners of his mouth are cut open?

You want to feel a joke, girl?

Just say it and I will push. I will cut.

You wanted knife play.

I am a sadist.

You knew all that.

And still you agreed.

It is on your own head, sweet.

Your fault.

...

I remove the knife, carefully. I didn't cut you. Not a drop of blood is spilled.

"Fuck!" you swear. "You fucking bastard! You evil f-"

I grab your head with my hand and between my spread fingers I put the point of the knife just under your left eye.

You freeze instantly.

It is pretty hard to cut out an eye. But it can be done.

You want me to do it?

"You want to stop?" I ask. "Just say so, and we will stop."

Yes. No.

"Please," you whisper.

"Please, go on?" I try.

"Yes," you whisper, very small, full of shame of your dark desires.

I am not the kind of guy who goes for "Yes Master". I am a sadist, not a Dominant. There is a difference.

"Good," I reply.

I take away the knife, and my hand.

We hug. She cries. We sit like that for a while.

Finally, I dry her tears and look her in the eye. "Are you okay?"

"Yes," you answer, still a little bit shaky.

"Lay down on your back. You are doing very well. You are wonderful."

I am sweet to you. The knife skates lightly over your skin, my fingers caress and massage. Bring back the trust, bring back the peace, built up the desire all over again.

Nipples, sweet nerve end volcanoes, I treat them well. Only a few pinpoints and light scratches.

I put my lips on your belly button and blow as hard as I can. You scream and laugh, arms and legs high in the air. "Noooo."

Between your legs. The knife circles your vulva, lightly, slowly, teasing, non-threatening. My fingers and lips, and tongue and teeth join the dance.

Around and around we go, not entering. Not yet.

My fingers spread your lips, revealing the inner sanctum.

No tongue. No fingers.

Knife? Yes.

Verrrrrry lightly. Verrrry tender.

Yes, that is also knife play.

The steel point dances around your clit.

I pull back the hood.

Steel kisses the little sweet spot.

It's terrifying and hot as hell. I know, I know.

We go on. There isn't much of 'me' and 'you' anymore. It's 'we'. We move together, we feel together, we get hot and hotter together. Steel on hot flesh, wet flesh. Never ending, little earthquakes, lighting bolts under your skin race towards our brains.

On and on, endless sweet torture.

Little Fears, building up. And up. And up.

I put the knife on the side table, it has done it's work. Now we don't need it anymore. We grind, we use nails and our mouths and our dick and pussy. We fuck.

It's great.

The best fuck in ages.

Thank you, knife.

...

We're lying together in bed. I feel your heartbeat, you feel mine. Your sweat is my sweat. We are both satisfied. Damned well satisfied.

I can reach out and take the knife.

I can, but I don't.

Knife play is enough.

For now.

Other HellBound Books

For You To Enjoy

All available now in paperback and eBook from Amazon, iBooks, Barnes & Noble, Kobo etc.

For full details, visit our official website
www.hellboundbookspublishing.com

Or

Download our App from iTunes / Google Play – or simply scan the QR Code below

The Big Book of Bootleg Horror

Twenty tales of terror, darkness, the truly macabre and things most unpleasant from a delectably eclectic bunch of the very best independent horror authors on the scene today!

S.E. Rise, Kevin Wetmore, Paul Stansfield, Craig Stwewart, Shaun Avery, Jeff Myers, Marc DeWit, Timothy Wilkie, Quinn Cunningham, Melanie Waghorne, Marc E. Fitch, Stanley B. Webb, Tim J. Finn, Ken Goldman, Ralph Greco Jr, Roger Leatherwood, Vincent Treewell, David Owain Hughes, J.J. Smith and the inimitable James H. Longmore

In this superlative tome, HellBound Books have embraced the taboo, gone all-out to horrify and have broken the flimsy boundaries of good taste to make The Big Book of Bootleg Horror the perfect anthology for those who take their horror like we take our coffee - insidiously dark and most definitely unsweetened

Shopping List

A simply superlative collection of spine-tingling horror from the very best minds in the business!

We decided upon the shopping list theme for this particular volume as an antithesis to those wildly successful writers (they know who they are) of whom it is often said *'we would read their damned shopping list if they published it!'*.

Well, we have given twenty-one of the hottest authors in the independent horror scene the unique opportunity to have their own shopping lists read by you - along with their most terrifying tales of course!

Stories of gut-wrenching terror from: Kathy Dinisi, Robert Over, Christopher O'Halloran, Eric W. Burgin, Russ Gartz, Mark Slada, Jeff Baker, Tim Miller, Nick Swain, JC Raye, Jovan Jones, Ben Stevens, David F. Gray, Brandon Cracraft, M.S. Swift, Kevin Holton, David Owain Hughes, Bertram Allan Mullin, Jeff C. Stevenson, Sebastian Crow and S.E. Rise

Sángre: The Color of Dying
By
Carlos Colón

Carlos Colón's first published novel is the story of Nicky Negrón, a Puerto Rican salesman in New York City who is turned into foul-mouthed, urban vampire with a taste for the undesirables of society such as sexual predators, domestic abusers and drug dealers.

A tragic anti-hero, Nicky is haunted by profound loss. When his life is cut short due to an unforeseen event at the Ritz-Carlton, it results in a public sex scandal for his surviving family. He then rises from the dead to become a night stalker with a genetic resistance that enables him to retain his humanity, still valuing his family whilst also struggling to somehow maintain a sense of normalcy.

Simultaneously described as haunting, hilarious, horrifying and heartbreaking, Sángre: The Color of Dying is a breathtakingly fun read.

Nightly Visits
By
Stephen Helmes

When you close your eyes, where do you go? What do you see? The moment you drift off into that world of the unknown, you are on a rollercoaster ride, speeding down a track that takes you anywhere it wants to take you.

Often it takes us to places that we would never voluntarily go when we're awake, into a world of darkness, tragedy, and fear. In this virtual reality world, you do things that you would never do when you're awake, such as jumping from a plane without a chute, or opening the door to a room when you know there is something behind it waiting for you to enter.

But dreams can also tell you stories of love, wit, and treasures. You may wake laughing, crying, or screaming, because your dreams know your weaknesses. They know your every thought, and they know how to attack.

That's not what Nightly Visits is *about*. THAT'S WHAT *NIGHTLY VISITS* IS!

**A HellBound Books LLC
Publication**

www.hellboundbookspublishing.com

Printed in the United States of America

9 780998 636962